Through Shade and Shadow

Through Shade and Shadow

Shades and Shadows Book 1

Natalie J. Case

To my dedicated cheerleaders: Cassie, Lisa, Nicole
To the women who inspire me: Victoria, Karla and so many more

Thank you for being with me on this journey!

Chapter One

"*It is now being reported that this man, this serial killer, is in fact a Shade, Alec.*" Mason Jerah turned from his grandmother's bedside, lifting the television remote to increase the volume. "*For those of you just joining us, we are covering the recent arrest of late night DJ, William Darchel, from Salt Lake City, Utah, for the murder of as many as 25 women over the last ten years. Darchel was found drinking the blood of his latest victim, Marisel Deboi.*"

Mason watched as video played of the arrest, with Darchel being led out of a house with blood on his face and painting his shirt. "*Until very recently, Shades were believed to be nothing more than folklore, brought over with immigrants from places in Europe.*"

"I told you they'd find us."

Mason turned back to find his grandmother pushing herself up to lean back against the headboard. "They didn't find us, Nana. They caught a killer."

Her lined face clearly showed her disgust. "It's always the worst of us that they find. Mark my words, Mason, this is not going to do us any favors. Bad enough as it is."

He let her words go without protest. It wouldn't do any good to argue. She had lived a life he barely knew about, had seen things he never would. She had earned the fear that had kept them separate, hiding from a world she knew would never understand or accept them.

"I'll bring you some tea."

"No, boy, help me up. I'm tired of this bed."

He sighed, but pushed his chair back while she pulled the blankets off herself. He offered his hand as she put her feet on the floor, letting her use it to steady herself and pull herself upright. Once she was steady, he let her set the pace, taking them out of her small bedroom and into a spacious kitchen.

His father had grown up in this house, and his Nana had helped build it when she was in her teens. Mason had spent a lot of time in the house as a boy, and since the fire that had destroyed his own house and killed his father, he too had considered this place home.

"I'll make some tea." Mason said as they reached the kitchen.

"That's my good boy." She patted his arm and shuffled into the living room. He heard the television come on and sighed. The more she saw of the world outside, the more she was afraid.

Not that he could blame her.

They were the last of their line. He was a few weeks shy of eighteen and he had never met another Shade who wasn't family.

Mason set the kettle on the stove and set up the tray for his Nana's tea. He'd always thought they were the last, until they had received a letter from a Shade on the east coast, the daughter of one of his Nana's friends.

If it was true that Darchel was a Shade, things would change for any living Shade. They had always been a thing of myth and legend, stories told around campfires and written about in books with other fantastical creatures like dragons and unicorns and witches.

Darchel had been found three days before in a house in Utah with blacked out windows and bodies of missing women, all hung upside down and bled dry.

Clearly the man was deranged.

Mason filled the teapot from the kettle and set the tea steeping before putting a couple of cookies on the tray as well. He headed into the darkened living room.

"*Of course, liberal media is going to say there is no such thing as Shades,*" a man on the television was saying as Mason set the tray down. "*They will try to tell us that this man has some sort of disease, that he should be pitied. I'm here to tell you that William Darchel is the son of the devil himself. How else do you explain him?*"

Mason poured tea and handed the cup to his Nana, sitting beside her on the couch. "Do you think he really is one of us, Nana?" Mason asked.

"I think he might be. Look how pale he is. Never seen a sunny afternoon, that one."

Mason watched the footage again as they replayed it, Darchel being dragged out of the house by two men, his face a mask of rage and blood. He flinched as the sun found his skin, pulling back instinctively, only to be dragged forward again.

"*We are joined now by Utah senator Norman Douglas. Senator, thank you for being here.*" Mason didn't recognize the man in the dark suit, but one look told him the man was a politician. His thick brown hair was sprinkled with gray and styled in a typical rich man's haircut. His gray eyes belied the serious set of the man's face. Something made him happy, probably the free publicity.

"*Thank you, Alec, I'm glad I could be here. Let me tell you something. This is not something we could have predicted, but rest assured that we are prepared to do whatever it takes to keep the people safe.*"

"What an ass." Mason glanced at his grandmother, smirking at her use of the pejorative. "That man..." She shook her head, never finishing the thought.

They sat in silence for a while, watching as the news cycled through to other stories and came back to Darchel. It was all of his Nana's worst fears come to life.

Her fear had kept him isolated. All he knew of his heritage as a Shade he had learned from her, and most of what she taught him had been to teach him how to hide what he was from the world.

There was a lot more to who and what they were, he knew that. He knew how to find clean water and to avoid salt and sunlight. He knew how to use the energy within him to ease aches and pains. But he also knew from the memories inside him that there was a lot he didn't know.

The fullness of those memories wouldn't unlock until he turned eighteen. They were his mother's, hers and her line's, taken with her last breath when he was only nine and locked away by his father until Mason was of age, when presumably he would have learned enough to understand them. His education in his heritage ended two years after that, however, when his father was killed in the fire. His grandmother had forbidden him to use his gifts outside of the house, refused to teach him how to use the healing energy inside him to affect others.

She was terrified they'd be found and killed. Or worse. Listening to some of the people on the television now, he couldn't say her fears were unfounded.

* * *

His birthday was a somber event, there was no cake, no presents. He sat beside his Nana in the shadows of her bedroom, holding her hand as if his grip could hold her in her body.

"There was a time, Mason, when we did not have to hide what we are. We were sought for the gifts we can give, and not feared for them." She coughed weakly. "But those times have long past, and you need to be safe. You need to protect yourself from them that would use a Shade to evil ends."

"I know Nana," Mason said softly, blinking away the tears. She had told him the same thing over and over for most of his life.

There had been a great uproar about Shades since Darchel's arrest. Old myths were pulled out and then debated on every news channel, along with talk of medical research. People were scared. Darchel had people believing the old stories about Shades drinking blood to survive.

It wasn't true. Shades *could* survive on blood, but it wasn't a first choice. Like anyone else, they required nutrition, food. But a Shade's physiology required liquid and lots of it. Preferably good, clean water.

"If they know what you are, they'll kill you. And if they don't kill you outright, they will torture you, make you do things, make you a monster." Her old, wrinkled hand lifted, one bony, arthritic finger poking into his chest. "You hold on to the heart the gods gave you, boy. I won't be there to remind you." She took his hand again, squeezing it tightly. "You take what I'm giving you."

He shook his head. "No, Nana. Not yet." He wasn't ready to let her go, and he certainly wasn't ready for what she was giving him. He was too young, too inexperienced.

"Yes, now, before it's too late." She pulled him closer with a surprising strength for one about to die. "Close your eyes, open your mouth. Take the strength of our line. You're the last of a lineage, Mason."

Tears slipped past his eyelids as he closed them, opening his mouth and leaning over her. Her body vibrated and she breathed in deep, holding it for an impossibly long time before she grabbed the sides of his face and pressed her open mouth to his.

Mason pulled away involuntarily, but she held him, breathing out into his mouth while her voice filled his head. "*Swallow it, Mason.*" It was too much, too hard, like a giant rock formed from her breath, getting bigger as he held it in his mouth. "*You must.*"

He sucked in and forced himself to swallow and the rock moved into his throat, then slowly down, until he could feel the fingers of it stretching out, pulling itself into him, expanding as it filled him. She fell back to the bed, panting. "There's my good boy."

His throat burned and he reached for the water on the side table, swallowing rapidly as the lump melted into him. It was different from when it was his mother. More, somehow. Images started leaking into him, memories from down their line, the heritage of his people, the root of their gift.

They had been a proud clan once, and his Nana had always told him that once he was the last of the line, all the power, all of their history would be his to safeguard.

She was the keeper of their line, and that hard ball of power and memory would bloom and flare in him... It was the right of the leader of his line: the power to lead, the memory of the world from which they came, the parting gift of every Shade, every life collected.

It was meant for an elder, for someone trained, someone who knew what he was.

It was never meant for someone like him. "Nana?"

Her eyes were closing and he could feel the cold creeping into her. "You be a good boy, Mason," she whispered. "Make me proud."

He felt her letting go and clung to her a little harder. "Please don't leave me."

"*I'll always be a part of you.*" He couldn't tell if that was her actually thinking in his head or the part of her that was inside the gift she'd given him. Her death rippled through him, activating parts of him that were meant to be dormant until he was old enough to handle them.

Mason stood, his stomach churning with grief, even as his body grew hotter. There was too much light in the room suddenly, the last rays of a late spring sun slanting through the closed slats on the wooden shades, and he ran, down the stairs into the basement, drowning himself in the dark, stripping down and immersing himself in the cool waters of the soaking pool.

The water welcomed him, and he sank deep into it, clinging to the feeling of her until it slipped away and he was alone. He surfaced slowly, as his body shifted inside, as it accepted those that had come before, the memory rippling through him of times past, of ancestors tormented, chased into hiding.

Some of it he knew from the stories his Nana would tell them, some he had guessed at from her silences. His line was long, stretching all the way back to the days when Shades were the healers and shamans, before the coming of the Church had bred fear. There was too much to follow coherently. It exploded in small bursts of information, memories. It prodded at the barrier his father had put in his head to keep his mother's last breath safe, breaking it open and doubling the effect.

Mason inhaled and sank deep into the pool again, willing the water to ease the transition. Knowledge came alive inside him and he tentatively stirred the water with his hands, letting energy stimulate the water, which in turn warmed against his skin.

He would stay there, in that cool pool of water until it had unrolled inside him, until his brain had sorted it into some sense of order and his body had adjusted. Then he would see to his Nana's body, and decide what to do next.

* * *

Mason pulled himself up out of the pool, a little dazed, but driven by hunger. He wasn't sure how much time had passed, but he knew he needed to eat.

He dried himself and pulled his clothes back on, climbing the stairs wearily. He opened the basement door cautiously, checking for sunlight, but all was dark. He eased through the door and stopped in the kitchen. It was too quiet. Not that she had been loud, exactly. Her presence could fill the house and now that she was gone, the silence was empty. He pulled bread from the cupboard and ham from the refrigerator, throwing together a sandwich to satisfy the hunger inside him.

His time in the dark had given him insight into what was possible, but did nothing for his practical knowledge. There was more to learn than he had ever imagined. It all bubbled there inside him, and he had no idea what to do with it all.

Once he was done with his sandwich, he checked the time. It was nearly one in the morning. It gave him time to do what needed to be done.

He let himself out into the night, pausing to appreciate the smell of damp earth and pine sap. It was the smell of home. Grabbing a shovel from beside the house, Mason headed down the dirt path into the woods. The clearing that was home to the Jerah family's earthly remains was small and well hidden.

His mother was buried there, her stone small and carved by his father's own hand. Her father and a brother Mason had never known lay there as well. His great grandparents both were buried in the center of the plot, the only formal headstone adorning their grave in the tiny cemetery. Mason paused in respect, closing his eyes and feeling inside him for the lingering presence of those who were buried there.

His Nana would want to be buried with her husband. Mason turned to his grave, marked simply with a small cairn and set his shovel to the earth.

It was hard work, the earth heavy with recent rains, but Mason found it comforting to lose himself in the physical labor, and he dug his way down to the linen shroud wound around his grandfather's remains.

Mason had loved spending time with the old man when he was small, following him around as he worked in the garden and, later, learning to fish and hunt at his side. Like his mother and father, his grandfather had died far too early. Mason cleared the dirt from what was left of his body and climbed out of the hole.

He trudged back to the house, feeling a little guilty for tracking mud onto the gleaming floors, and into the bedroom where his Nana lay. She was beautiful, looking peaceful, as though she had only fallen asleep. He knelt beside the bed, reaching up for the talisman she wore around her neck. It was a dark stone, barely the size of a half dollar and carved with a symbol that represented the Jerah family. His grandfather had carved it before they were wed, the stone taken from the family hearth in the old country.

Mason removed it carefully, kissing the stone before lifting the leather cord and sliding it over his head. The stone sat heavily against his chest as he stood and prepared his Nana to join her husband.

When he had wrapped her securely in a sheet, Mason carried her out to the graveyard and gently lowered her in to lie atop his grandfather's remains. For a long moment, he knelt beside the grave. Memories spilled through him of other graves, other losses, back through time.

The sun would be rising soon. Gathering himself, Mason stood and covered the bodies with dirt. He was weary as he returned to the small house, his heart heavy with loneliness. He showered and crawled into his bed, closing his eyes against the pain.

"*You are not alone.*"

Mason sat up, half certain the voice had been spoken, but he was alone in the room. Slowly he lay back down, reaching inside him for the voice. In the dark he could see others, Shades. They were scattered, each line had taken its own path centuries before, but they weren't all broken.

"*You must find your Book of Line. You must carry the line forward.*" The voices inside whispered to him, carrying him off to sleep, to dream of times when whole families came together to learn and teach, when the gifts a Shade can bring were welcomed into the world and not feared.

Mason woke shortly before the sun went down, filled with an urgency to find his grandmother's book. She had kept it hidden from him, afraid he would learn from it and somehow expose them. He dressed quickly and went into her bedroom. It still smelled of her as he turned on the lights. There wasn't much in the room that he wasn't familiar with – her bed and nightstand, her antique dresser and mirror. All had stood in their place since she had been a girl.

Mason crossed to her closet and opened the door. There was a small stool against the back wall. He pulled it toward him and stepped up so that he could see the shelves on either side. There was a dusty photo album and an old pair of dress shoes that had been his mother's. Behind the photo album was a beat up cardboard box.

He pulled the box to him and stepped off the stool. The lid was loose and came off easily, revealing something wrapped in an old quilt. Mason set the box down on the bed and unfolded the fragile fabric.

He had seen the book once before, when the mourning time for his father had passed and his Nana had pulled it out to record his death.

It seemed smaller somehow than he remembered it. The leather that covered the book was hand tooled, the same symbol that adorned the talisman around his neck etched into the cover, and the name Jerah was stamped underneath. He ran his hand reverently over the cover before opening it.

Inside it was a history of his line, his family. It was incomplete, of course. In part it was because his Nana had refused to update it after his father's death, and in part because the ancestor who had copied it from the original had been rushed so it wasn't fully transcribed.

He sat and slowly paged through the book, marveling at how much there was to learn. The first pages were filled with the family tree and marked where the branches expanded onto other pages. There were stories of lives lived in other times and other places as well as remedies and recipes in the writing of varied hands.

Now that he was alone, it was his duty to copy the book into one of his own. It was meant to help him learn his history and fill in the gaps of his knowledge of Shade work and lore.

Near the last half of the book, he could see his Nana's handwriting. She had made notes on various pages, changing measurements on a remedy to ease mouth pain and breaking down the ingredients in a family blend of herbs. Later pages she wrote herself, a recipe for honey wine flavored with honeysuckle and infused with Shade healing to be given as a wedding gift.

Mason stood and took the book out into the kitchen. He would need to go into town to get a book of his own. He could take care of the business of his Nana's accounts and the like while he was there. They didn't have much, but there was a small bank account and he would have to record her death with the county.

If he left early enough, he could get to town before sunrise, and only his walk home would include daring the sun. Mason left the Book of Line on the table and began making a list of things he would need.

Near to four in the morning, Mason pulled an empty backpack onto his shoulders and headed out. In the dark, he could take the fastest route, down the dirt road. Shortly before he reached the town of Naft, the road would become gravel and at the town limits, it became paved. The maps told him that the paved road would lead down to a two-lane blacktop highway that would take him out into the world.

Mason reached the start of the gravel and stopped to check the lightening skies. Sunrise wasn't far off. He pulled down the sleeves of his flannel shirt, covering his arms and adjusted his old floppy hat to make sure his face was shaded before he set out again.

The town of Naft had been growing in recent years. Since he was fourteen, he'd made the trek into town once a month to pick up what they needed, the things they couldn't hunt for or grow. His first memory of it was of single building that housed the post office, town hall and a dry goods store. Now it had a bank, a coffee shop that opened at four in the morning and stayed open until nine at night, a grocery store, and a gas station in addition to that one building.

He nodded a greeting to old man James, who was always up with the sun, sweeping the walkway in front of the town hall building and getting ready for the day. He could feel the heat from the sun, though it still sat low enough in the sky that only it's red glow was visible over the trees.

Naft was named for Maxwell Naft, who was the first to settle here. His Nana had always told him that Naft had been a Shade, but if he was, no one else seemed aware of it.

Mason let himself into the coffee shop, lifting a hand to Brandy, the early morning waitress. There were only two others in the place this early, men who likely worked in one of the larger towns down the mountain and had to get an early start.

"Wasn't expecting you this morning, Mason." Brandy said as she came to the table he snagged in the corner.

He nodded. "I know. Nana passed. I need to handle a few things."

"Oh, I'm sorry to hear that."

"Thank you. I'll take a cup of coffee when you get a minute, and a glass of water."

"Sure thing." She walked away and Mason looked up at the television over the counter. Early morning news was talking more about Darchel.

"If you are just joining us this morning, we are talking about the news that a medical exam has confirmed that suspected serial killer William

Darchel is, in fact, a Shade. We are joined by Dr. Anthony who has examined the suspect."

Mason glanced at the two men at the counter, then back at the television. The doctor being interviewed was a big guy, at least next to the morning news anchor, who seemed tiny beside him. His dark red hair was just starting to grey at the temples and his face was a little pink, as if he'd just been running.

Brandy delivered his coffee and water and momentarily blocked his view of the television. "Can I tempt you with a bagel or something?"

"No, I'm fine. Just killing time until the bank is open."

She followed his gaze to the television, shifting her weight to lean lightly on the table. "Can you believe this?"

Mason sighed and sipped at his coffee. "Yeah, crazy, right?"

"They're saying he was drinking the blood of the last victim when they found him."

He looked up at her, nodding. "I heard that too."

She shook her head. "Scary, thinking those things are out here walking around with the rest of us."

Mason swallowed. "There can't be that many of them, or we would have heard of them before now."

"That's what the news was saying this morning," Brandy agreed.

One of the men at the counter held up his coffee cup and Brandy left Mason to go fill it. The doctor was gone from the screen and instead the senator he'd seen before was there. *"Of course, we are concerned that there are more of them out there. Darchel insists that he acted alone, but as we find out more about him, I am convinced that there are Shades living among us, just as he did. I think we need to begin by rooting them out and expose them for the evil that they are."*

Mason shook his head and turned to look out the window. He drank his coffee and watched the town come awake instead of watching the talking heads on the television. At least it was more entertaining.

The door chimed as a small family came in and the two men at the counter left. Brandy came to refill his coffee and turned the television to cartoons for the kids. When the clock turned past eight in the morning, Mason rose and dropped a five-dollar bill on the table.

He pulled his hat down to protect as much skin as he could and dashed across the street to the store. He walked past the canned goods and aisles of groceries to the counter in the back, reaching for one of the catalogs. He found what he wanted and filled out the order form before taking it up to the front where the owner was stocking a shelf with bags of potato chips.

"Early in the month for you, isn't it?"

Mason nodded and handed him the order form. "Needed to do some business. I need to order that and cancel our usual grocery order."

The older man looked at him with knowing eyes. "I'm sorry for your loss."

Mason nodded. "Thank you."

"Do you need help with her body?"

"No, thank you. I've already buried her in the family plot. I just need to register the death."

The man nodded. "Manny's away visiting his sister. But I can take the information. Let me get you the form."

When he returned from a back room with a piece of paper, Mason took it and filled in the requested information. Filing the form would leave him with no regular income. His grandmother had been collecting government money since her husband's death. He could manage with what he could hunt and grow on the land, at least for now.

"How long for the book?" Mason asked, pulling his wallet out to pay for it.

"About a week, if I get the order in today. I'll have Andy bring it out to you."

"Have him leave it on the porch if I don't answer the door."

"Will do."

Mason sighed and headed next door to the bank. Closing the account would give him enough money to get through the next few months while he decided what to do with his life.

Chapter Two

"I think recent events illustrate my point well enough," Councilwoman Bethany Flanders said.

"Are you suggesting that we should be racist and xenophobic?" Anson Lambrecht asked the councilwoman. Alaric touched his father's shoulder in warning.

"Is it racist to defend yourself against murderers?" the councilwoman argued. She bristled and put both hands on the table in front of her. "My husband and several other state assemblymen are drafting a bill that would require all Shades to register so that they can be monitored. All I am suggesting is that we consider a local ordinance to protect our children."

"*This is not going well.*" Alaric thought to his father over their psychic connection.

"*Steady,*" his father replied, his thought warm and familiar.

"While I recognize that your concern is for the children, I fail to see how the proposed ordinance would do anything more than turn our citizens against one another." Alaric looked up at the speaker, caught a little off guard. Townsend Marley was not usually the voice of reason.

Councilwoman Flanders held up a file folder. "We're talking about people who kill. I got this from Chief Kalin. We have had three bodies found in two weeks, drained of blood, Shade symbols carved into their skin."

Alaric sat forward, his hand on his father's shoulder. He hadn't heard anything about any Shade related deaths. His father's surprise told Alaric he hadn't either. "Why is this the first we're hearing of it?" Anson asked.

She stood a little straighter and lifted her chin defiantly. "The police are afraid that if it came out that we had one of these killers here there would be mass panic."

"So, because we may or may not have a serial killer who may or may not be a Shade, our logical response is to put anyone who might possibly be a Shade into some ghetto?"

Next to Councilwoman Flanders, a slight man with almost delicate hands cleared his throat and stood. "I believe the point to be made here is that people who are different, who can kill us without a weapon, should be segregated, for the protection of our citizens. I would take it a step further, and include any person with extra-human ability."

Alaric sat back in his chair, his eyes on the newest member of the city council. He was a local minister, the kind that had always made him nervous.

"What exactly do you mean by extra-human, Roth?" Anson asked, crossing his arms. Alaric could feel his concern and outrage at the idea that Roth might mean them.

Alaric did not like the way Roth looked at his father then. "I'm sure *you* are aware, Councilman, that the Bible counsels us to expel evil. Even now, in this age, there are those among us who receive nefarious powers from the devil and use them to ensnare the godly."

His father actually snorted. "You can't be serious, Reverend. This is a city council, not a church meeting. You've been warned before to leave your religion at the door."

"Three months ago, you would have argued that there was no such thing as a Shade, Councilman." Roth said, an eyebrow lifting. "And yet, here we have found that they do exist and that they are evil. If such an evil being, with powers beyond our own, is real, how can we deny that there are also Witches and other beings that can bring about our destruction?"

"So…what?" Anson asked. "You want to outlaw psychics and herbalists now?"

The corner of Roth's mouth lifted into a sort of half smile. "It would be a start." There was a smugness about him, a sense that he was pleased with Alaric's father's objection. But he couldn't know the truth. For generations, his family had kept their secret, their tribe, like the Shades and others, hidden in plain sight, not out of malice, but for self-preservation.

Anson shook his head. Alaric looked around the council chambers, mentally trying to tally those who would support the ordinance currently under discussion, which would limit the locations where a Shade could legally live. He scanned the surface emotions of the those he could, coming back with a nearly fifty-fifty split with at least one member of the council still very undecided.

He glanced at the clock. There wouldn't be a vote now. The session was nearly over. "I suggest we table this discussion until everyone has had a chance to review the ramifications and legality of what it is being proposed." Councilman Marley said.

Alaric's father nodded. "Seconded."

Harold Mackey, the recording secretary held up a hand. "All in favor?" A chorus of "Ayes" shuffled around the room. "So moved. The allotted time for this session is at an end. Do I have a motion to adjourn?" Several people raised a hand. "Moved and seconded. All in favor?"

No one waited for him to say approved. As one, they all began standing, turning to aides and heading for the door. Alaric's father put a hand on his arm, drawing him to the exit. He put his copy of the proposal in Alaric's hands as they headed for his office. "Get me numbers."

Alaric nodded, holding the door for his father. "Should I tell Mom you're going to be late?"

Anson smiled and nodded. "She knows."

An aide for one of the other councilmen came running toward them. "Turn on the news, right now."

Alaric darted around his father and turned on the television in his office. The screen came to life, instantly filling with flames as a voice tried to relay what was happening.

"We are in downtown Sacramento right now, where a fire is blazing after witnesses say that five men claiming to be the 8th Battalion beat a man and dragged him into this building, where they reportedly set the man on fire."

Alaric sank into the chair, his stomach tightening as his father moved to stand beside him. He could feel the comfort his father was sending his way, but underneath it he could feel his father's own fear.

"We have received footage that is supposedly from the 8th Battalion, a militia group that has taken credit for several attacks across the US. I warn you that this footage is graphic."

The burning building faded and in its place was shaky footage of four men in navy blue from head to toe, ski masks obscuring their faces as they dragged a bloody black man to a column in a dark building where they stood him up and tied him. *"We are the 8th Battalion. We are the mighty right hand of God. This is justice."* Two of the men doused the man with liquid from gas cans, trailing a puddle away from him. A third man lit the puddle as they all jumped back.

Screams filled the air as the fire raced up the man's body. Alaric looked away from the screen as his hand found the button to turn the screen off.

"That's right here." Alaric said to his father.

"I think it's time to go home, Alaric." Anson said, his hand warm on Alaric's shoulder. "We can work on this tomorrow."

Alaric nodded, standing slowly. "Thanks, Alison."

She nodded. "I thought you should know."

"Tell your mother that the preserves were appreciated." Anson said as Alison started to leave. "And we'll have you over for dinner sometime next week." He shut the door behind her and turned to Alaric. "Perhaps we should call a meeting. Things are starting to get hot."

Alaric nodded. "I'm starting to think that maybe Riley was right." None of them wanted to believe that things would get as bad as Riley had seen them in his premonition, but each day something new happened to make him wonder.

He felt his mother reaching for him, her thoughts warmly caressing against his shields as she checked in to make sure they were okay. He returned the affection as he gathered his things. His father joined the link and for a moment they just shared in the familial bond, before information was relayed and his father reached out for the other members of his clan.

They left the office then, needing no words as they made their way to the car and headed for home. It would be a tense night for all of them.

* * *

"We have to be prepared for where all of this is going," Riley said, his voice quiet, but intense. Riley James had married into the family a year before. He was younger than Alaric by about five years. The product of a mixed marriage, Riley's mother was a Vodon priestess from Ghana, his father a police officer in Virginia who was a part of the clan. His skin was a soft brown, his eyes a deep, dark blue. His hair changed often, but was currently dyed blond and gelled into spikes. His gift was not the most active, but it was strong. It had been Riley who first suggested that the current tensions would lead to war, and that their kind would be among the casualties of that war.

"We don't know where it's going," Bryan countered from his place near the front door. Bryan Wagner was one of his father's best friends; they'd known each other since they were kids. His chin was covered with dark blond hair that was shot through with gray. His skin was deeply tanned, all but the stark white of the scar that ran from his hairline down onto his cheek and into his beard. He was a good fifteen years older than Alaric and together they were two of his father's three Keepers.

Alaric glanced across at the third of those Keepers. She was older than all of them, a distant cousin with a depth of gifts he couldn't begin to guess at. Victoria Olson was the epitome of what he supposed a wise woman looked like. Her long silver hair hung in braids and her colorful clothes were as playful as the sparkle in her eye. Alaric had known her since he was four or five, and she never ceased to surprise him. Her gifts were plentiful but never on display, and she was known to be as wise in the ways of herbs and stones as she was in her counsel.

Victoria raised an eyebrow at him and Alaric smiled. As Keepers, they shared a fairly intimate bond, but he didn't want to intrude, so he withdrew.

"We need to watch our step." Alaric's father said beside him. "Riley's premonition seems to be pretty close to the truth."

"That has never been the most reliable of gifts." Bryan said. "We've worked hard to pull this clan back together. I don't want to see us run off by a vision that may or may not come true."

"You want to wait until the person burned alive is one of us?" Riley asked, his hand coming to rest on his wife's shoulder.

The only child of Alaric's aunt, Abigail was only twenty-two, and was nearly six months pregnant with their first child. Of all of them, she was the only one who was publicly known for her gifts, making a living as a psychic, reading cards and palms out of the parlor of the house she had inherited from her mother and sometimes from a local metaphysical shop.

"The 8th Battalion **is** a problem, even if they haven't turned their eye our way. It is pretty clear my fellow council members have, however." Anson said. "Tonight, Reverend Roth suggested that his proposed ordinance should apply to more than just Shades."

"It isn't just here either." Victoria said, her sharp eyes sweeping the room. "The winds bring news of violence erupting all over. This business with the Shade murderer has opened a door to a very dark place, and that darkness has found its way out."

Bryan crossed his arms and leaned back against the door. "The racism isn't new."

The face of the man who had been killed filled Alaric's mind, the footage playing as though he was back in his father's office watching it. He could almost feel the pain as the flames caught. He turned away, trying to keep his discomfort from derailing the conversation.

"Perhaps it isn't new." Victoria said. "But once it was shoved behind a door and we tried to pretend it was gone."

"I don't want to be the one to say that it isn't our fight..." Bryan said.

"Yes you do." Anson answered with a shake of his head. "But you're wrong. Bigots seldom focus on just one group of people. And when it gets dressed up in religion, we're all fair game."

"Roth made it pretty clear tonight that he wants to see anyone his religion brands as evil contained, at the least." Alaric said, pushing the fiery images in his head away.

"But Roth is a councilman, not a member of these militias that are committing the violence." Bryan insisted.

"You sure about that?" Alaric asked. He licked his lips and drew in a deep breath before glancing aside at his father.

"You've been quiet so far." Anson said. "Speak your mind."

"When you asked him if he wanted to outlaw psychics and herbalists tonight, his reaction was...it was like you validated something for him. He is hiding a lot more than he's showing."

"Did you read him?" Riley asked.

Alaric shook his head. "No, just surface stuff, emotions. I wasn't close enough...and I'm not sure I want to read beyond the surface with him."

"I think we need to be vigilant. And we need to be prepared." Anson said. "I will be increasing my time with the globe, see if I can spot trouble coming. I want the rest of you to be alert too. And if you see something, tell us."

Alaric sensed his mother's approach and turned to her as the room slowly emptied out. She smiled and took his hand. Her touch was soothing. She was worried, he didn't need to read her to know that.

When the room was empty but for his parents and himself, Alaric sighed and tried to stifle a yawn. His father was going to go out into the yard, to the grove of trees where the orb waited. It was one of the few remaining artifacts of their ancient tribe in existence. It was a source of energy, a means of connection. The appointed leader of the tribe could use it to instantly reach any and all with gifts, no matter where they were. Since his father had taken on the mantle to lead the tribe, they had used it to unite the displaced families, bringing them together in a way the tribe hadn't known in over a century.

His father had been chosen because he was one of the few remaining with a bloodline that went back to the old world, back to a time when their tribe had been whole. Anson had inherited the role from his uncle and he had chosen Alaric to stand with him, though at the time Alaric had barely been an adult. Nearly seven years had passed since that day when he had stood with Bryan and Victoria to support his father's initiation.

Alaric had learned a lot since then. In some ways the ritual that had connected him to the others had opened him up, brought his gifts to the fore. He'd been a skilled empath even then, though he seldom exerted influence, preferring to use his gifts to gather information. It made him good at reading people, at seeing through lies. But in the years since the ritual, his ability to read far more than emotions had become stronger.

His father saw it as a sign that Alaric would follow him as leader. It was part of why he delegated authority to Alaric regularly, hoping he would become familiar with the work of leading the tribe. As his mother walked with his father out into the yard, Alaric turned for his room.

They had been a fractured tribe, scattered across the world, the gifts waning as they intermarried with those without gifts. Since his childhood, Alaric had helped his mother trace the lines, contacting people, offering them connection, family. Some had moved to be closer, and they had begun training again.

Together, he and his mother had designed a series of tests to help determine which gifts were strongest in those that came to them wanting to learn. Using the knowledge his father collected from the memories of the ancestors, they were building customized courses of study and intensive practical trainings.

He sat at his desk and ran a hand over his face. All of it could come crashing down around them. He had been skeptical when Riley told them of his vision. As Bryan said, precognition wasn't ever the most reliable of their many gifts. The future was always in motion, and telling the future was like trying to pin it in place.

But he was starting to feel like, just maybe, Riley's vision of the future was closer to true than any of them wanted it to be.

Chapter Three

"The FBI is now indicating that the explosion this weekend outside a crowded Catholic church in New York City was not, in fact, the product of foreign terrorism as was originally speculated. Two suspects are in custody after exhaustive investigation. The bomb was set in the predominantly Hispanic neighborhood by a white supremacist group. Twenty-two people died in that blast and another thirty were wounded. We will have more information following coverage of the press conference due to begin momentarily."

Mason turned away from the television and turned his attention back to the books on the coffee table in front of him. He had nearly completed copying his Nana's Book of Line into one of his own. It wasn't as complete as he had once believed, with gaps indicating that none of his most recent ancestors had gone back to the original in generations.

To complete his book, he would need to take a journey across the country to the grave of the first Jerah to land on American soil.

Secreted in a compartment in a gravestone in what was now Washington DC was a much larger Book of Line, one that tracked all of the family lines. As the last of his branch of the Jerah line, it was his duty to go back and update the book, and take from it any updates left by other Shades paying homage to their origin.

It was a rite of passage passed down from the days when the journey involved was far more arduous than his would be. He merely had to navigate the hardships of his natural sensitivity to sunlight and figuring out the confusing maze of transportation through cities he knew nothing about. He glanced toward the television and amended the thought. He'd also need to steer clear of the gun-toting, Shade and minority hating, right wing crazies who were popping up everywhere. The number of hate crimes had been rising in the last weeks, spurred on by Darchel's arrest and the xenophobic rhetoric that was being spewed by several of the presidential candidates now that the race to party nominations was getting contentious.

"*No, at this time we do not suspect any Shade involvement.*" The words made Mason look up. There was a man in a suit behind a podium with at least twenty microphones in his face. Behind him stood an array of similar men in suits and in front of him a sea of reporters, each clamoring to ask the next question. "*The men responsible are a part of a white militia group known as the 8th Battalion. As far as we know, this attack was purely motivated by hate. The suspects have confessed and indicated that there will be more attacks to come.*"

A suspected Shade had been beaten to death in Montana the week before. A homosexual black man and his Hispanic partner had been found dead in their car, which was covered with spray painted swastikas and racial slurs. Three Islamic centers had been burned following political rallies in their cities.

He'd always believed his Nana was paranoid, but since her death, he was beginning to wonder if she wasn't right after all. The world outside his quiet mountain home was a terrifying place.

Mason closed his Nana's book and got to his feet to return it to the hiding place where he'd found it. When he returned from his trip he would update it and then bury it where it belonged.

He returned to the living room as a clip was playing of Norman Douglas' rally in New York the week before. "*I'm not saying that we should kill... you know, but we shouldn't be afraid to take back our country. They take our jobs, they take our lives, they force their beliefs on us. Islamic terrorists, black and Mexican gangs, Shades, the gays... they are all here and they are killing us. We need to stand strong. We need to deport all the illegals. We need to keep the bad element out!"*

Mason turned the television off. He didn't want to hear any more. Instead he went to his room, pulling his old hiking backpack out of the closet. It had been his grandfather's. They had used it when they went hunting or camping up in the mountains overnight.

He packed a few changes of clothing, an extra pair of gloves and went into the bathroom to pack up the necessities. He wanted to travel light. He'd keep to the woods until he got down the mountain, and from there he could catch a bus traveling east. He wasn't sure how long it would take him.

He stopped at the hall closet for the pup tent and sleeping roll, checking them before securing them with the straps on his pack. In the kitchen, he pulled out the old cast iron skillet and packed up the last of the canned goods and cleaned out the fridge to make a couple of sandwiches. He put his new book into a smaller canvas bag and stashed it in his pack before he got his hunting knife and kit. The knife fit into his boot, the kit fit into the pack.

Mason slipped on his jacket and settled his hat on his head. It was early evening as he stepped out onto the porch, pulling the door shut and locking it behind him. He adjusted the pack on his shoulders and took up the hand carved hiking stick that he and his grandfather had made.

He paused at the tree line, looking back at the little house that had been his home for years. He had never dreamed he would leave it. Not like this.

Mason set out into the gathering dark of the night, moving through the familiar woods at a steady pace. He had hiked through these trees all his life. In fact, the town at the bottom of the mountain was the furthest he'd ever been from home. He kept to back trails that steered clear of people and houses. He stopped close to midnight, in a dense thicket where he couldn't see the sky, to eat a sandwich. Out this far, the world was quiet. He could almost pretend he was alone.

Near dawn, he stopped and pitched his tent, crawling inside to sleep. It was made of thick canvas so it would protect him from any sun that could find its way through the heavy tree cover above him. The familiar confines of the tent were comforting. He unrolled his sleep roll and lay down on it. In the recent days, as he'd worked on copying his book, he'd taken to practicing things he'd read about. It was something he should have been doing all along, if he'd been allowed to follow the traditions, starting his own book as he reached puberty.

He closed his eyes, taking his grandmother's talisman from around his neck and holding it in his right hand as he started with a simple routine: breathing in slowly and out just as slowly, bringing his focus out of the outside world and down into his own body, feeling through his limbs and organs for any signs of disease or damage and directing energy to heal anything he found.

It was calming, if nothing else. As he lay there, he directed energy to his feet and legs to prevent any soreness that might develop in his muscles. He swept his inner eye over his vital organs, through his stomach and intestines. He didn't actually expect to find anything, but the text had said that it was a good practice daily so that anything that did begin to develop could be caught early and dealt with before it became a problem.

Besides, he figured it was a good thing for a Shade to know his own body. He'd never had any schooling in human anatomy, so he would have to learn it through the study of his own. Once he'd completed his review and centered his thoughts again, he reached inside him for the network of thoughts and memories that had grown from the joining of his mother's last breath and his grandmother's.

The memories were all scrambled, far from any coherent story line, something he could look through for the knowledge he needed. He picked at a thread of memory and let it play through him, filling his mind with another time and place, a young Shade with a young wife and a baby on the way, building a place for them in a small village.

Fear shot through him as men in uniforms and priests came to find him, and the memories jumped around as he was named and questioned before escaping with his wife into the mountains. There wasn't much to learn from those memories, but they left him cold and shaking.

"*Do not be afraid,*" a voice said inside him.

Mason let go of the memory and smiled into the face of his grandfather. It was his own memory that bubbled up then, one of their trips up the mountain. They were beside the pond where they would swim. Mason stripped down to just his underwear, nervous because the water was deep. His grandfather was in the water already, beckoning Mason to join him.

"*Do not be afraid, Mason. Shades are made for the water.*" With a sudden clarity, Mason remembered the day and as he moved through the memory, knowledge filled him. His grandfather had taught him how to use the water to speed healing. Mason had twisted an ankle on the hike. As he reached his grandfather in the water, Mason could feel his energy moving around them.

His grandfather had helped him float, telling him to pay close attention as he used his hands to bring the energy to the inflamed tissue around his ankle. After a few minutes, it was Mason's turn to try. He wasn't as graceful as his grandfather, his small hands less adept at bringing the energized water where he wanted it, but he realized that he could direct his own energy into the water, not just try to use his grandfather's.

Mason let the memory go and drifted toward sleep. His dreams were jumbled memories, snippets of lifetimes not his own, and lessons learned from his parents and grandfather in his early childhood, all jumbled together with news images and his grandmother's fear filled words.

He woke in the late afternoon and lay listening to the stillness of the woods. By nightfall he would be well into the civilized world and that peace would be a memory. He wanted to soak it in as much as he could.

Mason stretched as he climbed out of the small tent. Long shadows and hints of golds and reds through the thick tree cover told him the sun was beginning to sink in the distance and he should be on his way. It didn't take him long to strike camp and set out in the general direction of the town he'd only been to a handful of times in his life, and most of those had been before his father had died.

The dark in these woods was deep, making them difficult to travel at night for anyone who wasn't accustomed to the dark. He knew it meant he wouldn't be likely encounter anyone.

Several hours after starting, Mason could feel the pull of water and altered his course. He wasn't sure how long it would be before he would find clean water again.

Beside a small mountain pond, Mason stripped down and waded out into the water. Life teemed in the water; fish and plant life and as he sank deeper he could sense the lingering touch of another Shade. He stopped and scanned the area, but if there was another Shade he was too far away for Mason to sense him.

The water still carried his energy though and Mason almost wanted to seek the Shade out. He hadn't met a Shade who wasn't family since before his father died.

Mason soaked only for a few minutes, restless now and eager to be moving again. He dressed as quickly as he could and pulled an apple from his pack to eat as he walked. As he resumed his hike, he noticed a path worn into the ground. Again, he felt the lingering presence of another Shade.

He continued cautiously, scanning around him more thoroughly than he had been before. The path curved to the east, and even though his destination lay in the south, Mason followed it a little further. Just as he was about to abandon the path and return to his own journey, he spotted a small cottage with a vegetable patch beside it.

Here, the feeling of another Shade was stronger. He stopped, watching the cottage uncertainly. An aging black man rounded the corner of the building, his eyes finding Mason and he stopped. "You lost, son?" he asked when Mason didn't move or say anything.

Mason took a step closer. "No, sir. I'm sorry if I'm intruding. I just…" He gestured vaguely behind him in the direction of the water.

The man nodded. "Ain't never seen one of your own?"

Mason shook his head and stepped closer still. "Family. We live further up the mountain, near Naft. I was just curious is all."

The man's dark eyes narrowed and swept over him. "You headed somewhere?"

"Back east. Family business."

The man stuck the shovel in his hand into the dirt and came toward Mason, wiping his hands on a bandana from his pocket before reaching that hand out. Mason hesitated slightly, then shook the hand. "I'm Paul Raymon. Clan Oamra."

"Mason Jerah."

"Don Jerah's boy?"

Mason was surprised, but he nodded. "Yeah."

"Was wondering what happened to you after his death. Figured you'd been shipped off to your mother's sister."

Mason frowned. He didn't know anything about a sister. And he realized slowly that this man had to have known his parents.

Paul nodded, smirking a little. "Yeah, I knew him. We were little hellions together. Stood with him when he married your ma. I moved away a year or so later so I wasn't around when..." He looked away, nodding. "I'm sorry."

"Thank you. It was a long time ago." He felt awkward standing there and gestured back toward the trail. "I should probably..."

"I was just going to have something to eat. Do an old man a favor and share a meal with me?" He wiped the bandana over the dark black skin of his face.

"I don't know."

Paul nodded. "I understand."

"No offense." Mason said, blushing a little as he realized it probably was offensive. "I've never...my Nana warned me..."

"Ah." Paul seemed to suddenly get what Mason's discomfort was. "Your Nana. She was a powerful Shade, but she was afraid of her own shadow. Not that I blame her, she didn't have it easy."

"I wouldn't know." Mason said, shifting on his feet. "She never told me much about…anything. Just that I needed to be careful of…" he rolled his eyes, "pretty much everyone."

Paul nodded. "Yeah, she was like that even back when we were kids, your dad and I. She didn't trust other Shades because she was afraid they'd be like the one that killed her brother. She didn't trust humans, because of what happened to your grandfather during the war."

Mason shook his head. He didn't know anything about the events Paul was talking about. He wondered for a moment if he could find the details in the memories that lived inside him now.

As if he could sense Mason's thoughts, Paul asked, "Did she give you her last breath?"

Mason nodded. "Yeah. I just wish she'd trained me how to …." He waved a hand at his head. "It's a jumbled mess. And my mother's is in there too…Dad locked it away because I was too young…but it's all open now and it all bleeds together." He stopped, closing his eyes and chastising himself for saying too much. Here he was, telling some perfect stranger things he had no business sharing. "I'm sorry. I'm sure I'll figure it out."

Paul touched his shoulder softly. "It's okay, Son. I imagine it's a right mess." He pressed his lips together and seemed to consider something before he took a deep breath. "I could help, if you'd let me."

Mason narrowed his eyes. "How?"

He offered a smile. "Well, I could train you to handle all of those memories that aren't yours. Maybe give you some basics on other skills that she should have taught you, but didn't."

Mason's breath caught in his throat. He had no reason to trust this man, and his heart thundered with fear as he considered it. Something inside him wanted him to run, but he recognized it as her fear, not his.

"I think…I think I'd like that." Mason said.

Paul smiled, a deep smile that smoothed out some of the wrinkles on his face and made his eyes sparkle. "Well then, take that load off your back and let's have a meal. We can start after."

* * *

"Are you ready?" Paul asked as Mason settled to sit in the grass beside the pond where they had spent some time soaking and building up his energy.

Mason swallowed tightly and nodded. "As I'm ever going to be."

"Relax."

"Easy for you to say." Mason muttered. He pushed the fear aside for probably the tenth time since they'd started just after the sunset. Up until now, everything had been talk. The last three nights Paul had walked him through the theory of a number of skills he should have already known. Now, for the first time, he was going to let Paul touch his mind, something no one but his father and grandparents had ever done.

He inhaled slowly and closed his eyes. His hand tightened around his talisman and he exhaled just as slowly to center himself. He took a few moments to breathe and center and clear his mind. When he was ready, Mason opened his hand, palm up on his knee.

Paul's hand was warm as it slid over his. There was a moment of pressure in Mason's head and his hand began to tingle under Paul's. "Relax." Paul breathed.

Mason focused on not fighting against the unusual intrusion, and with an almost audible pop he could hear Paul's voice. "*That's good.*"

Panic raced through him, but Mason held it at bay, forcing himself to stay open. "*Now what?*"

"*Remember what I told you about last breaths, and how they are meant to become part of you. The memories are real, organic, they belong to you.*"

Mason reached into the place where the memories were lumped together. "*Begin with your mother's.*" Paul said and Mason shifted through until he latched on to the moment that his mother had breathed into him. The ball of her last breath was largely unchanged from the day he had received it and he metaphorically dragged it out into the center of his mind-space. He had accessed memories within the ball, but it had never really been incorporated as part of him.

"*Good.*" Paul said. "*Remember.*"

Mason nodded, hoping it was as easy as his lessons had made it seem. He had to go back to that moment, when she realized she was going to die and told him to be strong before she had opened her mouth and pressed it to his.

Tears burned on his cheek, but he didn't move to wipe them away. Instead he stepped into the memory, once again becoming that nine-year-old boy. Fear and pain filled him as he clung to her hand and she whispered into his mind to swallow it, keep it safe. "*You are a Jerah, Mason, but you are also a son of Clan Leighis. Don't be afraid.*"

Her hands were shaking as they reached for him. Her face was pale, ghostly white. "*As my mother once gifted me, I now give to you. Carry forward the Magena line, Mason. It is part of you.*" Her thumbs rubbed away his tears and she drew him close. Her mouth opened and he wasn't sure what to expect when she covered his mouth with her own. "*Open your mouth, Mason, and take the gathered knowledge of my line.*"

He opened his mouth dutifully and she pushed the ball of memory into him with her breath. She lingered a few minutes more before her heart stopped, her hands sliding away from him as she died.

Mason held the memory, the image of her face as she lay there, the shock of it all. It had happened quickly. His father was away, tending to family business. They had gone into town, taking the beat up old truck down the dirt road and eating ice cream at the ice cream shop. It was on their drive home that she had noticed something wrong. By the time they had gotten to the cabin, she was fevered and in a matter of hours, she was dying.

Paul's presence intruded on the memory and Mason remembered he had a task to perform. "*There, it began to open before your father returned to hide it away. Can you see it?*"

Mason did see it and he nudged at the ball of memory, pulling on the strings that bound it until it opened, spilling out into him, washing through his mind in a sudden tide. "*Stay centered.*" Paul warned and

Mason nodded. He anchored himself and let the tide wash around him, observing memories and moments as they settled.

"You're going to want to soak for a while, let the water help you integrate it all." He could sense Paul pulling back, the touch of his hand leaving.

Mason lingered inside his head a while longer, feeling the nearly forgotten touch of his mother's hand and the smell of her hair. When he finally opened his eyes, Paul was gone and Mason was alone.

He stood and waded out into the water, sinking quickly into the dark depth and letting the energy they had charged the pond with earlier in the evening help even out the edges of his experience.

Inside him the memory was alive, shifting into place, showing him his own life in his mother's eyes, and back to the day she had married his father, her own life as a child, her father, a stern man that seemed angry, and back further even.

Mason discovered names bubbling up to attach to faces, people he had never known, but family and kin. He surfaced only when his lungs needed air, sinking quickly once he had filled them again.

For hours he soaked and lived through the lives of those who had come before him. It was better than any movie he'd seen, and he was reluctant to let it go, even though he knew he'd be best served by not letting it exhaust him.

Knowledge, at least theoretical, filled him; ideas of what was possible spawned and a hunger to learn grew.

Most of the night had passed without his notice when he finally swam toward the shore. He dried and dressed. Paul met him at the door of the little cottage with a large glass of water. Mason nodded his thanks and drained it.

They didn't speak. There was no need. Paul set the table, ladling a rich stew into two wooden bowls. Mason sat and pulled a bowl to him. His pack still stood beside the door where he had put it down when he decided to stay. It reminded him he still had a duty to see to, maybe even more so than when he had originally set out. He had never known his mother's family, not even their name. It must have been locked up with the rest of his memories of her death. But now he had a name. Her memories told him it had been complicated, and there was a reason they had never visited with them, nor had they come to visit her.

"Did you know my mother's people?" Mason asked suddenly, looking at Paul.

"Not so much. I'd met them, of course. Community as small as ours, but her daddy was not a pleasant man."

"She was angry with him." Mason said, though he hadn't figured out why.

Paul chuckled a little. "Might say that. Neither of his daughters were ever very happy with him."

Mason nodded. "Any idea where the family is?"

Paul shook his head and raised his glass of water, draining most of it before answering. "Last I knew, her sister had married and was living in Ohio. The old man must be dead by now."

Mason finished eating and pushed the bowl away. "So, tomorrow we can work on integrating Nana's last breath better?"

"You really should give it a few days." Paul said.

"I've already been here longer than I meant to." Mason replied. "I want to get to Washington, get the Jerah Book of Line. Then maybe see if I can find my mother's family." He knew Paul was probably right. Even with as much as he'd learned, he was woefully ignorant and he'd learned more in these few days with Paul than he had in the last five years. "I can come back, after."

"Okay. If you think you're ready." Paul's voice was doubtful, but he'd agreed, turning his attention back to his food.

Mason wasn't sure he was ready, but he knew he didn't want to wait. He was beginning to feel like all he had done his whole life was wait. "I'm going to call it a night. I'm wiped." Mason filled his glass with water from the pitcher on the table and excused himself to the small room he had been passing the days in. He stretched out on his sleeping bag and closed his eyes. He slipped into sleep quickly, gliding along dreams of strangers who shared his blood.

Chapter Four

Alaric looked out the window of his father's office, watching the gathering throng on ground below. Tension filled the air following the failure of the police to find the vigilantes responsible for the recorded deaths of another black man, and a woman of middle eastern descent who wore a hijab.

The videos had been posted online, picked up by news sites and shown around the world. Similar deaths had happened in Atlanta, Detroit, and Chicago in the last week. There were rumors that the 8th Battalion was becoming an organized threat, not just a scattered ideology shared by random militia groups.

"There's going to be trouble." Alaric breathed as his father joined him at the window. The mood of the crowd was fiery; anger and fear broiled with grief and pain. Even from this distance, it was nearly suffocating him.

The crowd was teeming in the space in front of city hall, pushing against the barricades lined with police officers. It wasn't going to take much of a spark to set off the fireworks. There was a swell of emotion and the crowd was shifting. Alaric squinted as he moved to get a better look. Behind the crowd clamoring for justice, there was a counter protest forming. "This isn't good," Alaric's father said beside him.

The new group was smaller, but still growing. They were loud, screaming some chant he couldn't hear clearly enough to parse through. The front line was filled with signs with big letters spelling out exactly who they held responsible for their problems. The nearest sign had a list with a circle around it and crossed through: Muslims, Shades, Witches, Blacks, Immigrants.

The first group was turning its attention away from the police and city hall and was screaming back at the new group. "This is going to get ugly." Alaric said.

"Yes, it is." Anson agreed.

Suddenly, his father grabbed the back of his neck and pushed him down. Alaric went to his knees, the question on his lips, but before he could ask, something slammed through the window and into the opposite wall. Outside, the yelling became screaming. Shots rang out, the measured beats of a high-powered rifle answered by scattered gunfire from automatic weapons. Alaric dared a glance up, trying to sense what the target was, stretching his gifts out as much as he could.

Both crowds were running, their panic overthrowing their anger as they ran for cover. Alaric spotted cops and others running toward a building to the east, heard people screaming for help and others yelling that the shooter was a terrorist. Emotional chaos washed over him and he dropped his head back down, shaking it at his father' unspoken question. He couldn't see any clear sign of who was shooting or who they were shooting at.

"Anson!"

They both turned to the door, gesturing from the secretary to get down. She crouched and moved across the room toward them. "Are you okay?"

Alaric nodded. It was starting to quiet outside and he could hear sirens approaching. He eased up, peering carefully out the shattered window. There were a number of bodies on the ground. The crowd had dwindled to handfuls of people huddling together behind press vehicles and police cars. Police were moving slowly, guns drawn as they tried to find where the shooter was shooting from.

His father shifted upwards as well, his eyes scanning the streets. *"Did you get anything?"*

Alaric shook his head. His own senses were too blown open to make sense of anything, fear and pain reverberated through him and he forced himself to take a deep breath and tried to retreat behind his shields, walling off the growing grief as people outside the window began to wail for their dead.

There were gunshots now in the distance and the sounds of people moving through the scene below, radios echoing as police and emergency medical personnel began to assess the fallout. Alaric stayed clear of the window as he crossed the room. Outside the open office door, people were coming to see if anyone had been injured.

Alaric stepped into the outer office to further distance himself from the chaos outside, only to be confronted by an odd mix of emotions from the people crowding in around him now. There was a flood of worry and concern, a flash of anger and fear. His hands lifted to rub at his temples, trying to block out the input. His elbow brushed someone, and the emotion coming from him was not what he expected. Where the others dripped with worry, there was smug self-satisfaction, a thought about learning lessons.

Alaric started to turn to figure out who it was, but hands were grabbing him and pulling him out of the crowd, spinning him away down the hall and pressing him against the wall, a soft barrier going up between him and the others.

He swallowed and blinked, forcing his focus back inside and blinking up into Bryan's worried face. He took a few deep breaths and centered himself, nodding his thanks for the reprieve. Once he was sufficiently guarded, Alaric stood up a little straighter and Bryan eased down on the mental wall.

"You were leaking out all over the damn place."

Alaric nodded. "I know. I'm not sure what happened."

Bryan's face softened and he took a step back. "First time you've ever been shot at, it's to be expected."

"What is?" Alaric asked.

"You over extended, how long has it been since you used that actively?"

Alaric glanced at the people who were close enough they might overhear, if they weren't more concerned about finding out what had happened. "A while," he conceded.

"Well, I suggest you start practicing, or this will happen again." He crossed his arms and looked over those who hadn't ventured into his father's office yet or wandered off. "Did you manage to get anything useful?"

"No, just... too much emotion between me and whoever was doing the shooting." Alaric said softly. "What are you doing here?"

"Your father called me."

"He's inside. One of the shots just missed us."

Bryan frowned. "Do you think it was meant for you or your father?"

Alaric shrugged, his eyes scanning over the remaining crowd. "I didn't. But..." He replayed the overheard emotion and its accompanying thought, opening up enough to share it with Bryan. "I'm not sure who it was though, you grabbed me before I could find him."

Bryan's eyes narrowed and Alaric could sense him reaching out. "Whoever it was is gone." Alaric said. "He kept moving."

"You sure?"

Alaric nodded. "I don't sense him anymore." He pushed off the wall. "I should check on Dad." Bryan followed as Alaric eased past an aide and several clerks.

"I'm fine, Alaric is fine. Please, let's focus our efforts on the people outside who need help," Anson was saying as they entered the office. Several of the city office administrative staff were there along with Councilman Marley.

"I'm sure that the police will want to ask a few questions," Marley said, putting a comforting hand on Alice Hanely's shoulder. "Alice, why don't you see if you can get maintenance up here to board up this window. Thom, can you coordinate with security to have a detective come up here to get Councilman Lambrecht's statement?"

"Thank you, Townsend." Anson said, his eyes finding Alaric's and checking in. Alaric sent reassurance that he was okay. Alaric moved to the window, first looking over the dismal scene where paramedics were tending to blood soaked victims and police were still combing through buildings. His eyes moved up then to the hole in the window, not far from where his head had been moments before the impact.

Cracks radiated out from the hole, spider-webbing across the glass. The hole was big. Alaric turned, tracing the likely path of the bullet, finding the spot in the wall where it had impacted. He crossed the room, ignoring the voices around him and focused his attention on the remnants of the bullet. It wasn't likely that he was going to be able read anything from it, especially not in the charged atmosphere around him, but he thought it worth the try.

Blocking out everyone around him, Alaric extended his senses toward the wall, starting outside the hole the bullet had made to give himself time to adjust to the inherent violence he knew he would get from any connection to the actual metal.

Slowly he moved his attention closer to the actual hole, then to the metal that protruded slightly from the wall. He almost recoiled physically from the heat that hit him first, but kept steady and tried to read past it. There wasn't much left of the bullet and nothing left of the last person who had touched it.

He felt the approach of the police and stepped neatly away from the wall, moving to his father's desk. Bryan's unspoken question caused him to look up, making eye contact, followed by thought. "*Not enough left.*"

Bryan nodded. There was no way to know if they had been targeted or not. Alaric was inclined to think not. If it had been another act perpetrated by the 8th Battalion, they had not shown any signs that they were even aware of his kin. And if it wasn't the 8th Battalion, they had even more to worry about.

* * *

Alaric finished answering the police officer's questions and stepped out of the office. It had been hours since the shooting. The death toll stood at seven, two of whom were police officers. The injured numbered around twenty, some with gunshot wounds, others injured in fights that had broken out or by flying debris.

His father was on the phone with his mother and they were still waiting for the maintenance men to come board up the window, but Alaric needed to move.

He headed down to the coffee cart on the first floor that he assumed was doing heavier business than usual. As expected, there was a line. He sighed and resigned himself to waiting, settling into line behind two police officers.

"We need to be careful, Minister."

Alaric turned his head, startled by the clarity and loud nature of the voice. It wasn't spoken. It was a thought.

He stepped back, out of the line and back against the marble pillar that was in the center of the room. He slowly scanned the room, spotting Councilman Roth near the hallway that lead to the council chambers. The man with him was unfamiliar.

He started to reach out, but hesitated. If this man was gifted, he'd be exposing himself. Alaric pulled his phone from his pocket and pretended to be answering texts as a cover for watching them.

They seemed to be talking normally, but he was sure that this was the same man he'd just heard mentally. Alaric couldn't tell what the warning had been about, but the fact that he had called Roth Minister and not Councilman said that his purpose had more to do with the man's profession outside of city hall, and that was concerning.

Roth's church had long championed some of the strictest laws on moral issues. He was anti-abortion, anti-birth control, anti-LGBT, anti-Shade (although that seemed to be a new addition to the repertoire) anti-sex, and anti-pretty much anything that could be interpreted as part of the "liberal agenda" or that the religious right decided was against the will of God.

Alaric turned his face back to his phone as they looked his way. He could feel them watching him. He thumbed a link on his phone to call Riley. He lifted the phone to his ear, smiling as he pushed off the pillar and headed past Roth and the other man.

"Hey, Riley." He kept moving, hoping they would decide he had no clue what they were up to. He snorted to himself. It was true. He knew they were up to something, but he hadn't a clue what it was. "No, we're okay." He stepped out into the main entryway, stopping before he would be visible to the press outside. "I just was wondering if you'd be up for a visit this evening. I thought I'd stop by."

"Which means you need to talk without your father listening in." Riley said with a dark chuckle. "Should I be worried?"

"I don't know." Alaric glanced back over his shoulder, but Roth and his companion were gone. He sighed and shook his head. "I want your opinion on something, before I bring it to Dad."

"Yeah, come on over. Abigail's got a client coming, but we can sit out back."

"Great. See you in a bit."

Alaric lowered the phone and put it back in his pocket. He carefully walled off his concerns and the overheard bits of conversation before reaching for his father mentally. "*I'm heading over to Riley's for a while. See you at home.*"

His father acknowledged the thought with little feedback, so if he suspected Alaric wasn't telling him something, he'd kept it to himself.

Alaric knew that it would be next to impossible to get out of the area through the main entrance, so he let himself back into the lobby and headed back toward the council chambers, taking the south hall and the private back door that only councilmen and their staff had the key to. It let him out onto the shaded south side of the building, away from the chaos of the shooting, and let him bypass the cordons of police and press.

He took the side road out to the main road and hailed a cab. The house that Abigail had inherited was on the end of a dead-end road, set back from the sidewalk with tidy flower beds along the front porch. Alaric paid the cab driver and bounded up the front steps to knock.

Abigail answered, one hand smoothing over her rounded belly as she smiled at him. Alaric kissed her cheek, rubbing his thoughts along hers affectionately. There was an answer that wasn't Abigail's and he raised an eyebrow. She chuckled and looked down at her stomach. "He's going to be a handful."

"I'll say." It wasn't unheard of, but Alaric had never felt an unborn child quite that strong. There were no thoughts, of course, just presence that let him know the child was there, mimicking the emotional waves of his mother.

Riley emerged from the kitchen, two beers in his hand. He passed one to Alaric before kissing Abigail's cheek. "We'll be out back."

There was another knock on the door as Alaric followed Riley, past the staircase and into the kitchen before they emerged out into the small back yard. He took a drink from the beer, wishing that it would wash away the doubt and concern flooding him.

"So..." Riley asked, dropping onto an outdoor chair and gesturing to another. "What's this about?"

Alaric sighed, sitting and looking down at his beer as he gathered his thoughts. He wasn't sure he could even articulate what he was worried about. "Aside from the racial tension and this whole mess with the council?"

Riley shrugged, watching him. "Hey, it's me. I'm the one who said six months ago that civil war was going to come, before we had any of this."

Alaric looked at him. "I'm sure it's crazy." He huffed and took another drink from his beer before he nodded. "So, after the protest and the shooting, I was in the lobby of city hall and I *heard* something."

Riley lifted an eyebrow and sat back in the chair. "I take it that whoever you heard wasn't one of us?"

Alaric shook his head. "No, at least not a face I know. And it was said to someone who I think actively despises us. That's what stopped me cold." He thought back to the moment, the thought. "He said it into Councilman Roth's mind. Just like I would to you or Dad. It was familiar, and Roth didn't seem to react."

Riley frowned. "Maybe he's controlling Roth?"

Alaric didn't think so. "I suppose it's possible, but to what end?"

"Can you show me?" Riley asked, offering his hand.

He put his beer down on the ground and wiped his wet hand on his pants before reaching across to take the offered hand, clearing his mind and centering before he reached out to connect their minds. Once he had a steady rapport, Alaric let the memory play several times.

Riley didn't let go right away and brought up a memory of his own, from the prophetic vision he'd had months before. Alaric was startled to see the same face, this time in military uniform. Whoever the man was, he would play a part in what was to come.

Alaric worried at his lower lip with his teeth, a bad habit his mother had been trying to get him to break. "I don't like this, Riley." Alaric said after a long moment. "Not any of it."

"I'm beginning to think that reading Roth is going to be something one of us has to do." Riley responded.

Alaric shuddered. "I don't know. All that hate is bad enough. He reeks of it. I'm not sure I want any contact with what's underneath it."

Riley shrugged and drank his beer. "You're going to have to tell your father."

Alaric shook his head. "He's got enough on his plate. The protest today, the counter protest, whoever did the shooting. The emotional fallout is huge, and there's going to be more violence before it gets better."

"If it gets better." Riley countered. "You know there's an anti-Shade rally planned for tomorrow night?"

Alaric closed his eyes. "Where?"

"In the park by Roth's church. They're going to release a list of people in the community they claim are Shades and other 'undesirables,' I hear."

"Yeah, that should be a mess." Alaric lifted his beer, draining the last of it. "Do you have any idea if their list actually contains the names of Shades, or are they just pointing fingers?"

Riley shrugged. "I haven't seen anything clearly, and Abigail needs physical contact to do her thing, but I don't want her getting involved."

"No, I don't either. You need to protect that baby." He stood and paced a little. "We should see if we can get the list before they publish it."

"Abigail can give you the name of someone to start with." Riley offered. "You got anything resembling a plan?"

"Nope." Alaric pulled a hand through his hair. "I'm completely playing this by ear. Want to come along?"

Riley grinned, standing. "I'm always up for some craziness. But shouldn't you have someone along with actual gifts that can help you? My random bouts of future glimpsing aren't exactly helpful."

Alaric smiled and clapped a hand to his shoulder. "You're coming to be my lookout."

Riley didn't respond, just led Alaric back into the house, poking his head into the parlor where Abigail was sitting with her client. Alaric felt her response to the interruption, then a name floated to him, along with an image and an address.

It was someplace to start.

Riley grabbed a set of keys and led him out to the beat up old Chevy sitting in the driveway. They headed out for the address Abigail had given him, pulling up in front of an unassuming small house a few minutes later. Alaric could sense at least three people inside. One of them was the woman they were looking for.

He could see her through the window, setting food out for her husband and a son. He found himself wishing he had more active gifts. Empathic ability was great for reading the temperature of a room and knowing when someone was lying or hiding fear, but when it came to reading actual thoughts, it wasn't particularly helpful.

His ability to hear other people's thoughts was mostly due to the intense connection he had with his father and his Keepers. He had only tried to read someone without any of the gifts a few times, and they had all been volunteers who knew what he was doing.

This was different. He wasn't even sure he could read anyone without touching them first. There was only one way to find out. With a glance aside at Riley, Alaric closed his eyes and stilled his mind, setting aside his anxiety and fear. Slowly he reached out for the house.

Immediately, he got love, dedication, family bonds that were very strong. He pushed past the emotion. The woman was tired. Her husband was focused, his attention on the boy who was recounting his day. It was the man that pulled his attention.

He was disciplined, strong willed. Alaric tried to read beyond that wall, but there was a resistance keeping him from getting more than vague impressions. He couldn't be sure if it was his own limitations or if the man had passive shields.

Alaric pulled back into himself. He was shivering, sweat covering his skin, soaking into his clothes. He shook his head to answer Riley's unasked question.

"What do you want to do?" Riley asked.

What he wanted to do was to knock on the door, get a hand on the man and really read him, but he was exhausted, the day's events dragging him down. "Can you drop me at home?" Alaric asked, wiping his face. "I'm not up for much more."

Riley nodded and they pulled away from the curb. Alaric watched the world outside his window, letting the motion of the car lull him. He didn't stir until they were outside his house.

"I'll call you tomorrow." Alaric said, opening his door. "We should be at that rally."

Riley leaned over the seat as Alaric climbed out. "You know what Bryan would say."

"Yeah, I know." Alaric sighed. "So we keep it to ourselves for now. This may be about Shades, but that doesn't mean it isn't also about us."

Alaric shut the car door and headed for the house. Now that the adrenaline of the day's events had burned off, he was physically worn out. He wanted to just go to bed, but he knew his mother would worry if he did, so he made for the kitchen instead.

As he took his place at the table, Alaric pushed all of his concerns behind a privacy wall in his mind. There would be a time and place when he would tell his parents about those things, but for now he preferred to keep them to himself.

Chapter Five

Exhaustion pulled at his limbs, clouding his mind as he moved from the body of a child he couldn't save to a woman who was dying. The disease was spreading faster than even Shades could heal, and it had even started to affect them as they attempted to halt its spread. The medicines they had were ineffective and the number of dead continued to climb.

"It isn't any ordinary disease," he heard someone say and he looked up. "A Shade did this."

He wanted to deny it, but it was the only explanation. Someone had planted this disease, like a spike that would leach out into the body and spread. Already people were afraid and pointing fingers.

"Gavin, get some sleep." A hand came down on his shoulder, the older Shade frowning at him. "You'll do us no good if you succumb."

Fever burned in his skin, starting where that hand touched him and eating into him. He staggered to his feet, pulling away and pointing as he stumbled. The illness was already inside him, blackness soaking into his organs. He fell, grabbing for water, but his hands shook too much and he couldn't get enough to his mouth.

Staggering out of the makeshift hospital, he grabbed at the first person he found, grabbing her and pulling her close so that he could breathe his last into her mouth, hoping the truth would find its way out.

Mason broke the surface of the water, disoriented as he cast about him for something to hold on to. He was panting as he started back toward shore, his head a jumbled mess of memories that terrified him.

It was something he'd never really considered, that a Shade who could heal disease could also spread disease.

It made sense he supposed, and it certainly helped him understand his Nana's fears. She'd warned him about being used for evil, but never really explained what she meant.

He was shaking as he climbed out of the water to grab at the towel he'd left on the shore of the pond. He dried himself and sat, slowly pulling the memory back to him. The Shade was familiar somehow. He held the man's image in his mind and tried to call up more information than just his first name.

"Gavin." He spoke the name out loud, hoping it would spark something. The village was old, something from the old world, back in time and in a place where Shades were obviously accepted for their gifts.

Mason closed his eyes and focused the way Paul had taught him, slipping back into the memory without losing himself in it as he had the first time. A part of him stayed separate to observe, looking at the people and the buildings as Gavin staggered out the door. The clothing suggested some time in the early eighteen hundreds.

Gavin's view of the village was limited and Mason could only guess it was somewhere in Europe. After running through the memory twice, Mason dressed and headed back for the cottage.

Paul was in the garden when he approached, looking up expectantly. Mason didn't say anything, just walked past him into the house. He stopped in the small kitchen, looking at his pack by the door. He had planned to leave, he was packed up and ready to head down the mountain, but a voice inside him said he wasn't ready.

"You okay?"

Mason looked up at Paul in the doorway, shrugging a little. He opened his mouth to respond, but shut it again and shook his head. He didn't know how to broach the subject. "The more I learn, the more I don't know." Mason said quietly.

"More blocks?" Paul asked.

"I'm not sure." Mason sat slowly. They'd taken several days working to overcome the blocks his grandmother had inserted into her own mind, blocks that kept many of the memories of his line suppressed, even once they had been passed on to him. "Gavin Frach." He said the name slowly, the image of the man's face filling his mind.

Paul nodded and moved into the room, pulling out a chair at the table. "I know of Gavin. My mother's grandmother died around the same time."

Mason nodded, his hand idly tracing the lines of the wood table as the memory played through again. "I never…it never occurred to me…"

"Oh." Paul sighed and sat back. "You never realized that what we can heal, we can also cause?"

He shook his head. "It helps me understand why people are so afraid of us."

"There are many reasons they fear us, Mason. Shades like Darchel, for one. And yes, there have been those of us through the centuries that have used the gifts we have to spread disease. There are those that believe the great wave of the black death began with a Shade who was jealous of a man who had won the affections of a girl he loved."

That wasn't the history he had learned, but then, history was mostly written by humans, and until recently, history had relegated Shades to myths and legends, alongside unicorns and werewolves.

"Your grandmother did you no favors refusing to educate you." Paul said.

Mason agreed now that he had a glimpse of how much he didn't know. "How do you fight it?"

Paul frowned a little. "Fight what?"

"A sickness a Shade creates?"

Paul bit his lip, crossing his arms. "It sometimes isn't easy. These are the old ways, lost to most of us." He narrowed his eyes at Mason. "We can…manipulate a disease. In little ways that aren't always easy to spot. It can make it difficult to get rid of. Even if we can heal them, the victim can end up with symptoms that last the rest of their lives."

Mason could feel his grandmother inside him, warning him away, telling him to be a good boy. He held his breath and looked up at Paul. "Can you show me?"

Paul met his eyes, his face stern. "I thought you wanted to go get your book dealt with."

Mason nodded. "I do. But if I leave today or a week from today, or a month. The book will still be there."

"What you're asking isn't easy." Paul said. "It requires control that you don't have yet, and education in things that go beyond what we can do physically. It isn't something I can teach you in a week. Or a month."

There was an urgency inside him, pushing him, despite the warnings of his grandmother's voice. "I'll stay. If you teach me, I'll stay."

The room was quiet for a long moment before Paul stood up. "Okay. Make some dinner. I'm going to go finish in the garden. I need to go into town for some supplies after. You can ride along if you like."

* * *

The sun had been up for nearly two hours by the time they emerged from the trees in an old Chevy truck with dark tinted windows. The town that lay below them was bigger than he remembered, spreading out to fill the valley. It was picturesque as they descended the mountain and headed toward the town's center.

Mason unrolled the sleeves of the flannel shirt he'd donned for this adventure, buttoning the cuffs to ensure most of his skin was covered. Paul handed him a list and a stack of bills. "Get the groceries. I'll handle the hardware store." He dropped Mason outside a Safeway and headed off down the street.

The store had been open for hours, but was still quiet as he pulled a cart from the corral and headed inside. A stock boy looked up, stifling a yawn to smile and say good morning as Mason cleared the automatic door.

He stopped in the main aisle to look over his list, then up at the aisles to get an idea of the layout. Most of the list was canned goods, things that they would use to round out meals that came from the garden, fishing and hunting.

It felt strange, being in the world outside of their little mountain. He'd seen so much of it from the television that it was familiar, and yet it was completely foreign at the same time. Mason pushed his cart toward the aisle, his eyes skipping around him, half expecting someone to be watching him. It was ridiculous.

He hurried through the list, filling the cart with canned goods and cleaning supplies, flour and sugar and spices. He was on his way to the checkout when his eye caught on the headline of a tabloid.

"KILLER SHADES AT LARGE IN AMERICA"

Mason frowned as he reached for the tabloid. There was a picture of Darchel, clearly taken from the day of his arrest, blood covering his face. Under the picture was an article. He skimmed through it, frowning harder. It was filled with flat out lies, including a list of traits to help identify potential Shades hiding in your community, things like pale face due to lack of feeding on human blood, demonic symbols protecting their home or their person, lack of children, and other nonsense.

He shoved the paper back into the rack and continued to the one checkout lane that was open. The magazines that lined the lane were more variants on the theme, including one that promised pictures from inside Darchel's home with the headline, "Inside the Lair of a Killer Shade" and another touting a movie in the making based on some hidden diary of Darchel's. On the cover of Time was that Senator from Utah with a caption that indicated that Norman Douglas was behind a rash of panic-driven laws aimed at Shades specifically.

Mason pushed the fear that surfaced from within him away and unloaded his cart onto the belt, nodding hello to the young man behind the register.

"Did you find everything okay, sir?"

Mason glanced up and nodded again. "Yeah." He watched the man's hands as they scanned his items. A teenage girl appeared at the end of the counter to bag his things. It all seemed remarkably normal. He handed off the cash when the man gave him his total and thanked them both.

Paul hadn't returned yet, so Mason found a place in the shade to wait for him, leaning against the wall of the building. He kept vigilant, his eyes scanning around him. Something had him on edge. It was probably nothing more than the spotlight on Shades, but he wasn't sure.

His stomach lurched, the odd tickle of another Shade filling him. He turned toward the feeling, expecting to see Paul and his truck, instead, he saw a strange figure coming from the corner of the store. He was burned and bleeding profusely, leaving a trail of blood on the concrete and along the wall as he stumbled toward Mason, holding out a hand in desperation.

Mason took a hesitant step toward him, grabbing at him as he started to fall and easing him slowly to the concrete. His skin was burned both from exposure to the sun and something more, his skin charred black. He was bleeding from multiple wounds, more blood than Mason had ever seen. His breath came in wheezing gasps as his hands fisted in Mason's shirt.

"*Help... me...*"

Mason pulled back involuntarily from the non-verbalized plea, his hands moving to the gaping wound in the man's side to try to staunch the flow of blood, but already he knew it was too late.

"I'm sorry." Mason said, pulling the man's hands off him. "I don't know how...it's too..."

But the man was gone, his eyes darkening. Mason blinked as someone screamed, looking up and around him. He stumbled back, into his cart. There was blood on his shirt and hands. People were gathering and he heard sirens in the distance.

"What happened?"

It took a second for Mason to realize that the man beside him was talking to him. He blinked and looked at him, trying to reconcile it. "I...he just came from over there." Mason pointed, though the trail of blood made it obvious. Someone was kneeling beside the victim.

Like someone slowed time, Mason watched as police arrived, then an ambulance. People were moved, and he found himself getting dragged back out of the way as the scene filled with uniforms.

"Mason?"

He tore his gaze from the scene and up to Paul who was suddenly beside him. He distantly recognized that he was standing in the sun and shuffled a little to his right to move into the shade.

"What happened?"

Mason shook his head. "I should have...his line..." It hadn't even occurred to him to take the man's last breath. His line would die with him. Paul grabbed his arm and dragged him further away from the scene.

"Are you saying...?"

Mason nodded. "He was...it was too much. I couldn't..." Even if he'd known where to begin with injuries that catastrophic, he doubted there would have been time to save the man.

"Okay, we need to go." Paul said, his hand firm on Mason's elbow.

"Excuse me."

"Shit." Paul breathed the curse and turned them to face the officer approaching them.

"I understand you were the one who found the body?"

Mason sort of nodded, then shook his head. "He was alive. He found me." The memory of it played in his head, the smell of burnt flesh and blood, and he held his hands up, feeling them flush with the heat that had seeped from the wounds.

"I need to take your statement," the officer said.

"Can't you see how upset he is?" Paul said beside him, his hand moving from Mason's arm to his back.

"I'm sorry, but this is important." The officer made eye contact with Mason. "Did the victim say anything to you?"

"*Help...me...*" Bile rose in his throat and Mason tried to swallow it, but as the words repeated, he lost the fight, doubling over to vomit.

Paul's hand was warm on his back, gently pushing energy into him to calm the physical symptoms of his shock. Mason wiped his mouth and turned back to the officer. "I'm sorry. No. He didn't say anything. He...fell and I caught him, then he died. That's all."

"Sir, do you have reason to believe this victim was a Shade?"

Mason looked up sharply. "What?"

The officer licked his lips and glanced over his shoulder. "This is the second victim with the same types of injuries. The first was a Shade, or so the note said. She was beaten, stabbed, burned and left in a park. There was a note tied to her body that indicated she was a Shade and that this would be the fate of all Shades."

Mason's stomach rumbled and he turned to Paul. "How is he supposed to know if the man was a Shade?" Paul asked. "He just died. It's not like Mason knew the man."

The officer's eyes swept over Mason, fixing on the bloody handprints on his shirt. "Did he touch you, sir?"

"What?" Mason asked, pulling back.

"Did he touch you?"

Mason shook his head. "No, he grabbed my shirt."

"I think it would be best to have you checked over."

Mason pulled away as the officer reached for him. "No, I'm fine. I just want to go."

"We may have more questions."

Mason stepped away. "I told you already. I don't know anything." He could see Paul's truck and headed for it, hoping the officer would take him at his word.

A few minutes later he heard Paul loading the grocery bags in the back of the truck. The door opened and Paul slipped behind the wheel, starting the truck and pulling out of the parking lot before he said anything. "You okay?"

Mason didn't answer right away. He was trying to decide why he was so shaken up over it. It wasn't his first time witnessing death.

Only this Shade couldn't have been much older than Mason himself...
and someone had done this to him, for no reason other than he was
a Shade.

"He asked me to help him." Mason said finally, his eyes on his bloody
hands. "In my mind."

"From what I saw, you couldn't have helped him."

Mason knew that at some level, but it didn't ease the guilt twisting
in his stomach. "Maybe Nana was right." He said it quietly, not even
fully out loud.

Paul's hand touched his shoulder. "The whole world isn't like that."

"Not what I'm seeing." Mason responded. "They're publishing lies
about us, and telling people how to kill us. Hell, they're making a
movie about Darchel." He rubbed his sticky palms together. They were
cold now, the heat of life gone from the blood. "He was one of us. I
could have at least taken his last breath...so his line could go on."

"Don't beat yourself up about it. Lots of us die with no one to take
their last breath. He won't be the last."

"He wasn't much older than me." Mason said, finally glancing up.

Paul didn't respond, just turned them onto the road that would take
them back to their mountain safety, away from a world that seemed
to increasingly hate them for no other reason than their existence.

Chapter Six

Alaric stayed near the back of the park, his eyes sweeping the people around him. Beside him, Riley was a solid center of calm compared to the crazy emotion of the crowd. They were riled up, chanting "No Shades" while foot stomping and fists in the air. The fury was twisting in his stomach.

Near the stage, he could see Councilman Roth, and beside him was the man Alaric had seen him with at city hall. Alaric nudged Riley's elbow and gestured toward them with his chin.

A woman he didn't recognize was with them as well, though her attention seemed to be completely on the crowd. At some unseen signal, she nodded to Roth and he stepped up on the stage to an upswell in sound from the crowd.

Roth held up his hands to quiet them, and eventually they settled, though it wouldn't take much to have them screaming again. Roth looked at the crowd for a long minute before he leaned slightly in toward the microphone. "Americans! Thank you for being here today! Your presence sends a message to the state government that we will not tolerate evil in our midst!"

There was a cheer from the crowd and Roth waited for them to settle. "We have seen what Shades are and we do not want them in our communities." Another cheer went up and Roth beamed out at them. "And once we have dealt with the Shades, we can turn our eyes to other evil, to the things God tells us we must eliminate. The witches,

Muslims, and those who communicate with demons… the fornicators and unbelievers! We must take back our community for God!"

More cheers. Alaric had to reinforce his shields as the emotion swelled and rolled over him. He grabbed Riley's arm and sent his intentions to get out of the park. They started moving backwards, picking their way through the crowd.

"Now, before you leave today, make sure you stop by our table over by the fountain. You can sign up to be on our mailing list, volunteer to help with our initiatives, and get a list of known Shades, witches and other evil doers in your neighborhoods."

Alaric changed their direction, determined to get a copy of the list. If the news from around the country was any indication, someone on that list would be assaulted before the weekend was over.

"Hang back here." Alaric said to Riley as they cleared the back end of the crowd. "I'll be right back."

He headed toward the fountain, skirting the crowd. Three women manned a table under an awning, all smiles as he approached. "Hello, sir. I hope you will volunteer with us."

He offered a tight smile and hoped his voice sounded genuine. "I already do. I was just looking for a copy of the list. I need to know who in my neighborhood needs to go."

"God bless you, sir." The woman in the middle handed him a piece of paper. His stomach was twisting and a sense of urgency filled him.

Alaric took it with a nod and headed back to where Riley was waiting. "Let's get out of here."

Riley nodded, and together they headed for the street. Alaric folded up the paper and shoved it in his pocket. He wanted to get to safety before he looked at it because he felt something coming.

"Where you going, boy?"

Riley froze beside him. Alaric was the one to turn and look. Two middle aged men were approaching them from the park. "Look, guys, we're just leaving." Alaric said, urging calm toward them.

"We didn't say he could leave." The taller of the two was nearly six foot, with broad shoulders that spoke of a lifetime of physical labor.

Alaric could tell that they were furious, whipped up from the rhetoric at the rally and looking for someone to blame. "You one of them Shades, boy?"

Riley turned slowly, his hands clearly out to his sides. "No, boys. I'm no Shade." Riley said, glancing at Alaric. He was afraid, but in control. "I'm just a blue collar guy trying to make a living for my family."

"Bet he's Muslim, Cal. Look at his skin. He look Muslim to you?"

Alaric didn't like how this was playing out. It was clear these two were just fishing for a reason, any reason, to attack them. He took a step forward, pushing calm more strongly at them, but he could tell it wasn't penetrating. He eased between Riley and the two men, putting the car keys in Riley's hand. "*I'm going to give you a head start. Go get the car started.*" Alaric sent to Riley. "Let's talk, gentlemen." He held out a hand as if to shake, knowing one of them was likely to respond automatically. He wasn't disappointed as the shorter one took his hand. "*Now.*"

He used the physical connection to shove a jumble of emotion into the man: confusion, doubt, calm, happiness. Behind him he felt Riley take off running. Alaric released the first man and grabbed at the second who was starting to shout. Alaric knew he only had seconds to subdue him enough to get away before others came to investigate. He grabbed the man's arm, moving with him as he started to follow Riley. He did the same as he had to the first man, then let go and ran for where they left the car.

It wouldn't buy them much time, but it was enough. He jumped into the car and was still pulling the door shut when Riley stepped on the gas.

They were both quiet for a long time as Riley drove them away from the rally and toward Alaric's home. "That was..." Riley shook his head.

"It could have been really bad." Alaric responded, rubbing a shaking hand over his face. "They were..." He had gotten a little bit from them as he'd touched them, enough to know he wasn't wrong about them itching for any reason to beat the shit out of them.

"You exposed yourself." Riley said, looking at him.

Alaric shook his head. "No, they won't realize I did anything. Their heads are too fucked up."

"I think we need to tell your father."

Alaric agreed. "Yeah. It's already worse than we thought."

"And it's just going to get worse." Riley said.

As much as he didn't want to believe that, Alaric knew it was true. Whatever this was, it was just beginning. He pulled the list out of his pocket with hands that shook a bit. The adrenaline of the situation was still flushing through him, and he forced himself to breathe in deep and center, exhaling slowly before he unfolded and smoothed the paper.

There were twenty or so names on the list, and he scanned them for anyone familiar. There were a handful of businesses as well, particularly porn shops and a metaphysical book store. He could feel Riley looking at him. "I don't recognize any names." Alaric said.

"That's good, right?" Riley asked.

Alaric shrugged and folded the paper back up. "Someone on this list is going to get attacked this weekend." There was nothing he could do to prevent it, and he knew it. Knowing didn't make it easier to deal with. "And it won't be long before names of people we love are on lists just like this."

"Do we take it to the police?"

"We can try, but I'm sure they're already watching things. How could they not be?"

"Doesn't seem to be stopping anything," Riley countered.

Alaric sighed and thought through the various ways this could play out. None of them sat very well, and all of them ended bloody for someone.

* * *

"Two men suspected of being Shades were arrested in Georgia last night. An astronomy club made up of homeschooled teenagers was attacked by a mob of people in Louisiana because they were convinced the kids were Shades," Abigail said, her hand soothing over her stomach.

"They haven't come after us," Bryan insisted.

Alaric nodded, putting the paper with the list on the table and smoothing it out. "Yet. Two of them might have attacked Riley simply for the color of his skin today." He glanced up at Bryan. "They aren't the most discriminating group of people."

"It will spread." Abigail said, not looking up at them. "Every day I see the signs. It's like a disease, spreading out around us. If you show no signs of having caught it, you are suspect."

"If we sit idly by and do nothing, they will eventually turn their violence on us." Victoria said quietly. Her hand touched Bryan's shoulder. "You are all too young to remember this within your own lifetime. I am not."

"It's not like we can actually do anything," Bryan countered. "Not without making ourselves targets."

"We can leave." Riley said, drawing all of the eyes in the room. "I said it before. As a clan, we've done it before."

Bryan snorted. "You want us to run? Go into hiding?"

"It doesn't have to be like that." Riley said. "Jordan reminded me of a place."

"The camp," Anson said, "that we have used in recent years as a place for education, where we could practice our gifts openly."

"It's perfect." Riley said. "There are already cabins built, electricity. There's running water and a town within walking distance."

"So not just run and hide," Bryan said. "You would have us separate ourselves from everything."

Riley sighed and looked at Alaric.

"Do you have a better idea?" Alaric asked, looking to Bryan.

His father lifted a hand. "I'll have Jordan head up to the camp, start laying in supplies. I'm not quite ready to say we run, but I want the place ready if we decide we need to." He looked around the room. "I'll spread the word. Anyone who wants to go now can go with Jordan."

Alaric let himself out the back door onto the porch as the others spoke quietly. The impending sense of something coming sat heavy on him.

"You've been spending too much time with Riley," his mother said beside him, her voice soft. "You've started to take on his gifts."

He smiled and held out his arms to her. She moved into them, laying her head on his shoulder as she hugged him. The night was warm, the air still. She kissed his cheek before pulling away and moving to sit on the porch stairs. Out in the yard, behind a series of hedges, he could feel the pull of the orb, pulsing lightly.

Alaric joined his mother on the steps with a sigh. "I'm pretty sure I will never have Riley's gift."

She patted his knee. "One day, you will take your father's place, and then you will have access to all of the gifts."

He tried not to make a face that would give away his distaste for the idea. He should have known she'd know his feelings on the subject anyway. She patted his knee again and smiled. "I'm not saying that it will be anytime soon, Alaric, but the time will come."

"Maybe."

"You are maybe better suited to it than even your father. Your primary gift gives you a head start."

His primary gift was empathy, the ability to read emotion, to feel what others did. It was also said to be able to take emotion from others, to influence the emotion of others, and, in a well-trained and powerful empath, that could become the ability to influence thought as well as the ability to assume the gifts of those around him. He was still working at the first part, using it to affect the emotions of others and reaching beyond emotion to read thoughts and intentions. He sometimes doubted he'd ever be half the empath his father was.

"Your time will come." Her hand caressed his face. She smiled at him and turned her eyes back out into the dark yard. "Trust your heart, Alaric. It knows the way'."

She stood and left him then, returning to the kitchen. He sat for a long time before he stood, following the pull of the orb.

It had been a part of their tribal memory for as long back as any of them could recall. At its center was a core of quartz crystal, clear and round and nearly twelve inches in diameter. Around that core was energy, the energy of a thousand lifetimes poured into it and the legacy of a people once whole, now scattered around the world.

The hedges that protected it from view were only some of its protection. There was a glamor that the orb itself produced that reduced its footprint, shaping the image in the minds of those who were not of its tribe.

Alaric made his way through the brief maze of hedges, stopping as he entered the clearing and the sense of the orb washed over him. It knew him as the third of his father's Keepers, and it welcomed him, warmth flooding his skin.

None but the leader of the tribe could enter the orb, to journey psychically to its center and commune with those who had gone before, but to those who supported the leader a certain level of accessibility was granted. He could draw energy from the orb and he could open himself to it, let it draw out his hidden thoughts, memories he had forgotten. It was calming, just standing there in its presence. Alaric closed his eyes and drew in a steady, centering breath, exhaling slowly as he opened his shields that had been tightly buttoned up since the rally.

The energy rushed into him, filling his senses so that the world outside of the orb faded and there was nothing but him and the orb, pulsing together to the beat of his heart. He gasped as it scrubbed through him, cleaning out the collected muck of emotions not his own. Alaric almost felt as if he was floating off the ground as he relaxed into the embrace of the orb, letting it flow through him and back to the crystal before returning to him again.

Words whispered in the back of his mind, murmurs and secrets he couldn't quite understand, faces passing through as a parade of things he didn't fully see.

"The tribes must unite."

The words were as clear as if they had been spoken and Alaric started, pulling back and stumbling until his back was against the hedge. There was a face in his mind, a man he didn't know, a man he somehow knew he would meet and their lives would become irreversibly intertwined.

Alaric turned from the orb breathlessly, surprised to find his father standing beside him. "What did you see?" Anson asked.

Alaric shook his head. "Nothing. Nothing clearly."

"The tribes must unite." Anson said quietly. "It has been telling me the same for most of the week, but it does not seem inclined to tell me how." They were both quiet for a long moment before Anson patted Alaric's shoulder. "Things are going to get worse."

"Riley's vision?" Alaric asked.

His father nodded. "I can't help but see it being the logical conclusion of the road we're on. Norman Douglas has made it official; he announced his candidacy tonight."

"Great. Just what we need." Alaric said. Of the eight or so men running for the Republican presidential nomination, not one had been unafraid to lay the blame for the economic and societal problems the country faced at the feet of immigrants, people of color, and now Shades and other people who were different. But Douglas was a tone darker than the rest. Already he advocated for separation, camps and prisons for Shades, Muslims, whoever he labeled as an enemy of the people.

Riley had seen war, a civil war that would divide the country and result in death and destruction the likes of which the United States had never seen. In his quiet back yard in a California suburb, it should have been hard to imagine, but all he had to do was remember the faces of those people at the rally and he knew it would come.

War would come and it would be devastating.

Chapter Seven

Mason sat up in frustration, tossing aside the blanket covering him. He wasn't sleeping. No amount of lying there with his eyes closed was going to change that.

He scrubbed over his face, rubbing over the barely there stubble of facial hair that had recently started to show itself. It had been nearly a week since the death of that unnamed Shade and he still couldn't close his eyes without seeing his burned face or hear his silent plea for help.

In that week, Paul had kept his promise, teaching Mason things he should already have learned. That too was frustrating. He felt like a defective machine half the time, uncoordinated and fumbling his way through things most Shade kids could do at nine years old.

Mason stretched as he stood, pacing the small room for a few minutes thinking through the things Paul had been teaching him. Some of the lessons were familiar, echoed by the memories inside him. He turned his attention inward, walking through the exercise of cleansing his energy, flushing out the anxiety before he started an examination of his physical body.

He worked through his organs and tissue, starting at his feet and slowly working through his body, paying attention to blood flow and functionality. It was similar to what he had done before he met Paul. He'd gleaned the knowledge from his book and the memories, but he understood it more now. He knew what he was seeing, knew what his systems did and how so that he could recognize when something was off. He finished with his head, opening his eyes to find himself much more centered than he had been.

He still wasn't going to sleep though, and he sighed.

A glance at his watch told him it was mid-afternoon, which meant he could probably get out to the pond if he was careful. He sat to pull on his shoes, then Mason grabbed his towel and opened the door to his room, walking softly through the house to not wake Paul.

He let himself out the side door of the small house, onto the shaded side, slipping into the trees. The pond was shaded by the stone wall of the mountain on one side, even if the other was in full sun. It meant he had to be aware of himself so that he didn't accidentally float into the sun, but it also meant he could sink into the cool, clear water in the deep part of the pond.

Keeping to the tree cover, he made his way to the water, stopping to drop his towel and clothes on the big boulders beside the water. The air was warm, and the water had heated with the sun so it wasn't as cool as it usually was when he climbed in.

Mason waded out until the water was at his waist, then eased himself down, swimming out to where the water was well over his head. With a deep breath, he sank down into the darkness, closing his eyes and opening his senses to the rush of energy that came from the water.

Almost immediately his mind filled with the image of that dying Shade. Mason pushed it away and tried to work on his focus. He forcibly pulled up the memory from the night before, when Paul had cut his own hand repeatedly to let Mason attempt to heal it.

By the time he'd managed to close it completely, he'd been shaking with fatigue and sweating. Paul insisted that he would improve with time and practice, but Mason wasn't as sure. He surfaced, wiping water from his face as he did. He thought he heard voices. He held still and listened, his eyes scanning around him. He could almost feel a presence.

Slowly, Mason moved toward the shore, his attention high, his eyes scanning the trees. He reached his towel and started to dry himself off. He froze as the voices sounded again, this time closer.

"It's over there." Mason pulled his pants on just as two people appeared on the sunny side of the pond. "See, I told you."

They were likely his own age, one man, one woman, both dressed for hiking and carrying large packs. Mason watched them as he pulled his shirt on.

The woman started as her eyes found him, her hand instantly on her companion's arm. "We aren't alone."

Mason raised a hand in greeting. He was cautious. Very few hikers ever came up this way, which was why both his grandparents and Paul had chosen to live there. He pulled on his shoes and circled the rocks, keeping to the shadows of the trees as much as he could.

"Don't see many folk out this way." Mason said in way of greeting. The man moved toward him, his hand out. Mason shook it, smiling.

"Yeah, we needed out of the city for a few days. Figured some hiking would clear our heads a bit."

Mason nodded, looking from the man to his companion and back again. "Hiking is good for that."

"I'm Matt, this is my girlfriend, Heidi."

Matt was shrugging out of his backpack, but Heidi still looked a little spooked by Mason's appearance. "Well, this is good for a cool off, but if you're looking for some privacy, you might want to head that way once you're done. Couple of cabins up this way, people using this pond all the time." He pointed to the north and east. "Good spot to post camp about two miles from here. There's a creek good for fishing."

"Appreciate it. Not sure Heidi has another two miles in her though."

Heidi was looking at Mason, her eyes narrowing as if she was trying to figure him out. "You live up here?" Heidi finally asked as she lowered her pack.

"Not really. My place is further up the mountain. I'm just visiting a friend." Mason smiled and pulled a hand through his wet hair. "Which I should be getting back to. You guys enjoy."

He didn't like them being so close, but it wasn't like he could just kick them out. It wasn't his land. He nodded and started back, listening to them set up camp until he was out of hearing range.

The sun was starting to consider setting as he approached the small cottage, and he wasn't surprised to find smoke curling up from the chimney. He opened the door, dropping his damp towel over the back of a chair just as Paul came into the room.

"I was just going to head out to the pond to join you."

Mason's nose crinkled. "We have company at the pond. Two kids hiking. They're making camp for the night."

Paul shrugged. "It happens. First time in a while, but it happens." He moved to the wood burning stove and adjusted the pot so that it was over the open burner. "Did you talk to them?"

Mason shook his head, sitting at the table. "Not really, tried to tell them there was a better camping spot north of here, but I got the impression the girl wasn't much of a hiker."

"Maybe we should go share our dinner with them, see if they can fill us in on any news."

"What?" Mason frowned. He had seen enough of the news on their trip into town.

Paul turned to him, crossing his arms. "It pays to be aware of the world, Mason. Especially if you're still planning on heading out into it to get your Book of Line."

"Yeah, every time I learn more about the world out there, the more I think Nana was right to hide away from it." Mason muttered.

"All the more reason we should go talk to these people. There's a basket in the closet. Get it for me."

Mason did as he was asked, putting an old fashioned picnic basket on the table. Paul spent the next half hour filling it with tin plates and utensils, fresh bread he pulled out of the oven, butter and a variety of vegetables he'd pulled from the garden. Lastly, he put a lid on the cast iron pot and they headed out.

Heidi and Matt had their tent up and were working on a fire pit as they approached. "Hey, look who's back." Matt said, looking up at them.

"Mason told me we had company in the area, and it's so rare, I told him we should be neighborly. We brought dinner." Paul moved to put the basket and the pot down near the fire pit, rubbing his hands against his jeans before reaching out to shake Matt's hand. "I'm Paul."

Matt took the hand with a smile. "Matt, this is Heidi."

Mason got the brief impression of Paul doing *something* to Matt, but then he was reaching a hand to Heidi. "You two are a long way from anywhere." He sat on the ground beside the basket, beckoning Mason closer. "I figure you have to have been hiking for a few days, and a meal that doesn't come out of a can probably sounds good."

Matt sat on the ground across the small fire pit from Paul. Heidi still looked a little suspicious, but she sat beside Matt, laying kindling and slightly larger pieces of wood into the pit. She pulled a lighter from her pocket and lit the fire.

Mason took the remaining space, between Paul and Heidi as Paul opened the basket and started dishing up food. "It isn't fancy, but it's good and hot."

"We appreciate it." Matt said, passing a dish of the pasta to Heidi. The food was hearty, a thick gravy covering pasta, with sausage and pheasant, plus onion and garlic.

Mason took his dish with a nod. "I told them we don't get many visitors up here."

Paul nodded. "That's the truth. The last time we had anyone in the area was deer season a year or two back. Couple of hunters got turned around." He stabbed at his pasta and smiled. "So, how is it you came to find out hidden little pond?"

Matt swallowed a mouthful. "My dad used to come up here when I was little. I remembered this pond. We camped here one year."

Paul nodded. "Headed anywhere special?"

To Mason's surprise, it was Heidi that answered. "Not really, just...not in town." She seemed to relax, her shoulders lowering as she chewed. "We have some time before we go back to school."

Mason glanced at Paul, wondering if he'd done something to her to make her more cooperative. "A friend of ours was killed." Matt said, his eyes on the flames. "He..." He shook his head. "It wasn't pretty."

Mason's thoughts flashed to the man he'd watch die. Paul's hand reached out to Matt's knee, touching gently.

"We just needed to get away." Heidi added, looking up at them. "There's so much fear in the air at home."

Paul nodded, pulling his hand back. "We went to town a week or so ago."

They ate in silence for a few minutes before Paul changed the topic. "So, where do you go to school?"

As Matt started to answer, Paul spoke into Mason's mind. *"I want you to read them."*

Mason frowned at him, unsure what he meant. *"If you need to, find a reason to touch her, but read her body."*

Mason let the conversation flow over him, shifting a little closer to Heidi until he could let his knee connect with hers. He focused inward first, calming the drumming of his heart and controlling his breathing before he let his attention move to her, first through the knee where they touched, then into her body.

It was disorienting at first, being inside a body that wasn't his own or Paul's, but he pushed that aside. She was fit, muscular. Except…something wasn't right. Mason could feel his face frowning, even as he tried to follow the trail of some illness.

There was something inside her that wasn't normal. He followed the pull instinctively, until he found a mass that didn't belong.

He realized that the conversation had stopped and opened his eyes, popping out of his trance-like state. Paul had his hand on Matt's knee and Matt's eyes were glazed over. Heidi jumped, as if just realizing something had changed.

Mason brought his hand down on her knee, pushing into her and inelegantly urging sleep onto her. She slumped against him as he shifted to support her. "What are we doing?" Mason asked, once he was sure she was out.

Paul just nodded toward Heidi. "What did you find?"

"I'm not sure. A tumor of some kind. Maybe cancer."

Paul moved so that he had better control of Matt. "Good. So tell me how you would treat it."

Mason blinked up at him. "I'd send her to a doctor."

Paul rolled his eyes. "You can do better. Close your eyes, follow what is feeding it, separate it from the source to start with."

Mason licked his lips and exhaled slowly before he closed his eyes and put his hand on Heidi's stomach, just over where the tumor was. It wasn't big, but something told him that it would grow in coming weeks. He felt his way around it, figuring out where it was attached and how.

"Good. Now, tell me if it's safe to detach it."

Mason wasn't sure. He had no idea what to do with it if he did manage to detach it. He urged energy into her body, watching it flow over and around the tumor. *"I think it's safe to detach it, but then what?"*

"Then you help the body absorb what it can and flush what it can't." Paul's hand covered his, his mind guiding Mason's to slowly pull the mass away from the tissue. It took time, but eventually it detached and Mason could pull it away, turning it over to determine how to do what Paul said.

Paul directed more energy at the detached tumor, penetrating it and slowly it began to break apart. Paul pointed out the parts that wouldn't just absorb back into the body and Mason watched as he encapsulated them inside an energy barrier, moving the whole thing through her intestinal track toward her bowels.

"She should pass that on her own now. The barrier should hold for at least twelve hours." Paul backed off and let Mason explore what he had done. Mason followed it up by flushing some gentle healing energy through her before he pulled himself up and out. Paul met his eyes and gestured to Heidi. "She going to stay out?"

Mason nodded. "For a few minutes at least."

Paul beckoned him, welcoming Mason easily into the light trance that had Matt enthralled. *"Now that you've seen how it comes apart, can you recreate it?"*

Mason frowned and almost pulled away, but Paul pulled him closer. "*Watch.*"

He looked on in astonishment as Paul used his memory of the composition of the tumor to call elements together inside Matt's stomach. He stopped short of making it malignant, but it was easy to see how he could.

"*Okay, I get it.*" Mason said.

"*Do you?*" Paul did let him pull out of the connection. "*It gets worse; can you tell how?*"

Mason's stomach churned and he wanted to tell Paul to stop, but a part of him knew this is what he needed to learn, and he had asked Paul to teach him. He exhaled slowly and let himself explore around and into the tumor Paul had created. He could clearly see how to make the tumor grow, how to take it from a fairly benign growth into something cancerous that would eat away at the man.

He was nearly ready to admit defeat when he realized what Paul was leading him to. Once the tumor was malignant, it would be, well not *easy* exactly, but simple enough to turn it from something that would kill Matt within a year into something he would spread to others before he died.

He got the impression of Paul nodding. "*Good. Now take care of this.*"

Paul pulled up and out and left Mason to clear out the tumor. He followed the same procedure Paul had shown him with Heidi, sitting back when he was done and looking up at Paul.

"Good. Now then, I think we should let them up. They should just think they dozed off."

Mason settled back into his place between Paul and Heidi and eased back his control of her sleep. Matt came up first, since Paul's touch had been a little lighter. He stirred, stretching and yawning with a sheepish grin.

"Sorry, I guess the hiking wore us out."

"No apology necessary." Paul insisted. He started cleaning up dishes and packing them back into the basket. "Mason and I will let the two of you get some sleep. Just remember to make your camp bear safe. We haven't seen any in awhile, but that's no reason to be stupid about it."

"Will do. Thank you for dinner. I wish we could repay you."

Paul smiled as he stood. "No need. Do the same for someone you meet along the way, and I'll consider it even."

Matt's smile was easy and wide and he reached out to shake Paul's hand. "That we can do."

Heidi was stretching and yawning as Matt shook Mason's hand. "I should get her into bed. It's been a long day."

Paul led the way and Mason followed, glancing back as Matt cajoled Heidi up and toward the tent. When they were out of earshot, Mason grabbed Paul's arm. "What was that?"

He turned to look at Mason, his eyes dark. "A lesson."

"You were playing with that man's life." Mason argued.

"I was completely in control. I wouldn't have pulled that trigger."

"What if it had gotten away from us?" Mason asked. "We didn't have permission to do any of that."

"No, we didn't. And if we'd left Heidi alone, she would have died of stomach cancer in the next two years."

"You don't know that." Mason argued.

"No?" Paul started walking again. "You don't know that maybe, but I do. I've been trained in how to be a Shade since I was five."

Mason had to concede that point. That was, after all, the reason he had chosen to stay, to learn. Paul stopped as they neared the cottage, turning to look at him. "You aren't wrong. It isn't something I would consider doing anywhere or anytime else. But living up here, we aren't going to get a lot of opportunities for hands on learning on anyone other than each other." He sighed and shook his head. "If it helps, they'll both sleep good, have a nice morning constitutional, and it will all be over."

"Doesn't make it right." Mason said.

"Unfortunately, with the way things are right now, it may not be right, but it's certainly safer if they never know you were there."

He could see that. The fear of Shades did make it unsafe to openly practice the most impressive of their gifts. Still, he wondered if maybe his time with Paul was done. He'd learned a lot. He had control of the collected lifetimes of memories inside of him.

It was time to move on to his family obligations. Before the world outside his mountain became scarier than it already was.

Chapter Eight

Business as usual felt anything but usual. The window in his father's office had been repaired, the hole in the wall plastered over and painted. You'd almost think nothing had ever happened.

Except, Alaric knew better. His eyes kept straying to the place where the bullet had penetrated the wall. He sighed and dragged his eyes back to the numbers he was preparing for his father.

The entire city was tense. It felt like everyone was walking on eggshells, afraid that one wrong word would set off a fire that wouldn't end without bloodshed. Nothing had happened in the last few days; well, nothing that the news picked up on.

South of them, in San Francisco, there had been a protest that had gotten pretty intense before it was broken up. Los Angeles was reporting a third day of riots after a measure had been suggested, an ordinance not unlike the one he was working on defending against. They weren't alone.

Most of the major cities, especially those in the south and Midwest, were considering similar measures. Of course, every one of them was being disputed, and even the White House had made statements about not ostracizing American citizens. The President himself had promised that he would not sign any law that came to his desk. He had even warned that these measures and ordinances on the local level were unconstitutional. Unfortunately, the sane voices were mostly getting shouted over by various conservative groups, and, in staunchly Republican states, the rhetoric was getting attention from state legislatures.

It was going to end up being something that would have to be challenged at the Supreme Court level.

Alaric sighed and turned his attention back to the information he had gathered. Councilman Roth's list of ordinances was nearly draconian. If he got his way, all of those he considered "undesirable" would be forced outside of the city limits and into what would amount to internment camps, complete with armed guards at the gates. Of course, that was outside the purview of the city council.

The measure to restrict Shades was likely to pass, no matter what numbers Alaric provided his father. It would start with registration, and then limit the locations where registered Shades could live. He had no idea how many Shades actually lived within the city limits, and estimates varied wildly. His father estimated somewhere under fifty in the suburbs, including the relatively quiet suburb they called home, based on what the globe could tell him.

Fear based estimates claimed at least fifteen hundred. It didn't help that as fear grew and laws got rammed through, small numbers of Shades were striking back. Several had been arrested for retaliating violence, and there were rumors about strange epidemics of illnesses that weren't usually fatal suddenly taking lives as they swept several states.

The movie about the killer Shade, Darchel, was being rushed through production, despite protests and the trouble they'd had early on with writers battling the studio who asked that the horror be amped up. Alaric knew that the violence would escalate in response when it finally came out. He sighed and stood, stretching out tense muscles and crossing to the coffee pot. The very air felt tight, tense, like anything could crack it open and make it bleed. He sighed again, filling his coffee cup and trying to decide if what he was feeling was an omen of something big waiting to happen or just the accumulated tension of a city on the edge.

He looked up as his father came into the room. Anson was angry, the emotion rolling off him despite his best efforts to contain it, but his mind was closed off, so Alaric had no idea what had angered him.

"Dad?"

Anson dropped into his chair, scowling. "Roth."

Alaric waited for more, but his father stayed quiet. "I've been working on those estimates you wanted." Alaric offered into the stiff silence.

Anson shook his head. "Doesn't matter now."

Alaric frowned. "What happened?"

"Roth and his cronies." He inhaled sharply, closing his eyes and visibly pushing his anger aside to allow him some clarity. "I overheard him. They've gotten an emergency bill into the state that makes his measures here look like playground politics... And they seem to think it's going to pass."

"It won't hold up." Alaric said, sipping at his coffee.

"No, but it will do a lot of damage before it's struck down. And it's just the beginning. They have a slew of other laws that they're going to push through riding on this morality wave." He shook his head and stood, moving to the window. For a long moment he stood there, staring out at the streets. "You know, I ran for this seat because I thought I could do some good. I'm beginning to think I would serve our people better if I stepped down and focused on leading just our clan."

Alaric put his coffee down and crossed to his father's side, carefully marshalling his own emotions behind his shields. "You know I'll stand with you, regardless."

"I know, son." They stood silently for a long moment, then Anson sighed. "In the meantime, show me these numbers. Maybe we can make reason overcome this put-on moral outrage that Reverend Roth is peddling."

* * *

"There was another one."

Alaric looked up from his computer screen to find his mother in the door of his room. "Another what?"

She sighed and crossed her arms. "Another fire. Another 8th Battalion attack. Two more people are dead."

"Where?" Alaric asked, though he was already flipping to his internet window to search.

"Just outside Sacramento. Young couple."

He typed the words "8th Battalion" into the search bar and held his breath as he hit enter. The screen filled with results, each headline worse than the one before. "Not just one." Alaric breathed, checking the dates and locations on all of the headlines. "In the last forty-eight hours, there have been attacks in fifteen cities."

Alaric turned his monitor so she could see it as he clicked through a link that seemed to be rounding up the stories into one article. His eyes skimmed the screen, picking out the pertinent details. "Fifteen people confirmed dead, another four wounded. Information at all of the scenes alleges that the 8th Battalion had killed someone they claimed was a danger to society. In New York and Boston, they labeled the victims as Muslim terrorists. In Salt Lake, Phoenix, Los Angeles, and Sacramento, the 8th Battalion claimed they were Shades. The rest were gang leaders, an abortion doctor, and at least one of them was said to have been a witch."

"It's getting worse." Her hand rubbed on his shoulder and she shook her head. "I've never seen this kind of hysteria."

Alaric took her hand and pulled her closer. "I know."

"Abigail called earlier. Someone vandalized the shop where she sees clients sometimes. They spray painted 'witches' across the windows and covered the door in notes that said, 'Thou shalt not suffer a witch to live,' and other threats."

Alaric frowned. "When did that happen?"

His mother shook her head. "They found it this morning."

"Does Dad know?"

"I'm sure he does." She caressed his head, then leaned it to kiss his cheek. "Dinner in an hour."

He nodded and watched her go. It was stifling, sitting there watching the world crack and unable to do anything stop it. His phone rang and Alaric picked it up from where it lay on his desk, swiping the screen when he saw Riley's number. "Hey, what's up?"

Before Riley even spoke, Alaric got a blast of anger and a good dose of fear from him. "You busy?"

"No, just finishing up some email stuff. Is Abigail alright?"

"Huh? No, she's fine. Angry, but fine." Riley fumbled with the phone. "I had a...I saw something."

When he didn't elaborate, Alaric nodded. "Okay. I can be there in ten minutes."

He hung up and bounded out of his room and down the stairs into the kitchen. "Don't hold dinner for me. Riley just called. Not sure how long I'll be."

He kissed her cheek and headed out to his car. He took the back streets as dark clouds billowed in from the west. Riley was sitting on his front porch as Alaric pulled up, and he could feel Riley's anxiety before he even got out of the car.

"Hey. You okay?"

Riley sort of shrugged and stood, gesturing into the house with his head. "Abigail is still at the shop helping them clean up."

"I heard." Alaric let Riley lead the discussion, following him into the living room.

Riley paced as Alaric leaned on the door frame. After a few minutes of silence, Riley stopped, looking up at Alaric and nodding. "I'm still trying to sort it out."

"Okay."

He huffed and scrubbed his hands over his face. "It was one of those really disjointed ones, where it was just flashes of things in no logical order."

Alaric nodded. Riley's gift was often the hardest to learn to understand and control. Often, when the visions came, if the seer wasn't prepared, they could be difficult to interpret.

"It's…I think it's something about the 8ᵗʰ Battalion. And Shifters. I think." He rubbed his forehead. "There's a building in Sacramento with labs of some kind. I think they have a Shifter… and others. Possibly a Shadow, one of us."

Alaric stood up straight. "Wait, are you saying they have prisoners?"

Riley crossed the room and held out his hand. Alaric could already feel his shielding rolling back and he followed suit as he set his hand on Riley's. The vision played out between them, first as it had come to Riley., Then Riley pulled it apart and attempted to put it into some sense of order.

Small basement room, men in dark blue. Symbol on a whiteboard of a cross superimposed on a burning heart. Map with red dots calling out targets. Flash. White lab, people in lab coats, medical equipment. Cages. People in cages. A woman cowering from a man in a lab coat, growling like an animal. "Conditioning isn't working." A half familiar mind, the touch of another Shadow. "Leave it to me."

Alaric stepped back, letting the vision replay in his head. It was hard to tell how exactly it was all related, but he could see why Riley thought it was. "Tell me what you think it is." Alaric said softly.

Riley went back to pacing. "Honestly? I think they have a Shadow, a real Shadow, working for them, and they're trying to make assassins."

"You got a sense of him? His strength?" Alaric asked, frowning. He hadn't gotten more than that the man was an adept. "And the woman, she's the shifter? How do you know?"

Riley shrugged. "I'm not sure. I mean, I just know."

"Shifters are rare. I haven't even heard of one in years."

"I know." He exhaled. "It isn't just the images. I got… more. That woman needs help."

"Whoever that man is, the one you think is one of us, he isn't a prisoner." Alaric said.

"I know."

Alaric moved to the couch and sat slowly. "And if they're using someone with abilities to condition people…" He trailed off, not even wanting to consider what that could mean.

"I know." Riley sank into the chair, hands on his knees. "And who were the men in that small room, and how do they relate to the rest. What was that map showing? This is ridiculous." His agitation was clear.

"You said it was 8th Battalion." Alaric said, attempting to direct his energy in a more productive way.

"Yeah, I got the impression that the men were 8th Battalion, and they were planning something…" His face took on the look of someone in an altered state and Alaric could feel him *reaching* to try to recapture the moment. "Can't see it clearly. And then, it's gone."

"It's okay, Riley." Alaric soothed.

"No, it isn't." Riley stood explosively and went back to pacing. "For fuck's sake. I have no more control of this than I did when I was fifteen."

Alaric knew Riley had been working at it. He had been for as long as Alaric had known him. It just wasn't an easily tamed gift. "Have you talked to Abigail about it?"

Riley shook his head. "She's stressed enough with the baby, and the stuff at the shop… I don't want to add to it."

"There isn't enough to go on."

"I know that." Riley snapped. He closed his eyes and pulled his frustration back. "I'm sorry. I got a full dose of that Shifter's fear. It's got me on edge."

"What do you want to do?" Alaric asked softly.

"I want to know where they are so we can do something." Riley responded.

"Well, we could try to bring out more of the vision." Alaric offered.

Riley's eyes narrowed. "How?"

"The orb. We'd probably need my father too, though."

Riley nodded slowly. "Yeah, that might be good."

"Not sure what you expect we can do about it, but it might help just to get a fuller picture."

"When?"

Alaric reached out for his father, who responded almost immediately. He relayed the pertinent information and felt his father's affirmation. "Now, if you're up to it."

"Let me leave Abi a note."

Riley left the room and Alaric stood, twirling his car keys. His sense of some impending storm had only grown. The man in Riley's vision felt familiar, yet he wasn't part of Alaric's clan. He wasn't convinced he was part of the tribe either. He was an anomaly, not unlike Riley's mother, someone who came by their gifts not by birth necessarily, but through other means. Not that it was any better.

They were quiet as Alaric drove them back to his parent's house. "Dad's out back already." Alaric said once he'd parked. "He wants you to take a minute, get centered. You've never gotten close to the orb before, and it can be pretty intense."

"Yeah, okay." Riley rubbed his palms down his legs.

"I'll wait for you by the back gate. Come to me when you're ready."

Alaric acknowledged his father's instructions and got out of the car, heading into the house to drop off his keys. His mother nodded to him, but didn't move to get close. Alaric passed through the kitchen and out into the back yard, cutting across the lawn to the start of the hedge. His father was already inside and Alaric hesitated briefly, letting his shielding adjust to the power of the orb and letting his father call him when he was ready.

Alaric stopped just inside the opening, closing his eyes as the orb surged, filling him up and momentarily blinding him to everything else. When it had normalized again, he turned to his father. "Are you sure about this?"

He shrugged minutely. "No, but it feels important enough."

"Is he ready?" Anson asked.

"I don't know."

"It's been a long time since anyone from outside the tribe has come to the orb." Anson shifted, holding up both hands to forestall the argument. "He's family, Alaric. But his father was barely kin and his mother was not. In times past he would hardly be considered a part of the tribe."

"Good thing we don't live in the past then." Alaric offered.

Anson nodded. "Okay then, bring him."

Alaric separated himself from the orb and headed to the gate that opened into the side yard. Riley was there when he opened it and Alaric stepped aside to let him in. With the gate shut behind them, Alaric put both hands on Riley's shoulders. "Okay, we're going to start with your shields up. I don't want it to be too much for you. I'm also going to shield you. We'll go in and let them down in layers, giving you time to adjust."

He could feel Riley's default shielding going up, followed by a more formal set of shields. "Good." Alaric bolstered those shields then nudged them into motion.

It felt strange, moving them in tandem back toward the hedge. The orb pulsed as they approached, pushing against the shields as it detected someone unknown. Almost like a person would, it explored around the shields, felt its way through Alaric and slowly Alaric began to release his hold, letting the energy wash against Riley's own shields. "*Slowly now,*" he sent, making sure Riley was fully in control as he pulled back.

Riley gasped as the orb embraced him, his shields dropping a little erratically and Alaric kept his hands on Riley's back to steady him. His father moved closer physically before mentally joining the light rapport between Alaric and Riley.

"*Relax, Riley. The hard part is over.*" He guided them both to sit as he built a container of sorts. "*No filters, just dump it all here.*"

Riley did as instructed, dumping the unprocessed memory of the vision into the container. The energy from the orb surged, encircling them even as Alaric's father tried to control the direction.

There was no guarantee that this would work at all, but as Alaric watched, the vision filled up the container, stretching out and becoming more experiential than just seen. He could smell the closeness of the room, the nearness of men who had not showered in a while, the sharp tang of an accelerant. Voices whispered around him, fervent, but just out of reach.

A man in uniform stood by the map, pointing to a place near Washington, D.C., then a spot in rural Oregon. "*Found her there. Could be more. Go find out.*"

The man in uniform moved and the room changed around him until they were in the lab. "*Show me.*"

"*She is most resistant.*" A man in a lab coat approached a cage, sticking a cattle prod through the bars. He zapped her several times and she screamed, her eyes taking on a gold hue as her body started to morph. Cat like features began to appear before she gained control again and pulled back.

"*Get her on the truck tonight. I want her taken to our compound.*"

Images of trucks and a road followed, through mountains and into high desert where there was a handful of buildings low to the ground surrounded by miles of fence.

Abruptly, the replay ended and Riley slumped a little, his eyes closed. Alaric looked up at his father, who was clearly replaying the images.

"*The tribes must unite.*" Alaric frowned, trying to find the source of the words. The woman's face filled his mind, her fear palpable. "*The tribes must unite.*"

Riley stirred under his hands, and his father was dismantling the container, letting the vision slip back to its place in Riley's mind. He nodded and Alaric understood he was to ease Riley out. He got them up and onto their feet, guiding Riley out of the grove and out into the yard. Alaric helped Riley sit on a deck chair and pulled a hand through his hair.

Riley looked up at him, still a little spaced out. "Mason."

"What?"

Riley blinked, shaking his head. "Mason. I saw a face. And something about the tribes."

"The tribes must unite." Alaric said. "Yeah, I've heard it before. Not sure what it means exactly."

"We can't leave her there." Riley said, his face showing his distaste.

"What do you suggest?"

Riley shook his head. "I don't know."

"Riley is right." Alaric's father said as he approached. "We need a plan." He crossed his arms and looked down at Riley. "For starters, we need to figure out where that building is. I need solid information."

"I wish..." Riley inhaled and stood. "I can't even tell you when, let alone where."

Anson smiled. "I know son, but the information is there. We just need to find a better way to access it."

"He's tried." Alaric interjected. His father put a hand on Alaric's shoulder.

"And now we'll try together. Riley, I need you to prepare for some seriously deep work. Make what arrangements you need to, but you and I are going to spend however long it takes to get the information out of that vision. Let Abigail know you'll be gone for a few days. Then I want you to get a solid eight hours of sleep. When you wake up, take a hot shower and eat a protein heavy breakfast."

"Yes, sir."

"Good boy. We'll see you in the morning."

They watched Anson walking into the house before Riley turned to head for the gate. "You should let me take you home." Alaric said.

"Abi's on her way home, she'll pick me up." Riley responded. "I'll see you tomorrow."

Chapter Nine

"You don't have to leave." Paul said as he pulled the truck to a stop beside the bus station.

"No, but I think I should." Mason countered. "I've learned a lot, and I need some time to put it into practice." He turned to look at Paul. "Thank you for everything. I promise to keep learning."

"Just be careful out there." Paul said. "Don't show your hand. Stay out of crowds. Don't trust water that isn't free flowing."

Mason smiled and nodded. "I'll be careful. When I get home, we'll have to get together."

"I'd like that."

Mason climbed out of the truck and pulled his freshly repacked pack from the back, shrugging into it before waving and heading for the station. He crossed dirty concrete to the window and smiled at the woman behind the glass. "I need a ticket to Washington D.C. please."

Her fingers tapped at the keyboard. "Our next bus on that route leaves at four and is two hundred and fifty dollars."

"Sounds good." He pulled his wallet out and fished out the money he'd taken out of his Nana's account when he closed it. A few minutes later, he had a ticket and a little over two hours to wait.

Mason walked toward what passed as a lounge for waiting passengers. There were a number of people there, clustered in small groups. There were a few vending machines with soda and snacks. Mason shrugged out of his pack as he approached an empty bench.

Nearest him were an older couple with a small suitcase looking at a map. By the vending machines was a group of kids he assumed were his age, all with the name of some college on their sweatshirts or backpacks. There was a family too, mother and father and three kids under fifteen.

Mason felt the father's eyes and looked up, feeling a familiar twist in his stomach. His eyes widened slightly as he recognized another Shade. He nodded tightly in acknowledgement and shifted a little uncomfortably on the hard bench. Nothing in his life had prepared him for what he was doing. If he thought too much about it, his heart would race and he would break out in a cold sweat.

Instead, he focused on double checking the ties that held his small tent and sleeping bag to his pack. Something about the way the man kept looking his way made him nervous.

"No, Hamblin is a wuss." A man's voice boomed into the room bringing Mason's eyes up to the entrance across from him. "He won't last until the first debate. He's too soft on Shades and immigration."

"Douglas has it wrapped."

Three men entered the lounge, tall and wide and dressed in jeans and flannel. They stopped just inside the room, eyes sweeping over the various people waiting there. One of them gestured to the benches between Mason and the teenagers and they moved that way, dragging suitcases with them.

"Douglas understands us." The speaker was dark haired, his face half covered in facial hair. "He's gonna defend our right to protect ourselves from those freaks."

Mason glanced at the other Shade, who looked as uncomfortable as Mason felt. He found himself hoping these men were waiting on a different bus. As they carried on, talking about a number of different groups they needed to defend themselves from, Mason slid down the bench a bit, away from them, then got up, hefting his pack and starting to walk to the end of the lounge, nearer the Shade and his family.

He put his pack down beside a chair and turned to sit. One of the men was staring at him. He licked his lips, trying to decide if he needed to worry. A tentative touch on his hand brought his attention closer to himself, and the little girl who was smiling at him, her grin missing two teeth. "Do you want a cookie?" she asked him.

She held up a bag with small cookies in it. Before Mason could open his mouth to respond, her mother was there, hands on the girl's shoulder. "Honey, don't bother the man."

"It's no bother ma'am." Mason replied, echoing the girl's smile.

"I like him," the girl said, looking up at her mother. "He's like us." She whispered the words, and Mason caught the fear on the mother's face.

"I tell you what," Mason offered, "if you share your cookies, I'll share the cake I've got in my pack." He met the mother's eyes, trying to let her know she was safe, that he wasn't going to alert anyone to what her husband and children were. He reached into his pack and pulled out the slices of carrot cake Paul had given him as they were leaving. It had been Paul's grandmother's recipe, something he made frequently while Mason had been staying with him.

"Laura, it's okay." The husband stood and extended his hand to Mason. "I'm Simon. This is my wife, Laura, and our kids Becky, Lucas, and Lila."

Mason took his hand and shook. "Pleasure. My name is Mason." He took the cake and moved to the table they were gathered around. "This is some of the best carrot cake I have ever tasted. A friend of mine made it." He sat in an empty chair as Laura and Lila came back to the table. He put the cake on the table and unwrapped it, breaking the pieces apart. "I only share this with really special people." He grinned at Lila.

"That's very generous." Laura said as Lila put her bag of cookies on the table.

Lucas, who was clearly the oldest of the three and looked to be around eight was frowning at Mason. Becky looked like she was trying to decide which of her siblings to trust. Mason chose to let them make up their own minds and looked at Simon. "I appreciate the friendly welcome." Mason said softly. "I've never…traveled like this. I can admit I'm a little nervous."

Simon nodded. "A lot of reasons to be nervous these days." His eyes skipped over Mason's shoulder to the men, who seemed to have stopped their loud and obvious discussion to talk much more quietly amongst themselves. "What brings about your first trip?"

"Family. I am looking for some of my mother's kin. Our side of the family wasn't good at keeping in touch."

"We're going to visit our grandma." Lila said. She scooted closer to Mason, moving his arm so she could climb up in his lap. "He's like Uncle Mark, Daddy."

That clearly made Laura uncomfortable. Simon reached for her hand. "Lila, honey, remember what we talked about? How certain things we should keep to ourselves?"

Her eyes got big and she nodded. "I'm sorry," she whispered.

"It's okay, honey, just remember." Simon responded. "Sorry, she's only five, and she doesn't always realize…"

Mason nodded. "No, it's okay. I understand." He glanced over his shoulder. "Unfortunately, not everyone would."

"Exactly."

Laura still looked uncomfortable and he had no idea how to put her at ease. Instead, he focused on the cookie Lila was giving him, making noises of enjoyment as he ate it. She giggled. Becky had clearly decided that he was okay, tentatively reaching for a piece of the cake.

Mason spent the next hour or so alternately entertaining Lila and Becky with funny faces or silly questions and talking with Simon about various topics, from the difficulties of homeschooling to the problems with relying on public transportation, all without speaking certain words out loud.

The problem with schools and public transport for a Shade was, of course, the sun issue. Mason had chosen the bus simply because the windows were darkly tinted, which Simon indicated was their reason as well.

"Flying is faster, but there is so little control." Simon said. "But, the kids get to see a lot of the country this way too."

"Yeah, I'm looking forward to it. I'm already further from home than I've ever been." Mason said, looking up as a woman in uniform came into the lounge. She announced the arrival of the bus and people began shifting and moving, gathering their things to board.

Laura stood and started getting the kids organized. Mason watched the college kids grab backpacks and duffle bags and head toward the bus. The older couple shuffled behind them. The trio of younger men didn't move, but Mason could feel them staring. He lifted his backpack onto his back and let Lila take his hand as they headed toward the bus. There was a patch of sun between the shade of the building and the door to the bus, but it wasn't much.

Mason let the family go ahead of them, glancing back to see if the troublesome men were still sitting. They hadn't moved, and Mason breathed a bit easier. He followed Simon up the stairs, picking a spot and shrugging out of his large pack. He put it nearest the window where it would help block the sun and sat.

He was impatient now to get moving, though they weren't scheduled to leave for at least a half hour. He closed his eyes, listening to Lila and her family get settled and missing his home. It seemed like a lifetime had passed since he left.

Sleep pulled at him and he was tempted to give in to it. The last few days he hadn't slept well, and he'd been up much earlier than normal to get down the mountain in the early afternoon, expecting to hike down. Paul's offer to drive was a welcome one. It meant he'd gotten to the station on the same day, rather than spending the night hiking and getting to the station in the early morning hours.

He felt the bus move and opened his eyes. His heart sank and his stomach tightened as the three men from the lounge got on the bus. The one with the dark facial hair squinted at Mason as they moved past him, headed toward the back of the bus.

Mason turned to look, catching Simon's eye. Simon nodded, and Mason responded the same. They would need to be careful.

* * *

The bus slowing pulled Mason groggily up out of rambling dreams that felt like being chased, blinking at the street lights that lit the bus up like morning as they rumbled to a stop outside a station.

"Bathrooms are inside to the back. The diner is closed at this hour, but there are bag lunches for sale at the counter and vending machines inside the lounge. Be back on the bus by ten after ten for departure," the driver announced.

Mason stretched slowly. In front of him the older couple was getting up and shuffling for the door. Behind him he could hear the college kids waking each other up. He stood, glancing back to where Simon sat with Lila asleep in his lap. Across the aisle from him, Laura had Becky's head in her lap. Lucas was the only one standing up, dancing a little as if he needed to pee.

"I don't want you going by yourself." Simon said quietly. He started to shift, trying to figure out how to put Lila down without waking her.

Mason leaned across the seat. "I'm going in. I'll keep an eye on him."

"Are you sure?" Simon asked, glancing up at Lucas.

"Dad, I don't know him." Lucas hissed.

"It's okay if you don't want to." Mason offered. "It would be sad if one of your sisters got woken up though." He headed for the door, smirking when he heard Lucas call out for him to wait.

They walked together into the station, passing the counter run by a tired looking old black man and through the lounge to the men's room. Mason headed for a urinal, watching Lucas choose a stall. He chuckled a little. The kid was cautious. It was probably a good thing.

He finished his business and moved to the sinks to wash up, taking a minute to splash water over his face and pull his hands through his hair. It had gotten long, nearly past his shoulders now. His grandmother would have chided him into the "barber's seat" where she could cut the dark locks back to something she deemed acceptable.

It had been nearly a year since she had been well enough to cut his hair. He'd gone into the town barber once in that time, but even that had been months and months before.

Behind him, the door opened and he glanced up instinctively. Two of the three men that had made him so nervous before came in, eyes narrowing as they saw him. Their eyes moved around the room, then back to him.

"You came in here with a kid," the blonde one said.

Mason sort of nodded. "Yeah."

"You some kind of pervert?"

Mason turned to look at him. "What?"

"You heard me." He moved closer. He towered over Mason, and it was evident he outweighed him too.

He swallowed and stepped to the left slightly, trying to move so he wasn't up against the sink. "I'm just helping his father out."

"We don't like no perverts," the other man said, stroking his full beard. "Do we Ben?"

"No sir, we don't."

Mason took a step back. "Hey, Lucas, you almost done?"

His answer was the flushing of the toilet. The stall door opened slowly and Lucas came out, his eyes wide and his face pale. Mason nodded to him, keeping himself between Lucas and the two men.

"Like I said, boys, just helping out the kid's parents." They both stood watching as Lucas washed his hands then moved to stand as close as he could to Mason, who put an arm around him protectively.

"We don't like you much," the one that wasn't Ben said.

"Sorry to hear that." Mason said, reaching with his free hand for the door. For the briefest moment, he wasn't sure they were going to let them leave, then he got the door open enough to squeeze them both out.

Lucas pulled away from him and all but ran back for the bus. Mason followed, his eyes casting about looking for the third man. He could feel the other two still behind him and decided not to dally, heading out the door and back to the bus. Simon was standing as Mason climbed the stairs, worry in his eye.

"Everything okay?" Simon asked.

Mason nodded as he returned to his seat. "Yeah, we're good."

"Lucas said that you might need help."

Mason looked to Lucas, who still looked scared. "Couple knuckle-heads looking for trouble. I handled it."

Simon bent down to look out the window. The three men were coming back to the bus. Mason settled into his seat, his hand slipping up to the talisman under his shirt. He let go as one of the big men, the one called Ben, took the seat across the aisle from him. The others sat in the next row and Mason turned his eyes toward the window.

"See, told you Jake." Ben said, leaning across the aisle toward the big man in front of Mason. He peered down at Mason from over the seat.

"Hmmm. He looks like one of them perverts all right." Jake said, pulling off his cap to scratch at his dark hair. "What do you think, Wade?"

Mason kept his attention on the window, hoping they would get bored and move back to their previous seats.

"I think he's got something wrong with him. Look at him. Ain't never had no woman. Maybe he's one of them homosexuals."

"Is that it, Pervert? You like men?" Jake asked, reaching over the seat to pull Mason's face back to his. "Or is it just little boys?"

Mason yanked his head back. He could feel Simon bristling. "Look, guys, I don't want any trouble, okay?"

"He doesn't want any trouble, Ben." Jake said, smirking.

"You know what I think?" Wade asked, standing and leaning over to grab Mason's chin, nearly yanking him up to standing himself. "I don't think he's into little boys. No this one here, he's probably just a loser that lives with his mommy and never leaves the basement. Look at him. Look how pale he is."

"Is there a problem here?" A big voice boomed from near the front of the bus.

Wade let go of him and stood up straight. The bus driver was staring at them, a nightstick in her hand. She was nearly as tall as Ben and clearly not afraid of them.

"Just having a conversation is all." Jake said, gesturing toward their seats in the back with his chin. Ben looked Wade over, then moved down the aisle with Jake behind him. Wade took a moment longer, and Mason wasn't sure he wasn't just going to charge the driver, but then he pulled on the hem of his shirt and followed his friends.

The bus driver came part way down the aisle, her dark eyes finding Mason's. He nodded to show he was fine and she turned her eyes to the troublemakers. "I will pull this bus over and leave your asses on the side of the road if you try any more of that shit on my bus. Understand?"

She returned to her seat, but Mason could feel her eyes in the mirror she used to see the bus stretched out behind her. He was pretty sure that the trouble was only postponed and he determined that he should be careful to never get caught alone with any of them.

Chapter Ten

"I can't believe we're doing this." Bryan hissed at Alaric as they both leaned under the hood of Riley's car.

"You didn't have to come." Alaric countered, reaching out to check with the others who were hiding along the road.

"This ain't some action movie." Bryan said.

"No, but right now, we're the only chance that Shifter has."

"You don't know that."

Alaric shook his head. "Just do what we talked about. No one will even need to know that we were here."

Bryan sighed but seemed resigned to the action now that it was upon them. Alaric felt the alert from their first spotter. The van was approaching, with one escort car – an escort in uniform. That wasn't going to go over well. Alaric sent the message to be strong, silent, and swift to everyone involved.

They had Riley's car pulled diagonally across the lane, with Bryan's SUV pulled up beside it, jumper cables and other tools for roadside repair on the ground and fenders. "Here they come," Alaric murmured. The van pulled to a stop less than a car's length away. Bryan stood from under the hood, lifting a hand in greeting.

The driver of the van leaned out his window and yelled, "You're blocking the road."

"Sorry, I can't seem to get it started. Just died right here."

The driver got out, frowning at Bryan as he came closer. "Move the SUV. Let us by."

"I could really use a hand here." Bryan said, inching a little closer.

"Dan, what's the problem?" The speaker was in the brown uniform of highway patrol, coming up the passenger side of the van.

Alaric stepped around the car and moved toward him. "My fault really, officer. I was trying to help and managed to just kill my own engine." He gestured at the SUV. Bryan was close enough, and the others were in place.

He sent the signal and felt a psychic blast of confusion that came from his father, who was behind the cop. Bryan took the van's driver down.

The van rocked, rage seeping out through the cracks around the door. Bryan came with the key from the driver's pocket and unlocked the door, ready to deal with the guard.

There was a roar and the guard came flying out of the van, landing with a wet sound on the pavement, his torso torn to shreds. Alaric moved down the side of the van and rounded the back, grabbing one of the open doors and looking up. Two women sat in chains, while a third was shimmering somewhere between a large cat and a human.

Her eyes glittered from gold to a more human brown and her skin rippled from golden fur to a deep tan. She was panting a little as her eyes lifted from the blood staining the floor of the van to meet Alaric's eyes.

Alaric held up his hands. "We're here to help." Beside him, Bryan held up the key ring in his hand.

"I assume one of these opens those locks." Bryan tossed the keys up and she caught them, moving toward the others, while still keeping an eye on them.

When they were free, they moved together toward the doors. Bryan and Alaric stepped back to let them out. The one who had been mid-shift when they opened the doors looked them both over and she lifted her chin a little defiantly. "Who are you?"

Her voice had a hint of an accent that he couldn't quite place, middle east somewhere maybe, which would echo the color of her skin. Her hair was dark brown, but with a streak of honey gold at her left temple. The other two were younger, with lighter skin and hair. His first guess was that they weren't related.

"My name is Alaric Lambrecht." Alaric said, meeting her eyes. "This is Bryan. There are others with us. We came here to get you."

His father appeared from the side of the van. "We shouldn't hang here long, we can only cover up so much time in their heads without causing other problems."

Alaric nodded. "Can you tell us your names?"

"I am Sahara Katan. I thank you for your assistance."

"Alaric, we've got movement on the road." Bryan said, glancing behind them. "We need to move now, especially since she killed one of them."

She looked like she was going to argue, but Alaric held up a hand and held it out to Bryan. "Give me your keys. I'll get Sahara and her friends to safety. You deal with this."

Bryan looked angry, but put his keys in Alaric's hand.

"Be careful, Son." Anson said with a pat on his shoulder.

"I will be. You guys clear out of here as soon as you've got this covered." Alaric nodded to Sahara and gestured toward the SUV. "Ladies, I don't mean to rush you, but we've got trouble headed our way, and we need to move."

Sahara glanced at the other two, then nodded. Alaric led them around the van and up to the SUV. They climbed in and Alaric got them moving, speeding up and turning them off the main road.

They were quiet for a long time before one of the younger girls spoke. "Where are you taking us?"

Alaric glanced at her in the rearview mirror. "Someplace safe, I hope. We have a... campground of sorts. It's off the beaten path, but there are cabins and plenty of fresh water and game around."

"They put us in cages," the other one said.

Alaric could tell now that she was the youngest of them all, probably not even eighteen. "I know. I'm sorry." He glanced aside at Sahara. "My friend saw you." He rolled his eyes. "We're… psychics, for a lack of better word. Shadows. His gift is prophecy. He saw you and we knew we needed to come help."

"There aren't many who would risk so much for people like us." Sahara said, her eyes narrowing at him.

"Well, if we did our job right, the two that are still alive will only remember stopping for a tree across the road, and the one who died should end up off in the trees somewhere, looking like he went to take a leak and got attacked by a mountain lion." He took the turn that would head them north toward the western side of the camp. He felt the distant all clear signal his father sent letting him know they had left the scene and acknowledged it. "So, can you tell me exactly who those men were?"

Sahara shuddered, crossing her arms, but the younger one in the back leaned forward. "The doctor's coat said Omega Labs. But the guards were 8th Battalion."

"Maddie, you don't know that."

"You weren't there, Mila." Maddie met his eyes in the mirror. "I'm telling you, they were 8th Battalion."

"What did they want with you?" Alaric asked, glancing aside at Sahara.

"What all human men want with those who are different." Sahara growled at him.

"They did things," Maddie said. "Like tested our blood and hurt us to make us change."

Alaric nodded. He'd expected that much.

"They said we shouldn't exist. That we were abominations," Mila said. Her fear was palpable. There was more, he could feel it, but the sharp looks between them were enough to tell him they weren't ready to tell the whole story.

"How did they find you?" Alaric asked. He felt Sahara bristle. "You don't have to answer any of my questions," he placated. "I am asking so I can know how to help anyone else they've found."

"It's my fault." Maddie said. "I'm not completely through the change. I can't always control when I shift." She hugged herself, pulling away from Mila. "This guy was being a jerk, and he grabbed me, tried to kiss me. I freaked and next thing I know, he's screaming and bleeding and Mila's there telling me to run. We got home, thought we were safe... Two days later, this van pulled up..."

"They used tranquilizers, brought us both down. When we woke up, we were in the lab."

Alaric nodded. "What about your parents?"

"It's just us," Mila said. "Mom died when we were small, Dad about a year ago. It's been just us since. We've been living in an old house with access to the woods, but Maddie's only seventeen. She's got another year, maybe two before she's fully in control of her shifting. It was stupid to go into town. I should have said no."

"It is not your fault, either of you." Sahara said, turning to look at them. "Your parents should have made sure there was someone to look after you. Especially with Maddie's condition."

"Condition?" Alaric asked, glancing at her.

"Puberty can be a difficult time for us. The animal within is strong and awakening for the first time. Our emotions are volatile and the animal can ride those emotions. It takes years to learn to control the shifts."

They were quiet then for a while, as Alaric drove them down forest roads dark with the shadows of old growth trees. The camp was tribe land, bought over a hundred years before and kept in the clan since. It had originally served as a place for those who had lost control of their gifts to be safe while they relearned to function. Over the years it had been a retreat, a hideaway and in recent years, a summer camp for the youth of the various families of the clan to learn more about their history, learn to use their gifts, and spend time exploring those gifts.

It was located in a forgotten canyon with very little access to the outside world. There were hiking paths that would take you there: two from the north, one from the east that could take you to a small town, and a few to the south that he'd never fully traveled. The only route in for vehicles was an old, barely-there dirt road that came in from the south. "We have a ways to go." Alaric said softly. "Feel free to sleep. You must all be exhausted."

Alaric knew the rest of his people were safe and home when his father reached out for him. It was barely more than a touch due to the distance, but it unspooled with images and the knowledge that the camp was ready for them, that Jordan had been there and stocked supplies, including fueling up the generator.

By the looks of things, they had gotten away clean. The men would wake up with altered memories, their prisoners and the guard gone. Alaric's response wasn't as controlled and would come across a little shakey, but he relayed the information he'd gathered about Omega Labs and their possible collusion with the 8th Battalion.

The more they saw, the more Riley's vision seemed like reality.

* * *

Alaric pulled to a stop in the small clearing that served as a parking lot, stretching a little as Sahara stirred, her eyes skipping around before coming back to him. "This is us, we walk in from here." Alaric said, opening his door.

The girls were waking and stretching as Alaric went to the back of the SUV to retrieve a bag his mother had given him with clothes she had collected. He slung it over his shoulder and pointed to the trail as Sahara and the girls got out of the SUV. "Our bunkhouse is about a half mile up this trail. There's a kitchen and full working bathroom there, with two bunk rooms upstairs. Further in there are cabins that sleep four to six."

He set out up the trail, glancing back once to be sure they were following. There was smoke curling up from the chimney of the bunkhouse when Alaric cleared the tree line and he felt the familiar brush of Jordan's mind. Somewhere in the distance the sun was starting to set and the smell of wood fire and some meat cooking wafted toward them.

Alaric led the way, up the steps of the bunkhouse and through the door, smiling when Jordan stepped into the dining hall from the kitchen. "Dad didn't say you'd stuck around."

"Wasn't planning on it, but I heard you had extras in tow. Figured I'd stay, help them get settled."

"Ladies, this is Jordan Collado. He's... a friend." Alaric settled on the easiest explanation, rather than trying to dig through the family tree. "He is kind of a fix-it guy. He runs errands for us, plays courier when we need it. Jordan, this is Sahara, Mila and Maddie."

"I've got food ready, if you're hungry. The generator is up and running." Jordan looked at each of them, then back to Alaric. "Right, I'll get food."

He headed back into the kitchen. Alaric put the dufflebag on the nearest table. "We didn't expect three of you. Riley only saw you, Sahara, so I'm not sure any of this will be helpful, but my mother gathered up some clothes. I'm sure that if you give Jordan your sizes, he can come up with something for you."

Jordan emerged from the kitchen with a tray loaded with four steaming plates. It was simple enough fare, steaks with baked potatoes and green beans on the side. He set the tray on the table.

Sahara nodded to the girls, who each took a plate and withdrew to a table away from Jordan and Alaric. Sahara nodded her thanks as she took her plate and joined them. Alaric sighed and sank to the bench. "I should hit the road. It's a long drive back."

Jordan handed him the last plate. "Eat. I made up a bed in the boy's room upstairs for you. Drive back in the morning."

Alaric took the plate and nodded. The ominous feeling that has plagued him for weeks was pushing in on him. Up here in the canyon cell phones didn't work and the distance between himself and his father was too great to be trusted. He was cut off. Jordan was probably right, however. Driving the mountain roads in the dark wasn't the best idea.

He ate alone, glancing at the women he had brought into their sanctuary. Bryan had been against the idea, but had fallen in line when Alaric's father had supported Alaric's plan. Alaric turned his thoughts to the plan, and the unexpected twist that the van had been escorted by Highway Patrol. None of them had seen that coming. He found himself wondering if his father had read the man while he'd been in his head building false memories.

If the 8th Battalion was in fact in league with this Omega Labs, and they had law enforcement working with them, they could be further along on the road to the war Riley saw than they thought.

* * *

Nearly as soon as he reached a place with cell reception, Alaric's phone started buzzing for attention. A string of text messages and voice mail urged him to pull over and find out what was going on.

He pulled off in a turn out on the side of the road and lifted his phone, expecting the worst. There were text messages from his mother, several from the night before and more starting early in the morning. The first urged him to stay at the camp, then increasing concern over violence that had broken out.

His father's voicemail gave him the gist of the situation. In what appeared to be coordinated attacks across the country, a mosque, a synagogue, several businesses owned by African Americans, and a Planned Parenthood in the greater Sacramento area had been burned and at least fifteen people were dead, some of them burned beyond recognition. Area news stations had gotten videos that tied all of it together, and tied it to similar video messages sent to news stations in other major cities.

Alaric put the phone down and got back on the road. The sooner he got home, the sooner he would know what exactly was going on. It was after noon by the time he reached his house, and he was unsurprised to find Bryan and Victoria there.

His father held up both hands as Alaric rushed in, sending calm to him. "We're okay."

"What the hell is going on?" Alaric asked.

"Good question," Victoria responded. "Last night was brutal."

"We still don't have all the facts," his father said. "But for now, they've instituted a curfew."

"Was it 8th Battalion?" Alaric asked.

"That's what it looks like," his father responded. "Did you get our guests settled in?"

Alaric nodded. "Yeah. Jordan was still there. He's going to get whatever they need."

"Still think we shouldn't have gotten involved," Bryan groused. "We could still get tied to that murder."

Anson put a hand on his shoulder. "We covered our tracks. It would take someone with skills detecting mind tampering to even suspect anything. From the impression I got regarding the man in Riley's vision, his skills lie elsewhere. We're probably safe."

Alaric's stomach tightened and he shifted his weight as a cold fear leached onto his skin. His father looked up at him in expectation. "I wasn't going to say anything until I was sure, but... someone who I've seen with Roth is... well, I don't know what he is, but he's got skills."

Anson frowned at him and crossed the room. "*Show me.*"

Alaric closed his eyes and centered, then opened to his father's touch, showing him the various memories he had of observing the man.

Anson pulled back, his frown deeper and his eyes filled with concern. "That is troubling." He shared the information with Bryan and Victoria quickly.

"That would have been nice to share before we went out there to play hero yesterday!" Bryan exclaimed.

"I'm sorry." Alaric offered. "I wanted to be sure, and I'm still not, but even if all they have is one adept…and it looks like we're dealing with two, so…"

"We could be screwed." Victoria finished for him.

They were quiet for a few long moments. Alaric shook off the fear that had gripped him. "What I don't understand is… If this guy is one of us, what is he doing with them?"

"He isn't one of us," Anson said. "At least not in the traditional sense."

"But he is skilled," Alaric said. "And he's clearly involved in whatever Roth is up to."

"I think we should reach out to anyone in the clan with similar gifts to Riley," Victoria said, looking at Anson. "Maybe it's time we get a better reading on what is coming."

Anson nodded. "I've already been trying to coordinate that. Unfortunately, the number of prophets in our clan is very small."

"It never was a prevalent gift." Victoria sighed. "Even in my grandmother's time."

"And in the meantime?" Bryan asked.

"In the meantime, we hold steady." Anson said. "And try not to draw attention to ourselves."

Chapter Eleven

"This is our stop," Simon said as he sat opposite Mason at a bus stop table in Columbus, Ohio. "You going to be okay?"

Mason nodded, his eyes tracking Wade as he stalked through the building. "Yeah, I can handle myself."

Simon held out a card and Mason took it slowly. "My contact information...in case...There aren't a whole lot of us left. We should look out for each other."

"Thank you."

Lila and her sister came running with their mother and Lucas following. "Daddy, it's still bright outside!"

"I know, Lila. That's why we're waiting inside for uncle Mike."

She climbed up into Mason's lap. "Are you coming to grandma's too?"

He smiled and bounced his knee. "No, darlin'. I am getting back on the bus and going to Washington, D.C."

"Is that where your grandma is?"

His breath caught a little and his chest was tight. "No, my grandma... She's gone."

Lila spontaneously hugged him. "It's okay, you can see her again," she whispered in his ear before she kissed him and jumped down.

Mason cleared his throat and offered a smile to the little girl as she rejoined her mother. Simon was looking past him and Mason turned to see Wade and his friends staring at them. "I've got a bad feeling," Simon said, his voice pitched low.

"They won't try anything out in the open like this," Mason said, though he wasn't convinced that was true.

Simon's eyes met his. "And if they do?"

Mason shrugged, looking away from the men. His eyes caught on a television screen in the corner. "You see that?"

Across the bottom of the screen was a scrolling banner: "*Breaking News: There are unconfirmed reports of Shade retaliation in cities where violence toward Shades has been rampant.*"

Together they moved closer to the television and turned the volume up. A woman addressed the camera from a news desk somewhere. "*An outbreak of a virulent strain of influenza has incapacitated the Nashville offices of anti-Shade presidential candidate Norman Douglas, already resulting in several hospitalizations and one death. Meanwhile, a similar plague has ravaged New York City police, who have failed to locate the men responsible for the deaths of as many as five suspected Shades and more than ten others that the 8th Battalion has labeled enemies of the state. Senator Douglas has suggested that Shades are responsible.*"

"That's not good." Simon said.

"No it isn't," Mason agreed. "Would one..." He checked around them for someone who might overhear, then lowered his voice. "I mean, I know it's possible...but..."

"It's hard to say. People are scared, Mason," Simon said. "Scared and angry."

Mason nodded, turning the volume back down. Soon it would be time to get back on the bus. At least his destination was only a few hours away. He held out his hand to Simon. "You look after that family of yours."

"I will." They shook hands and Mason went back to grab his pack, which was still leaning against the table. He watched the family move to a place where they were still in out of the sun, but could see the station parking lot.

His plan was to get into Washington D.C. and then walk from the bus station to the local commuter train to get closer to where the cemetery was. If they kept on the current schedule, they would get to Washington by late afternoon. If he was lucky, he would get to the cemetery early and be able to go find some water to soak in and a bed to sleep in before he started for home.

Mason settled into his seat on the bus, nodding as several new people joined him. Wade and his friends glared at him as they climbed in and moved past him down the aisle. The rest of the trip was straight through. All he had to do was keep his head down and not give them a reason to come at him.

Of course, he wasn't sure what exactly that would be. So far all he'd done was exist, and take a kid to the restroom. He sighed and did his best to keep himself out of the diluted sunlight that came in the coach's tinted windows.

The bus driver boarded, glancing back at the people on the bus before sitting behind the wheel. A few minutes later they were moving down the highway and he let his mind drift.

He could hear the voices of the others talking around him, though he paid no attention to the words. He closed his eyes and turned his thoughts inside, pulling up what he knew about Shades causing illness. Despite what Paul had shown him, it was still a foreign concept to him.

He could hear his Nana muttering about evil and keeping to himself. He wasn't sure anymore that she'd been wrong.

Mason floated in a place that was half inside the gathered memories of his line and half-awake as the voices fell into the white noise of bus wheels on blacktop and the quiet roar of the engine.

His next conscious thought came as the bus crawled off the highway and started navigating narrower streets, taking them into a much more urban landscape. His stomach rumbled, reminding him he hadn't eaten since he'd finished off the sandwiches Paul had insisted he take with him.

He added it to the list of things he'd need to take care of once he was off the bus, running a quick mental tally of what money he had left. He was fairly sure he had enough to get a room for the night and some food to hold him over on the journey back, though he wasn't sure he wanted to take that bus trip all over again.

Mason thought again about finding his mother's kin, but tucked that thought away as the bus pulled into the station. He needed to focus on the immediate needs: find the light rail, get to the stop closest to the cemetery, and find his forefather's grave. He could worry about everything else after that.

The bus rolled to a stop and all around him people were stretching, moving, gathering their belongings and heading for the front of the bus. Mason waited, watching because he didn't want to get off the bus before the three rednecks, Wade, Jake and Ben.

When they had finally moved past him, Mason stood, shouldering his pack. He was the last person on the bus but the driver. She stood as he approached, blocking his path and leaning down to peer out the door.

"You got someone coming for you?" she asked.

Mason shook his head. "No, I'm going to catch the light rail."

She nodded. "Give it a minute, then head into the station. Follow the signs for the train. If those thugs give you any trouble, don't be afraid to yell for help."

Mason nodded with a smile. "Thank you ma'am. I'm sure I'll be okay."

"Those boys are looking for trouble. Don't be their trouble."

He leaned over to look out the window, but none of the three seemed to be around anymore. "Looks like they've moved on. I'm sure there's a Douglas rally or something that they need to be at."

She stepped aside and let him by, and Mason stepped down off the bus. Like the bus driver had said, there were already signs he could see pointing him to where he could catch the light rail. He kept an eye out for trouble as he moved through the station, but the troublemakers seemed to have moved on.

He found the station and bought his ticket, then spent a few minutes studying the station map to make sure which stop he wanted. The sun was bright, but starting to sink. Mason rolled down his sleeves and pulled his gloves and hat from his pack before moving out to the platform to wait for the train.

* * *

It was nearly fall, the hint of a chill on the air that tasted of apples and leaves and wood smoke as he stepped off the train onto the platform and glanced around, taking in the threats, the openings, the exits, and the people. Even at this hour, with the sun setting in the west, there were a lot of people.

He hadn't been alone since he'd let Paul drive him down the mountain. The nearness of so many people for so long made him uncomfortable. What he wanted more than anything else was a deep body of water to soak in.

Mason pulled the hood of his jacket up over his baseball hat to protect his face from the sun, keeping his gloved hands in his pocket. He'd had more sun exposure in the last week than he'd had in the last several years.

It would be dark soon enough and he'd make his way to the cemetery where his family lay buried so he could do what he had come for: offer his respects at the grave of his forefather, retrieve the book hidden there for him, and perform the ritual that would secure in him the bloodline. The rest could come after – water, a meal, bed.

At least that was what he had planned until he recognized a feeling, that awkward lurch in his stomach that told him there was a Shade nearby. He looked around him, scanning the faces of the people until he spotted the man, pale skin, dark hair. His cold, black eyes lifted and Mason knew, just knew, that this man had malice on his mind.

Anyone on the platform or the approaching commuter train could be his target. Part of him said he shouldn't get involved, but he couldn't shake the feeling that he should and he found himself moving closer, easing around people, trying to get close enough to reach him. Mason was nearly arm's reach away, easing his hiking pack off, when the Shade reached out and grabbed a woman waiting near the tracks.

She screamed as he pulled her back. There was a malignant stir of energy air that felt familiar, and yet not. Mason jumped at them instinctively, knocking them both down and dragging the other man's hand away from her throat. She was already thrashing, her skin black where he had touched her.

He wrestled with the other man, yelling when a hand closed over the bare skin at Mason's wrist where his shirt sleeve had ridden up. The Shade snarled as his palm burned with dark fire, then his fist slammed into Mason's face. He scrambled as Mason rolled away, climbing over Mason in an attempt to escape.

Mason shook his head to free himself of the energy and dove at the man again, catching his foot as he tried to get away. Mason clambered over him, pounding his head into the concrete to knock him out. When the man fell limp, Mason turned back to the woman and the people surrounding her now. "No!" He yelled it, jogging back to her and pushing people back. "Don't touch her."

He could sense what the other Shade had done thanks to his lessons with Paul. He had spiked her with some common disease, amped it up and turned it in a way that she would spread the disease on contact. He knelt over her, then looked up. "Did someone call the cops?"

"Already here." He looked to the voice and nodded. The man was a little disheveled, like he'd had to push his way through the crowd. His suit marked him as a fed, which was more than Mason wanted to know about him.

"He did this…and he ain't gonna stay out long." Mason pointed, turning his attention to the woman. If he helped her, he'd out himself, and to a fed. If he didn't, she was going to die.

"What about her?"

Mason licked his lips. "Let me deal with her." He couldn't let her die. Even if it meant getting caught.

"Ambulance is on its way."

"Good, now back off and give me room." Mason leaned over her, stripping off his gloves before hovering his hand over the dark, mottled skin as he tried to feel out the exact form and nature of the illness. He was painfully aware of his inadequacy with this. There were any number of ways a Shade could infect a person, what Paul had shown him with that hiking couple was only one. This was a whole different thing though, and he wasn't sure what.

It wasn't fully set, and he got the impression that this woman was not the other man's intended target. He needed to draw it out of her before the ambulance arrived, because if anyone touched her they would be infected with some remnant of the darkness, and it would fester inside them and spread. He exhaled slowly and let his hand touch her.

He shuddered, his stomach twisting. He didn't actually know if he could fix this. The other man was powerful and this was a working beyond anything Mason had learned. He had always believed the old ways were mostly lost, and yet, here a woman lay dying because of them.

He lifted his head and fumbled in his pack for a bottle of water. He filled his mouth with it, infusing it with what he could through contact with his tongue, then lifted the woman's head and poured some of the water into her mouth, encouraging her to swallow by petting her bruised throat.

"How is she?" Mason looked up to find the fed squatting next to him. The platform was almost empty, but for the line of uniforms now between him and the exit.

"Not good." Mason inhaled and looked up at the prisoner who was now handcuffed and about to be pinned inside a spotlight, probably UV light. That was also not good. It meant this fed knew what he had.

"Can you do anything?"

Mason shrugged. "I don't know. If I knew for sure what he did, maybe." He reached for her again, but the cop stopped him, grabbing Mason's wrist.

"If you can't, she'll be killed, incinerated and disposed of before we've even processed this ass-wipe." He let go of Mason. "No pressure."

Mason licked his lips and looked the man over. "You've seen this before?"

He nodded. "I've been tracking this guy a while. He was in Chicago a week ago, hit in New York a few days ago. Caught a rookie cop on her way to work. The death toll is up to five, with another twenty hospitalized."

Mason's hand shook as he reached for her. He touched her skin, so hot it felt like blisters were forming on his fingers. He closed his eyes and reached inside himself.

"*They brought this on themselves.*" The words slithered into his mind with the man's rage. "*Too much for you, boy.*"

He ignored the voice and forced himself to concentrate on the woman. She stirred and he tried to calm her, making soft sounds like his Nana would sooth him with when he was upset.

"*Even if you save her, they'll only kill you for it.*"

Mason lifted his free hand, pulling the talisman that had been his grandmother's out of his shirt, holding it to help him focus. He hadn't learned enough and this was far too different than the tumor Paul had used to teach him. He closed his eyes and prayed he had enough power to at least render the disease non-contagious.

There was a buzzing in his ears, and his body swayed. The disease was strong, and it crept up his fingers, hot, turning his skin red. He gasped and felt a hand that wasn't there close around his throat. He opened his eyes and looked up at the other Shade.

"*Poor uneducated Shade. Can't even heal a nasty case of the flu. Told you I was too much for you. Too bad I can't come take that last breath of yours to add to my collection.*"

The disease was burning up his arm. Mason pulled his hand off the woman and turned his concentration to cleansing his arm, but the Shade's power was stronger than his, choking him without touching him. Mason managed to shed the disease, but he was spent, gasping for air and falling over backwards. A gunshot sounded. Then another, and Mason fell into blessed blackness.

* * *

The smell of burning flesh and the silence, the absence of the crowd met him when he fumbled his way back to consciousness. He wasn't alone, but he wasn't out on the platform anymore either. He was laying on something soft and there was a needle in his arm, feeding fluids into him. It was cool and mostly dark. For the moment, he was safe enough.

He opened his eyes. The fed was watching him, dark blue eyes narrow, his face tight. He still looked a little disheveled, though he'd tried to smooth his graying hair back. "Easy, you hit your head when you went down."

"She's dead?" He didn't really need to ask.

"Unfortunately. I couldn't risk it."

"And…the guy who did it?"

"Shot him myself. It looked like he was attacking you."

Mason nodded and slowly sat up, his eyes following the IV line up to the bag. It seemed they were in the back of an ambulance. "Thanks." At least the IV seemed to be pure water, and not saline. That too indicated this fed knew exactly what he was.

"Not necessary. It's what I do." The man held out a hand. "I'm Adam Darvin."

Mason eyed the hand, then reached for it. "Mason Jerah." He shifted, his hand rising up to check the back of his head. There was no knot, so he was probably okay. At least for the moment. The fed could be a problem though. He could hear his Nana's voice warning him. "So…who you work for?"

Darvin smiled. "You've never heard of us. We're a branch of the Federal government, Department of Inter-Species Investigation. I specialize in handling certain assets for the government, or eliminating certain threats, as the case may be."

Mason narrowed his eyes. "So you hunt Shades."

Darvin made a face and shrugged. "Not until recently. I will say that it has gotten trickier these days. I find people who have certain unusual skills and train them to do a job. Shades, Shifters, oh and I have a few Sages. Well, had a few, down to one. The other two retired last year."

"Shifters…and Sages." Mason frowned at him. "What exactly are they?"

Darvin stood and fiddled with the IV bag that was mostly empty. "I can hang another bag if you need it."

Mason shook his head. "No, I would rather just…find some water. And that doesn't answer my question."

Darvin nodded. "Better for you too. But first, can I talk to you about a job?" He grinned and as much as Mason didn't trust him, he found himself liking the man, even if he had dodged the question again.

"I don't need a job." Mason said. "I have family obligations to meet."

"Sure. I understand. Here." He pulled a card out of his pocket. "If you change your mind."

Mason took the card, frowning at him as Darvin leaned over to pull the IV needle. "You're just…letting me go?"

His thumb pressed down on Mason's arm as the needle slipped loose and he replaced it with a folded gauze pad, then a bandage to hold it down. "I have no reason to keep you." Darvin moved to open the ambulance door. "You tried to help, and that means that you are first, not a threat, and second, you might be valuable someday. But one thing I know from experience. People coerced into doing the job spend more time trying to get out of it than they actually put into it."

Mason stepped down out of the ambulance and looked around him. He could sense water nearby, lifting his face into the breeze that brought him the scent. Darvin sat on the bumper of the ambulance and pointed east. "Nearest body of water big enough to give you what you need is that way. I'd avoid swimming pools around here. People are scared. They've been spiking their chemicals even more since the vigilante Shades have been in the news." Mason looked back at him, not sure he knew what he meant. "Salt, higher levels of chlorine. Not enough to kill you, but enough to muck up the works."

"Thanks." He hefted his pack onto his shoulder and headed out, not sure what to make of the man, or the fact that he was letting Mason go.

He half expected to be grabbed as he cleared the train station, shoved into some dark van and hauled away into an unknown, hidden bunker or lab to be poked and prodded and forced into a life he didn't want.

He probably wouldn't have dared a swimming pool, even without the warning. The fear of Shades had grown in just the six months or so since William Darchel had proven their existence. The fanaticism and the attacks on purported Shades hadn't helped, and now there was this guy.

Current estimates had reached forty women, possibly more, that Darchel had killed before he was finally caught. It didn't matter to much of anybody that he killed them because he was psychotic. All anyone wanted to talk about was that he was a Shade and that he'd killed them by drinking their blood.

Shades had long been cast as boogie men by Hollywood, and now they had become blood-drinking, soul-stealing devils. When all was said and done, despite all of the bull-shit Hollywood made up to make their villains scarier, enough information on how to actually hurt a Shade had gotten out and paranoid people were trying to protect themselves.

All the more reason to see to his business, and get the hell out of the "civilized" world.

Chapter Twelve

As one of his father's Keepers, Alaric was expected to help hold space when the prophets gathered, to help contain the shared vision and the excess of energy that might be released.

He waited outside the hedges with Brian and Victoria while the three prophets who had answered his father's call were receiving instruction from his father. Of the three, only Riley had ever been in the presence of the orb. Alaric didn't know the other two at all. The oldest of them, Delma Reeves, was a woman from Minnesota, her thick hair still gold with touches of silver, her eyes dark, almost haunted. The youngest, Freddie, was barely seventeen, a young man that had traveled with his mother to be there.

Both had a gift at least as strong as Riley's, though neither of them were as trained. The basic idea was to introduce the three of them into the grove of the orb and have them begin by offering up their scattered visions about the topic at hand to the orb. In theory, the orb would then sort the various pieces and put them into a chronological order. Then Anson and his Keepers would pour energy into the orb and each of the prophets to more or less juice them into a shared vision to fill in the details.

Or at least, that's' what they were hoping for.

Alaric got his father's warning that they were coming out and stood, gathering Victoria and Bryan with a gesture and moving toward the opening in the hedge. The orb seemed to know they were coming, the pull of its energy stronger, the pulse of it making him tremble.

Victoria took the lead position, settling a gold circlet on her head so that the crystal rested on her forehead. Brian followed suit, the crystal on his headpiece about half the size of Victoria's. Alaric took a deep breath and exhaled slowly before he lifted his circlet, gasping slightly as the crystal touched his skin. They were all pieces of the same crystal that the orb was formed of, tying them to it and giving them the strength to control the streams of energy it would put out.

The prophets were all clad in white with hooded robes. The hoods helped isolate them from the mundane world around them and focus on the internal.

Anson took his place behind Alaric, and sent the signal that would begin their work. Victoria moved through the hedges, leading them into the clearing and progressing around it. The prophets held at the entryway, heads down and hands folded as the others moved in a circle around the grove.

On their second pass, Victoria stopped in the east, facing away from the orb. Bryan took his place in the south on the third pass, Alaric taking up the west on the fourth. Anson finished the fifth pass by beckoning the prophets into the circle, walking them all the way around and into his spot in the north.

Victoria's voice lifted on the still air, the chant one Alaric knew by heart, though he'd never learned what the words meant. Bryan took up the words next, and Alaric joined when it was his turn, then his father.

In an echo of the ceremony that had conferred the leadership role, Anson stepped forward, then processed to Victoria, leaning in to touch the crystal in his headpiece to hers. From there he continued to Bryan, then Alaric to do the same. Once he was back in his place to the north, he opened his arms.

"Enter and be seen." Anson said, leading the prophets around the inner circle before stopping Delma in front of Victoria and pressing on her shoulder until she sat. Freddie sat in front of Bryan and Riley in front of Alaric.

"Now we gather to see the future, to know the path we are to walk. Raise the shield."

Together, they lifted their arms to their sides, fingertips not quite touching, and they pulled energy up around them, forming a barrier of sorts the would keep them all focused inside.

Once they were effectively cut off from the outside world, Anson nodded to the seated prophets, who joined hands. The orb pulsed, and as one they closed their eyes, heads dropping back. Alaric could see the fluctuations in the orb as they each offered up their visions. In his mind's eye, he watched the familiar scenes of Riley's vision roll out, joined up with Freddie's and Delma's as everything shifted and re-organized.

The earliest images told of the public outcry over Shades with the arrest of William Darchel, then violence as protests grew ugly and counter protests brought more anger and fear. Then came the rise of the right, a bitter rivalry over the election cycle, pitting straight fear-mongering and obviously false morality against a candidate who urged common sense and rationality. The images predicted a very tight race, and accusations of voter fraud, culminating in clashes that required the military to step in. Martial law would lead to quieter times, but in the quiet the threat changed shape, became more insidious, working from within state governments, through churches and schools, building to critical mass when the war Riley had seen would finally come, fracturing the country.

The details were amazing, at least what Alaric could see. He knew his father was getting more than any of them, including the prophets themselves.

In front of him, Riley was starting to shake and the images being transmitted got darker. In the center of the chaos, Alaric saw a face he had seen before. The man was bloody and broken, chained to a post as fire was laid around him. He lifted his head, sea-green eyes looking directly into Alaric as he screamed.

Alaric almost broke the circle in shock, but he drew in air and held his place, though his arms trembled now with the effort. There was a voice inside him, whispering words he couldn't hear over the noise of the shared vision. Then it as though someone had grabbed his chin, pulling his attention to that battered face. "*He must be saved, Alaric. Without him, they will all die.*" Beside him, he could feel his father's concern, but he couldn't break free. "*Unite the tribes.*"

Alaric's whole body trembled and his vision was starting to go grey. He fought to hold the circle, but he couldn't split his efforts, all it did was push him closer to the dark. Then he felt the connection break and he plunged backwards, passing out even before he hit the ground.

* * *

The blackness was punctuated by flashes of images and the quiet roar of silence in his head was shattered with the sound of screaming. Then a blanket of nothing surrounded him, the feeling of his father's touch comforting him and letting him find his way up to consciousness without the overwhelming input that had caused him to crash in the first place.

Alaric opened his eyes slowly, feeling through his body for injury, even as his father wordlessly reassured him he was okay. They had taken him inside between his passing out and his waking up, which told him that some time had passed. He was on the couch, his father seated beside him, his hands on either side of his head as he held the still firing stimuli behind a wall.

Riley hovered nearby, his face telegraphing his worry. Alaric knew the others were there too, but he couldn't feel them thanks to the dampening his father was controlling.

"*Easy.*" Anson's thought echoed inside the hollow space that had given him the room to wake up. "*See what I'm doing?*" Alaric felt along the soft walls, finding the controls, and nodding a little. "*Can you process it now?*"

"*I can try.*" Alaric echoed what his father was doing, and felt his father slowly pull back. For a minute he wasn't sure he could hold it all, but then his hold stabilized.

"*Good. Now let it through, slowly.*"

Alaric swallowed and let a small opening part the wall, gasping a little at the intensity of the emotion spilled into him. He was able to differentiate the layers now though. The man tied to the burning stake's fear and pain was strongest, but it was propelled by the urgency of the woman telling him to save the man, to gather the tribes. The whispering words still weren't clear and he got the impression that they wouldn't come clear until he needed them to.

He was shaking when his father's presence pulled back completely and he let the last of the experience wash through him. The room was spinning as his father helped him to sit up, then offered him a glass of water. Alaric drank it down before he could face looking up at the others who were gathered there.

"Sorry." Alaric murmured, glancing to his father for support.

"Don't be." Victoria said, her voice oddly coarse. "It isn't every day we get to witness an awakening."

Alaric frowned, looking to his father who smiled gently. "I don't…"

"What happened, Son, was the orb connected with you and blew open a few blocks, kickstarting some of your dormant gifts."

Alaric shifted, not sure he believed his father. "Like what?"

"We may not know in full for a while." His father rubbed a hand down his back gently.

"One thing's for certain," Victoria said, "we don't have to doubt who is next in line. The orb has chosen. It's been awhile since that happened."

"Maybe it knows something we don't." Freddie said, hugging himself.

"Oh, it most certainly does." Anson agreed. "I think this would be a good point for us all to take a break. Alaric, your mother has food ready for you. I want you to eat and then go lay down. The next few days are going to be difficult for you, I think. Freddie and Delma and Riley, I'd like a few minutes with you guys before you go back to Riley's place."

Riley was at Alaric's side as soon as he tried to stand, offering him support until he was sure his legs were going to hold. He felt odd, warm and wobbly and unsure of himself, but then his mother was there, wrapping her presence around him and drawing him to the kitchen table to eat.

She isolated him from the living room, so he could eat in peace, sliding into a seat beside him with a glass of milk. She was quiet until he had eaten most of the sandwich and drank most of the milk.

"Did I ever tell you that my mother's mother was a Shifter?"

Alaric looked up at her, surprised. "No."

She nodded slowly. "Your father knows, but not many others. In their day, the tribes didn't mix. Too much built up animosity. There was a time when Shades helped humans hunt Shifters... and a time when Shifters helped them hunt us. There's a time too when we delivered both Shades and Shifters to those who would hunt them." She looked down at her hands, sadness radiating from her. "No one speaks of what any of us did to the Sages."

"So... you're part Shifter?" Alaric asked softly.

She shrugged a little. "Mom was. She could shift if she worked at it. But those genes seem to have skipped me completely."

"Why are you telling me this now?"

She took his hand and held it. "It felt right. Things are happening, Alaric, and you will be called on to do things you never imagined. You need to know who you are."

She held his hand a moment longer, then squeezed it and stood. "You finish eating. I have some things to do for your father."

He watched her walk away, then turned to finish his sandwich. Exhaustion pulled on his limbs, making him feel heavy. Dumping the food left on his plate, Alaric left his dishes in the sink and headed for his room. He was very aware of the presence of others as he climbed the stairs wearily.

As he closed the door to his room, he raised his own shields to offer him some form of peace and what quiet he could get in a house filled with people who lived with their minds intermingled.

* * *

Scenes from the collected visions played out in his dreams, all too real and vivid. Alaric tossed from a corporate lab to a prison, from the prison to the dry, arid heat of a desert. The man followed him, his face changing from the clean-shaven youth he saw the first time to a slightly older, scarred visage with several days' growth on his face, his black hair straggly with blood clumping in it. At times, he was joined by others, from all the tribes; Shades, Shifters, Sages and Shadows.

In the midst of his dreams Alaric suddenly understood the man he kept seeing was a Shade.

"*He must be saved, Alaric. Without him, they will all die.*"

The words echoed inside him, bringing him from the deep sleep where dreams led him to a place where he was still sleeping, but what he saw was more controlled. There was a woman there, an ancestor he knew somehow. She was young, with shining blond hair that was not unlike his own and wide blue eyes that sparkled with the wisdom that came from living a full life. "*He must be saved, Alaric. Without him, they will all die.*" She said the words, reaching out to him, though her lips didn't move. "*Unite the tribes.*"

"I don't understand," Alaric said to her.

She touched his face, smiling as she leaned in to kiss his lips gently. "*You will soon. Rest now. Sleep and let the gifts open. You will need them soon enough.*"

Her lips moved to his forehead and before he could ask what she meant, he fell over backwards, dropping into a deep dreamless place where time didn't exist.

* * *

It was fear that woke him. Fear that bordered on terror. It was everywhere, the city was alive with it. Alaric sat up slowly, trying to find the cause, but there was too much pain, illness, and fear.

He pulled on the pair of pants hanging on his chair and went to the door of his room, listening past it for a long moment before he cracked it open.

From the living room, he could hear the television…and he could feel his parents sitting silently watching, stunned. He moved down the stairs, still confused. The sun was down, and he got the impression that more than a few hours had passed.

"*This is the scene in downtown Sacramento tonight,*" a female reporter said into the screen before the camera panned to her right. "*After nearly forty-eight hours of rioting, death, and violence, the streets are closed and the only people to be seen are law enforcement and the national guard. The fire is still burning in the building behind us where we are told the 8th Battalion killed twelve people. Their bodies have not yet been identified. We are getting reports that some of those dead were in fact Shades. We have unconfirmed reports that in response, several Shades have gone on the offensive. Two bodies were found in a park nearby, completely drained of blood.*"

Alaric stood at the bottom of the stairs, staring at the TV. His father turned and saw him, standing and reaching out for him mentally. "I'm okay." Alaric said aloud, shuffling toward them.

His mother stood too, her concern palpable. "You've been asleep for two days."

He nodded, accepting that easily. "I had a lot to work through. Looks like I missed the fireworks."

"Sadly, I think they're just getting started," his father countered.

Alaric nodded, though his attention was on the TV. The picture had returned to the newsroom, where the usually calm news anchor appeared to be rattled and more somber than Alaric could recall seeing him.

"*Sacramento and the surrounding areas are under curfew, with military and law enforcement patrolling the streets. Emergency bills requiring Shades to be registered with the state have been pushed through and signed. Any Shade who is found that hasn't registered by the end of this week will be subject to up to fifteen years in prison and the confiscation of any property they might own. Critics of the measures argue that the wording of the law is so vague that it could be used to prosecute many people beyond Shades, to include anyone of different faiths or abilities.*"

"This is going to be bad." Alaric breathed.

"It already is." Anson said, urging him to sit. Alaric took the chair, sinking into it before gesturing to his father to go on. "There was a protest at city hall two nights ago, after word got out about the ordinances that Roth was trying to get pushed through. It was a mixed group... No one knows for sure if there were actually Shades there, but a bunch of people got arrested. Some were ours, some were Pagans, some were just angry that such a thing would be considered. After the arrests, a bunch of police got sick: high fevers, vomiting... one of them passed it on to his immunosuppressed son. He died in under twenty-four hours."

Alaric knew where this was going. "The council approved the new ordinances. All of them."

"In one swoop." Anson confirmed. "Starting immediately. People have already been evicted from homes that have been in their families for generations. Planned Parenthood offices have been shuttered, adult bookstores closed. All of the Muslim centers and mosques have been closed but one. Same with Jewish centers and synagogues."

"Abigail and Riley?" Alaric asked, almost afraid to know the answer.

"They're both safe at home," his mother assured him. "She was at the shop when they came to close it. She said the others wanted to fight it, but they didn't want to risk her getting caught in it."

Alaric nodded slowly. "It all feels so...raw." He was starting to be able to sort through the emotional input, feel individual people around them and their emotions more completely. There was still fear, but there was suspicion and doubt, and some of it was directed toward them. "We need to protect the orb." Alaric said, getting a full dose of their immediate neighbor's suspicion. "Mr. Gamble called the hotline Roth set up. They could come investigate..." He trailed off, picking up more information from across the street. "And old Mrs. Ivery...." He shook his head, it was starting to be too much. Reluctantly, he pulled his shields in tighter and looked up at his parents. "We can't wait."

This was how it would begin.

Chapter Thirteen

Mason found his way into a city park, following the lure of water. He wanted a lengthy soak but knew it probably wasn't wise. He felt jangled by the negative energy from that other Shade and its sticky wrongness. It clung to him, made his skin itch. He wanted to taste something cleaner. He found the pond and a place to stash his clothes and things before wading out into the water in just his underwear. This wasn't a place he wanted to be found completely naked.

The water wasn't as clean as he'd like, not like the mountain streams and lakes that he loved, but it would do the job. It was cold and deep enough to let him sink into the dark and he wasted no time in swimming out to where the water was over his head and letting himself drift down into its icy embrace.

It was another thing that the hype and gotten very wrong in their analysis of Shades. They painted it like Shades could breathe in the water. It wasn't so much that they could; it was more a matter of having a lung capacity that exceeded that of most humans. All of the stories were much more dramatic, making Shades out to be little more than vampires, craving the blood of humans to survive. The truth was much more mundane. Sure, a Shade could survive on almost any liquid, even blood, provided it wasn't any heavier in salt than human blood. Water was best, and a Shade required a lot of it, particularly in the heat or after exposure to the sun.

He wasn't sure he fully understood it all himself, with his decided lack of education, but he knew he needed liquid in large capacity to soak in, to drink. Part of it had to do with energy and part of it had to do with the differences in their bodies. He was hoping that he would understand it more once he'd gotten a chance to study his ancestor's Book of Line in detail.

Mason rose from the water and retrieved his clothes, determined to find what he was looking for before the dawn. It was one of the few traditions he remembered from before his parents died. Part of it was ritual tied to the old ways, handed down from generation to generation. The book was hidden in a gravestone, usually at the grave of the oldest known ancestor. It was meant to be the original Book of Line: the family tree, stories of generations past, the old ways of the line, rituals and treatments to enhance their natural gifts, to bring healing, to increase strength. Each time the line branched, a new book was begun, the tree and basics painstakingly copied by hand as a part of the learning process for the young Shade coming into their rightful place.

Then, it was that Shade's responsibility to update the original with all the information that had been gathered since the Shade before him or her.

Unfortunately, Mason's father's book had been destroyed in the fire that had taken his father from him. His Nana had told him that it was a sign, and that was when she had hidden the family book, the one his father had copied from, away. But there were pages missing and she had not updated it in many years, since his father was still a child. She had not wanted him to die young like the others in her life and thought that keeping it from him would protect him. As much as he hadn't wanted it at the time, taking her last breath had afforded him some of that knowledge, and he would be able to at least update the family tree.

He dressed in the dark quiet of the park, pulling his dark hair back and securing it with an elastic band before he checked his bag and his pockets, a routine drilled into him by his Nana when he was still small and notoriously forgetful. Assured he had everything that had been there when he undressed, and nothing significantly extra, he headed out of the park to get his bearings.

The train station was to the west, which put the cemetery somewhere to his right. The moon was almost half full, the cool light soft on his skin. He stood for a moment in its embrace, until he felt someone approaching.

He blinked and looked around him. Three men were watching him, their voices low. It brought to mind the three men on the bus and he was uneasy. It was nearly midnight, and no good could come of three men hanging in a city park drinking beer while Mason soaked up the comfort of the moon. So far they didn't seem to be looking to fight, but there was a smell of stale beer and Mason could tell it wouldn't take much to rile them.

No, it was better to get where he needed to be and then get cover. He set out walking, not really hurrying, but anxious to be away from the potential for trouble.

He passed through a quiet residential neighborhood, working his way east and north through streets lined by perfect yards and picket fences. It was surreal, like something out of a television show rather than reality. There was nothing like this in his own life. His neighborhood was filled with trees and streams and a completely different kind of quiet. At this hour at home, the darkness would be nearly complete, but for that moon above him and maybe a fire.

The neighborhood gave way to a shopping district and he had to pause again to look to the skies to determine where he needed to go. The storefronts were lit up with neon signs, their windows dark, their parking lots empty as he passed through them, finding his way to a second residential neighborhood. He paused in the darkness beneath a giant elm tree, listening to the night. It sounded so different here.

Clouds moved to obscure the moon and he shivered. The air felt colder there, and he glanced around him, half expecting to find himself being followed. He chided himself for his childish fear and moved on.

Another fifteen minutes' walk through dark streets brought him to the gates of the cemetery. It was an old one, no longer active. Parts of it were rotting and falling apart, and there was already the smell of decaying leaves and damp earth.

He was unsurprised to find the gates locked, but didn't let that deter him. He moved along the old brick wall that circled the graveyard, one hand gliding over mossy bricks. He ducked under trees that lined a section of the wall, finding in their shadows a place where the wall had fallen, making it easy to climb inside.

The corner of the graveyard he found himself in was old, dating back to the earliest days of the country. He squatted beside a leaning headstone, rubbing a hand over it to loosen the moss and dirt to read the inscription. He knew that something inside him would tell him when he'd found the right plot. This one was too old. His eyes scanned the stones he could see, feeling inside him for a memory of the last of his forefathers who had been here.

Standing, he made his way deeper, following row after row of crumbling headstones and crypts, which lead him through time until he started to encounter stones with familiar names. Thomas Victor Jerah. He stopped and turned to face the overly large plot with several smaller headstones to either side of the one he sought.

He inhaled deeply, stopping and taking his pack off, leaving it beside the raised plot. He centered himself and felt for the memory. It bubbled up and around him, filling him, and when he opened his eyes, he stepped forward, hand stroking reverently over the stone to the button that would open the secret compartment.

With a quiet snick, a door eased open in the side of the stone. Mason exhaled and leaned in to get a look. The book was dusty and right where it was supposed to be. He eased out and brushed dust and years from its faded leather cover. Hands from as far back in his line as could be remembered had held this book, written in it, used it to better the world around them.

Getting the book out was the easy part.

With the book in his hands, Mason knelt on the grave, where he could touch his forehead to the old marble where the symbol for his clan was carved. The talisman on his chest warmed as he brushed a finger over the stone. He opened the book, running a finger over the ancient pages and the names of his ancestors, tracing the branch that his line had come from. He recited them slowly, softly, like a sacred prayer to gods long silent, fifteen generations to the place where the branch broke off. None of his more recent ancestors had been back since then to update the book.

He dug into the memory given him by his Nana to name the others, men, women...people who kept their secret and lived their lives in peace. He stilled and let himself open to the night, to the moon and stars, to the voices inside him. He closed his eyes and leaned in to the stone, ready for the shock that he knew to expect.

Cold fire sought out the connections inside him, the gifts, the seeds of power that came with being the heir to not just a clan, but an entire line. It surged through him.

"Peace be upon you, Mason. We call you brother and son. Rise up as an heir of the Jerah line. Our family goes with you."

There was a rush of wind, icy and fast, then the night fell silent and he was once again alone, kneeling in the dirt. Breathing in deep, he moved to put the book into his pack alongside the one he had begun at home. He stood slowly, a little wobbly with the expense of energy to integrate everything and tired from the long day.

A hotel was next on his list, someplace he could rest in darkness and sleep without worrying about being found. He stepped off the plot and started to shoulder his pack. He'd be grateful for some real sleep after several long days of only dozing on the bus.

"Well, well, boys. Looky what we found."

Mason turned, spotting one of the men from the park. "I knew you were trouble." One of them said and Mason blinked, recognizing the man from the bus. "You know what we got here? We got us a genuine Shade, like in them movies."

"Naw, you know that's just a story they tell to scare folks, Wade. He's just a sick fuck who likes to jack off on graves." The other two were new, but Mason was pretty sure they would be just as bad.

"Maybe he was stealing. We should look in his bag." The third one came from behind the grave.

"I hear them Shades like to keep things in graves, they make their newly turned come and fetch them," the one called Wade said as he moved closer.

Mason held up both hands. "Look, guys. I don't want any trouble."

"You were in the lake, when it was freezing. We lost you twice coming here. These graves here? I hear they all Shades and here you are stealing from one. What's that make you?" The speaker was taller than Wade, big across the shoulders. He dwarfed Mason.

"Just a guy paying his respects." Mason said taking an experimental step away from them.

"You a coward too?"

He sensed the stick and ducked, but the movement sent him into Wade and the fist expertly aimed at his stomach. He swung out with his right hand to hit back, and missed, disoriented as he was spun around, and sent hurtling into one of the others.

"What are you waiting for!" Wade screamed and as Mason found his feet, he felt heat and pain exploding in his cheek as the stick landed solid and dropped him to the ground.

He pulled his pack close, determined to protect it even as he curled around it, trying to keep away from their feet and their makeshift weapons.

His fingers curled in the straps, held on even as they beat him, until he couldn't feel his fingers any more.

Once they got it from him, they dumped the contents and rummaged through them, picking out the book. "Please..."

"Is this it? This all you were protecting, some old book?" Wade kicked him hard in the stomach, then the face. "Some stupid book?"

He cracked the binding and dumped it next to Mason. The three of them kicked him and beat him as he alternately tried to protect his vital organs and defend himself, until a well-placed blow from the stick broke a rib and he collapsed. They kicked him until he stopped moving and then left him with loud whoops of excitement and talk of finding more Shades to do the same.

Mason grabbed the pieces of paper and the book, pulling the loose pages and hidden treasures tucked into the pages in against his chest shivering. He had a brief moment to be glad they didn't decide to burn him before the blows to his head made thinking too difficult and he fell into a dark hole.

* * *

The buzzing wasn't entirely in his head, though some of it was. His face hurt, his arms were heavy, everything felt thick. He dragged himself up out of the dark, wincing when he opened his eyes and there was too much light, too much noise, too much...

"Oh, sorry," a muffled voice said, then the lights were gone and the room was a much more manageable dark, with only the soft light coming in the door and the green glow of whatever monitor was beside the bed.

So... hospital.

He grunted and took inventory. He was on his side, both hands bandaged. Left ankle in a cast. His back felt as though he had fallen asleep on hot coals. There were multiple broken bones, various cuts and bruises. They were feeding blood and fluid into him from an IV. He would live, though recovery might take a while.

Mason opened his eyes a little more slowly, half surprised to find the chair by the bed occupied by Darvin, his black suit clean and his hair slicked back. He offered a smile. "They found my card on you when they brought you in. I got you transferred out of the ER to someplace that's a little more secure."

He moved to sit up, and Darvin reached out to stop him. "Take it easy. You're lucky. Your back got pretty burned. Now, the doctor says you should make a full recovery, but you need to go slow."

"Where?" Mason asked, settling back onto his side.

"Special ward at a hospital in DC. We got you stabilized locally, then brought you here."

"Special?"

The agent smiled. "Our lead doctor is a Shade. He knows how to treat you."

Mason nodded. That would mean he wouldn't need to worry about saline solutions and medications that were toxic to his system. "Good to know."

"How you feeling?"

Mason winced as he shifted and other pains made themselves known. "Like three fucking assholes kicked the shit out of me." He stiffened as he remembered. "My stuff."

Darvin stood and went to a closet. "If you had any cash, they took it."

"Not what I care about." Mason sat up, groaning as his back protested the movement. His pack looked a little worse for wear as it was handed to him, dirty and ripped. He set it on the bed and opened it. The book was torn and pages were stuffed haphazardly into it.

"I'm told they collected as much as they could, but I'm afraid some of it was lost." Darvin went back to sitting, crossing one leg over the other knee as he watched Mason sort through the pieces. "Your Book of Line?"

He was surprised how much the man knew about Shades. Mason nodded. "Our family branched more than ten generations ago, but our book was lost when I was younger."

"And you are now the last of that line."

Mason narrowed his eyes.

Adam held up his hands. "It's my job. I traced your name. The last Jerah alive that I could find."

Mason nodded slowly and turned his eyes to the book. "My Nana...grandmother died a few months ago."

"But it's more than that, Mason. I traced your whole line, all the branches off that tree, plus your mother's people." He pointed to the book. "Near as I can tell, you're the last."

Mason shook his head. "We've lost a lot the last few generations, but I'm sure-"

Adam stood, pacing. "No, Son. I'm afraid I'm very thorough. When you're up to it, I'll bring you the proof."

It was stupid to feel suddenly and completely alone. He had never known any of the extended line, not anyone in the family, really, other than his father and Nana. Still, something inside him was suddenly hollow and he couldn't get enough air into protesting lungs.

"I thought I told you he shouldn't sit up." Mason looked up at the sound of the new voice, a deep, rich baritone that was soothing.

"You say that like I have some control over the boy." Darvin responded, shaking his head. "Mason, may I introduce your doctor, William Anthony."

Mason looked him over. He looked familiar somehow, middle-aged, his hair a dark red, his hands large making the stethoscope seem like a toy as he lifted it. Mason could feel the accustomed sense of another Shade and it made him a little uneasy.

"Your back is probably not happy about the change in position."

He had to concede that point, the burned skin was cracked and screaming at him. Mason eased down slowly. "I'm told I'll be fine, Doc," Mason said warily as he approached, watching him closely.

The doctor's hand paused and his brow furrowed as he looked down at Mason. "You've never been treated by your own kind?" the doctor asked, his tone vaguely surprised.

"Never knew my own kind outside my family." Mason responded.

The doctor nodded slowly. "That is becoming more and more true, I'm afraid." He held up a hand. "I promise, I'm only trying to help."

Mason nodded guardedly. "I'm sure." He wasn't sure of anything, truthfully, but they hadn't done him any harm thus far. In fact, he was pretty sure he wouldn't be alive without them. He swallowed and exhaled slowly.

Dr. Anthony smiled lightly and moved closer, the stethoscope in his hand. He listened to Mason's heart, then his lungs, and Mason could feel something... more, a light touch inside him. After a long time, the doctor nodded and stepped back.

"Well, the good news is that your lungs and heart are recovering well, so I can move treatment on to that back of yours."

Mason squinted up at him. "What?"

"I take it our good agent here didn't give you the details?"

Mason shook his head. He knew he was in rough shape. He knew that much from what he remembered of the beating. There were drugs between him and the pain though, so he had no idea of the extent of his injuries, even if he was starting to think he could feel some of the work the doctor had done before he woke up.

"Well, young man, you are very lucky you were found when you were. It was nearly noon, the only thing keeping those burns from being much worse was the amount of shade in that cemetery. The burns, however, were of little concern compared to the broken ribs and the damage they caused. Internal bleeding, your lungs were both bruised, fortunately only one of them was perforated. You sustained a number of other injuries too, I'm afraid."

Mason frowned, trying to remember the specifics of the beating, but mostly just recalling the effort to protect the book. "How long was I out?"

"Three days, give or take, assuming you passed out before the beating was over. You probably wouldn't have made it if the ER hadn't found Adam's card and called him. They were already running saline lines when we got there to fetch you."

Dr. Anthony checked his IV as he said it. "Looks like you could use some more fluids. Now that you're awake, we can get you into a water bed for a few hours. And once we get that back looking a little better, I'll prescribe you some soaking therapy. We have some great soaking pools here." He circled around to Mason's back and he loosened the ties of the gown. "Hmmm... how's this?"

There was a cooling sensation that swept over the most painful area, not at all unlike the touch he remembered from his Nana. "Good." Mason said as it ended. "I can probably-"

His hand touched lightly on Mason's shoulder. "No, I don't want you trying to heal yourself. It takes too much energy. Leave that to me. In the meantime, I'm going to increase your anti-biotics and ease back on the pain meds. If the pain is too much though, you can always ask for more."

Mason wasn't sure he wanted to know how bad the pain actually was if he could feel the way he did with meds in his system.

"For now, you get some rest. Mr. Darvin can come back when we have you a little more stable. I'll be back after my rounds to give you a thorough treatment for that back."

Chapter Fourteen

It took him several days to get used to the increased input the newly awakened gifts were giving him. He found himself trying to find places to be alone, to isolate himself from even people he loved because their emotions were too much for him.

In those days, Bryan and several others had come to help crate up the orb and put it in storage under a false name, so that if the worst happened, it wouldn't be found and confiscated.

Alaric took a deep breath as they pulled into the parking garage at city hall, glancing aside at his father.

"*You don't have to come in.*"

He smiled and nodded. "Yeah, I do." Alaric countered. "If this is going to be my new normal, I have to adjust."

"Okay, but if it's too much, I want you to take care of yourself."

"I will."

"Good. Let's see if we can mitigate some of this disaster."

Alaric opened the car door, prepared for the blast of emotional input. It wasn't as overwhelming as he had expected, which he took as a good sign. Maybe he was learning to manage the expansion of his gifts.

He kept his shielding as tight as he could and still function, however, as he followed his father into the office. The whole place was quiet, and he noticed the absence of many people he would normally see on the route from the car to his desk. "Are they staying home because they're afraid, or..." Alaric asked softly as they settled into their desks.

"I'm not sure." Anson responded, lifting a stack of messages.

During the day, the world moved on as a paler version of normal. The streets were less crowded, and police and military vehicles were everywhere, but people went to work, went shopping, went to school. From what he'd gathered from the news and internet, something similar was happening in other cities as well.

The press was speculating in some cases because they had been forced out and were not allowed to cover what was happening. Salt Lake City was said to have closed its entire city to anyone, erecting military style gates across the entry points and turning back anyone who didn't have proof they resided in the city.

Alaric didn't think his own city would take it that far, at least.

Alaric sat at his desk, uncertain of where to even begin. They had less than an hour until they were supposed to be in session. That gave him little time to try to get a handle on any of the pressing matters stacked up on his desk. He felt as though he'd only started shifting papers around when his father was standing beside him.

"Ready?"

Alaric nodded and pushed back from the desk. He focused mostly on following his father's back and not feeling the people around him until they were in the council chambers. He took his seat behind his father as the others came in and tried to get a solid reading on their emotional state.

Roth was smug, confident, even arrogant as he came in and took his seat. Beside him, Bethany Flanders was simply oozing pleasure with herself, proud of what she had done. Dominic Guterson nodded to Alaric and his father as he took his seat beside them, leaning in to ask Alaric if he was feeling better. Alaric nodded blankly, trying to get past the layers of bland and bored and a random thought about blueberry cobbler that seemed to stir more emotion in the man than anything.

Townsend Marley came in through a side entrance, nodding in greeting. He seemed collected and calm, but Alaric sensed some urgency underneath, concern about someone close to him, and a healthy dose of fear as he sat.

Lea Barker was the council's youngest member at barely thirty. She was a mother of two young boys and a school teacher. Alaric almost didn't have to try to read her the way her emotions were leaking out all around her. She was scared for her boys, convinced a fellow teacher at her school was a Shade or something else. He could practically hear her frantic recitation of a prayer as one hand clung to the cross pendant around her neck.

Tasha Moore and Harold Mackey came in together, moving quickly to their seats. Tasha was an older woman who had been on the council a long time. Her husband had been a police officer, though now he was on his deathbed. Alaric was surprised to learn she was convinced the cancer had been caused by a Shade. He pushed a little, extending his senses toward her, feeling his way deeper into her emotional state. He was confused by what he found, almost as if the emotions had been manufactured. Like someone with skills he didn't possess had been there and changed things.

Alaric felt his father poking him and pulled back, blinking a little before nodding to his father. *"I'm okay. Just...reading them a little."*

Anson squeezed his knee and turned back to the council. After Harold stood and called the meeting to order, Councilwoman Flanders stood. "I am happy to report that the entire block of porn shops on Beuford has been closed down and the police crackdown on sex work has cleared 5th Avenue. All abortion providers have been evicted from their rentals, which leaves only the clinic on Alameda Avenue open for business. Unfortunately, they own the building they're in so we can't use the same tactics to get them evicted. Their business license is up for renewal next month though, so we should be able to shut them down then."

Alaric shook his head and sat back, scanning the room. The only people who weren't pleased were his father and Townsend Marley.

Flanders sat down and Roth stood beside her. "It is good progress, yes. We have also successfully closed any business that flouts God's law, including a number of so called Witch shops and several bookstores selling religious articles and such that do not meet the standards set out in our new ordinance."

"So much for freedom of religion." Anson muttered.

"What we must discuss today, my friends, is the practicalities of our plans to segregate the Shades and others. My aide is handing out the plans we have put together for your review."

Alaric couldn't stand the feeling of the room, so he turned his attention elsewhere. Everything still reeked of fear, everywhere he turned. He reached out for the comfort of familiar minds, smiling a little as Riley greeted his thoughts with warm affection. It felt like an eternity since he had seen his friend.

He asked after Abigail, then realized that with his new added range he could check on her himself. He reached for her, and was shocked when she pushed him away. He sat up a little straighter and tried again, sending a warning to his father that something was wrong.

Abigail tried to push him away again, but he latched on, following her as she tried to escape her own home. She was afraid... no, she was terrified. His heart took on the rhythm of hers, pulling on him until he was inside of her. It took him a minute to make sense of the input as he seemed to merge into her body: heat was the first thing that registered, and it was getting hotter... flames. He could see them as she turned her head. His stomach tightened as the baby inside her kicked and moved. Panic filled him, racing through his veins. He stood, not even remotely aware of the council around him.

Abigail ran to the kitchen door, and he felt himself moving too. The flames had taken the wooden table and the curtains on the door... She couldn't get close enough to open it. Through the window he could see there were people outside, but they weren't trying to help.

She screamed and he heard his own voice echo out over marble floors, distantly recognizing that he was in the lobby of the building. The smoke was thick and his breathing was ragged. He tried to force himself back enough to communicate with her, but the terror held him and he could do nothing but follow as she ran back to the front of the house. He could see more people out front, screaming something.

Flames licked all around the room. The skin of his face was hot, and he was having trouble seeing.

Time seemed to slow down as he watched her hands move toward an end table, shoving a lamp off and picking up the table. The fire seemed to be closing in on him. Flames licked over the wood, jumping to the worn wool of her sweater. The table crashed to the floor. Alaric screamed, batting at flames even as his connection started to waiver. He couldn't feel the baby moving. Fire ate up his arms, and he could feel his skin breaking open.

A window broke and the burning curtain flew toward him, the melting fabric and plastic hitting his hip and he turned away, staggering and falling to the marble. Hungry flames consumed everything around him. He was going to die with her if he didn't break free. Abigail was barely conscious and he could feel his own body echoing her pain.

Suddenly there was a blanket between him and Abigail, dulling the agony enough that he could pull back, crashing back into his own body where the cacophony screamed. He seized up, his body rigid and on fire. Someone was trying to help him, but the touch of a hand on skin that was cracked and bleeding made him throw up, retching out the contents of his stomach on the cold marble floor.

He rolled away from the vomit, pressing his hands against the stone in search of relief. The blanket dampening him constricted and he was suddenly aware of his father beside him.

Alaric opened his eyes, tears blurring his vision, but he could see enough to know he'd drawn a crowd. "Abigail..." Alaric gasped. He felt his father's acknowledgement, and his urging to get up. Hands helped him get up to sitting and he blinked until he could see. His hands were red and blistered, and he had a feeling that once he could see his legs and hip they would be as well.

"*We need to get you out of here,*" his father sent. "*Can you walk?*"

Alaric responded by lurching forward, keeping his eyes down while he got to his feet. The pain was excruciating, but he kept moving, his father's hand on his back guiding him out of the bright lobby and out into the garage.

By the time they reached the car, Alaric was ready to pass out. Anson opened the passenger side door and helped him in. His hands were too hot and his face too close as he helped move Alaric's legs into the car.

Reality was shifted funny as he tried to hear his father's voice, but all he could hear was Abigail and the sound of wood burning. He could tell his father was trying to get a sense of how badly he was hurt, but he had no way of communicating as his fuzzy consciousness dimmed toward black.

Voices pulled him up, followed by the anguish of being pulled out of the car and carried into the house. Cold water soothed over his angry skin as he was settled into the tub without stopping to remove his clothing.

Slowly, the pain and confusion receded and he became aware of things outside his body. His mother was nearby, gently scooping water up to wash over his shoulder and neck. His father was in the living room, keeping a wall up between him and whatever was going on. He opened his eyes to find his mother smiling at him. "Don't worry about any of that. Let's just focus on you."

"Abigail...she...I..."

She nodded sadly. "I know. You're going to be okay."

His mind was still sluggish, but he remembered reaching out to Riley. He had to know... Alaric started to try to get up, but his mother's hand on his shoulder held him down. "Riley is okay. Bryan is with him."

"He can't be okay... not after..." Alaric shook his head as it flooded back to him, her terror making his heart beat race. Then he remembered the people outside. "There were people there, Mom. They knew she was in there."

Her hand was soft on his arm, above where the skin was red and blistered. "I know."

"They burned her alive."

"I know." There were tears tracking down her face.

"Emily, Anson would like you downstairs." Alaric looked up to find Victoria filling the doorway of the bathroom. "I can take care of Alaric from here."

His mother kissed the top of his head, practically the only place that didn't hurt, and pushed herself up off the floor, ducking past Victoria on her way out. Victoria came into the room, closing the bathroom door before easing herself down on the closed toilet seat.

From the pocket of her colorful sweater, she brought out several jars of herbs and ointments, lining them along the tub's edge. She arranged them neatly, turning each so that the labels were facing her.

"Did I ever tell you that my great grandmother was a Sage? Beautiful woman, tall as an oak and just as strong. She could sing to a garden and bring forth the most bountiful harvest you have ever seen, even while the gardens all around us were struggling. She could find water without a divining rod, and if you were sick, she would mix up a tea or ointment or lotion or syrup that would have you right as rain in no time. My mother said I looked like her when I was younger." She picked up one of her jars and opened it.

An earthy sort of smell wafted toward him. "Now, I know those burns feel like the real thing, but they're not. They're a sort of blow-back that happens when we go too deep into someone else and can't disconnect. So we can't treat them just like a burn. We have to treat the mind as well as the body."

"Okay…" Alaric wasn't sure he cared how she made the pain stop, as long as it did.

She sprinkled the contents of the jar into the bath, mumbling some words he didn't follow as she did. The water cooled noticeably. She nodded and tucked the empty bottle into her sweater pocket.

"Now, I want you to close your eyes and find your center. Clear your mind. Meditate on the feeling of the cool water and only the cool water."

"For how long?" Alaric asked, his eyes already closing.

"Until your skin is the same temperature as the water." Victoria replied.

Alaric exhaled and pulled his attention deep inside, centering himself and blanking his mind. Sparks of memory and pain made keeping his mind blank difficult.

"*It's okay. Each time you get interrupted, start again.*" Victoria sent to him, which was the first time he'd realized she had taken over keeping him isolated from everything. "*I've got you, Alaric. You are safe.*"

He didn't know how long he sat there before he started to feel as if his skin's temperature was actually dropping, but eventually he could feel Victoria's affirmation and he opened his eyes.

The skin on his hands was less red and some of the bigger blisters had shrunk some. "Now, you're going to want to get out of those clothes. Then I want you to put this ointment," she held up a jar, "on all of the red skin and all of the blisters once you're dry.

"I want you to use this jar of herbs in a bath in the morning, followed by more of the ointment. Should have you healed up quick." She moved the jars to the counter by the sink and stood, rubbing at her knees as she did. "I'm going to go downstairs. You should come down when you're ready. Your mother has food ready."

Alaric wasn't sure he could eat anything. Victoria made *tch tch* noises at him before she opened the door. "You need to try at least. You need to heal, and to do that your body needs fuel."

She closed the door behind her, leaving Alaric alone in the bathroom. His clothes were heavy with water as he slowly lifted himself up. Muscles complained as if he had run a marathon unprepared, but he managed to get upright. He peeled his clothing off, starting with his button-down shirt, turning to ring out the worst of the water before he tossed it into the sink.

The pants were a little more work with his balance off and his feet yelling out their pain. He wrung them out as well, draping them over the shower rail before finally reaching for the towel that hung beside the tub.

He shivered a little as he stepped out, but the cold air was a relief to his skin. He wrapped the towel around himself, leaving his skin damp to the air, and grabbed the ointment before opening the door.

Alaric could hear voices, but they were muffled by the wall Victoria was still holding in place. He shuffled on aching feet into his bedroom. The heat was starting to return to his skin as he loosened the towel and swiped it gently down his legs. He found that patting his skin hurt less than rubbing, so he worked his way down to his feet, then up over his torso and out onto his arms.

Once he was dry, Alaric sat on the bed and opened the jar of ointment. It had a pleasant scent, sort of like fresh cut grass mixed with fresh turned earth. He scooped up a glob of it and started with his feet. It tingled a little as he eased it over the blisters and red skin, and as the air touched the places where the ointment was smeared, it cooled, as if it was ice and not ointment.

Alaric finished applying the ointment and pulled his worn flannel pajama bottoms from the nearby chair. He figured they would be loose enough to not increase the heat by pressing against his skin. He grabbed a T-shirt out of the dresser and pulled it on, running his fingers through his hair as he finished.

He imagined he could smell smoke, though he knew it was an illusion. If he closed his eyes, he'd be right back there. He wasn't sure how he was going to sleep ever again.

Pushing those thoughts away, Alaric left his room and headed downstairs. His father glanced up at him from where he was huddled with men he didn't know. Their faces were familiar, but he couldn't place why. Victoria appeared in the kitchen door, taking his arm to guide him to the table.

"I take it I'm not supposed to ask what's going on?" Alaric asked as he sat and his mother put a plate of pasta and meatballs in front of him.

"Not right now. Let's get you through this first."

He opened his mouth to say he was fine, but his mother cut him off before he could even make a sound. "And don't tell me you're fine. You forget, it doesn't matter how many shields and barriers you throw up in that head of yours. I see all of it. Eat, then I'm going to make sure you sleep. Tomorrow, we'll re-evaluate where you stand and if I think you're up to it, we'll update you on.…" She waved a hand toward the living room.

He looked to Victoria who was standing between him and the living room, blocking off any attempt he might have tried to read the situation. She raised an eyebrow at him and he sighed. "Okay. Fine."

He turned his attention to the food, hoping he could eat enough to convince the two of them to let him go back to his room and try to figure out how to block out the feeling of his skin burning.

Chapter Fifteen

It felt odd to be sitting in a hospital bed, alone and thousands of miles from home. Though, if he was being honest with himself, everything about his life at the moment felt odd. He hadn't been alone since leaving the mountain, and then it was only moments of alone time, an hour tops, for the better part of two months.

He longed for a quiet mountain pond, the silence of the forest at night. Instead, he had the sounds of people in the hallway, the scent of antiseptic, and a broken body.

At least the medication was affording him some sleep. In fact, if he sat still for more than a minute or two, he would doze off. He supposed some of that was indicative of the level of his injury as well as the medication.

He woke from a doze, wondering how long he'd slept. He could tell Dr. Anthony had been in to see him, he could feel the difference in his back. He wished he could see it, so he could track the progress. He settled for closing his eyes and trying to feel his way. He could barely trace the energy pattern before he was struggling, the pain intensifying even as he wanted to try harder.

"I hope you aren't trying to heal yourself." Dr. Anthony's voice pulled him out of his attempt.

Mason's breathing was heavy and a fine sweat had broken out on his face. "No, sir…just trying to…" He lifted a hand and sort of reached for his back. "I can't see it and…"

Dr. Anthony nodded in understanding. "So you thought you'd try to see it a different way. I understand that." He moved closer, setting down the chart in his hands. "And what did you find?"

Mason tried to hide his frustration. "Not much. I couldn't..." He shook his head.

Dr. Anthony's hand touched his shoulder. "I expect the drugs are getting in your way to some degree. They mess with control, make it harder to focus. We could take you off them completely, if you would rather."

Mason nodded and let the doctor move around behind him. Dr. Anthony untied Mason's hospital gown, and his hands ghosted over the surface of Mason's burned skin, only the lightest touch of energy feeling over the damage.

"I get the impression that you don't have much in the way of formal schooling."

"I got some." Mason said, grimacing a little as the doctor's touch intensified. "My Nana was terrified that I'd show off and get us locked up, so she didn't teach me much, especially when I started exhibiting signs of early development." He made a face and rolled his eyes at himself, glancing over his shoulder at the doctor. "I started early, because my mother... She made me take her last breath when I was just nine."

Dr. Anthony's hand moved slightly. "It's hard when it manifests young. Harder still when you're hiding from yourself. You weren't the only ones, let me tell you." His attention shifted, and Mason stiffened. "Sorry, I imagine that stung a bit."

"A bit." He closed his eyes and tried to follow the intricate energy flow that Dr. Anthony was using to encourage the damaged tissues to knit together and heal. "I... my Nana when she went... It was only a few months ago. Just turned eighteen when she died. I tried to learn what I could from what she gave me." He gestured to his head and shrugged. "But it was a bit like trying to follow instructions written in Chinese."

146

Dr. Anthony chuckled. "It can be confusing, so many voices. Without training it can be overwhelming. Close your eyes now and breathe in slowly. I'm going to go a little deeper."

Mason inhaled and closed his eyes, feeling the pull of attention that was the doctor's presence drawing him in. "*Can you hear this?*"

Mason nodded and licked his lips. He was starting to get used to that part at least, having other people in his head. "*Good, breathe and follow me.*"

Mason did his best to clumsily follow his lead, watching the flow of energy like water over his skin, soaking in, seeking out the damage. It was a completely different view than when he did it for himself, and somehow completely different from working with Paul. Dr. Anthony moved in patches, his hands not quite touching skin, feeling for the places that needed him most.

When he was done, Mason's back felt incredibly better.

"Very good." Dr. Anthony picked up his chart and scribbled some notes. "I'll pull back the pain meds, but we can still give you something to help you sleep if you need it. Give it twenty-four hours and you should find your concentration and control much improved. Then we'll see if we can't patch up a few holes in your training while patching up the rest of you."

At the door of the room, the doctor paused, his eyes tracing over the plaster that covered Mason's leg. "I think that this afternoon, we will get you into a water therapy bed, see if we can't speed things up a little bit.

Mason nodded vaguely, but he had no idea what the doctor was talking about. He lay back, closing his eyes and dozed, and eventually slept deep enough to dream of his Nana and their house hidden up in the mountains of California.

He woke a few hours later as Dr. Anthony appeared in his doorway again. He smiled and came into the room, with a nurse behind him with a wheel chair. "Mason, this is Nurse Liza. She is going to take you to a water therapy room, and I will meet you there in a few minutes."

He stepped around her and left as she came to the side of the bed with the wheelchair and helped him off the bed.

"Liza, eh?"

Black hair was pulled back neatly at the nape of her neck and green eyes sparkled at him as she smiled. "Liza Datonelli, Mr. Jerah. Let's see if we can get you into some water."

Mason moved to the edge of the bed, sliding his cast across the sheets until he could ease himself down with his good foot on the floor.

Liza helped him maneuver into the chair, then get his cast-bound leg onto the footrest, smiling at him as she stood and moved back to the handles on the chair. "Hold on. We wouldn't want you falling out."

"So why haven't I seen you around before? I thought I'd met everyone on the floor." Mason asked as she pushed him past the nursing station.

"I've been on vacation, spent the last week in Mexico on a beach." She turned them down a corridor and past the elevators. "I hear you got the living kicked out of you." Liza said, her tone playful. "Six guys or something?"

Mason chuckled lightly. "It was only three, but they were big guys."

"I'll bet they were. Good thing Dr. Anthony got to you. He's a great doctor, and I haven't ever seen anyone mix tradition medicine and Shade healing better."

They turned another corridor and she pointed out where they were going. "I've worked with some of the best too, let me tell you. Hey, Freddie, man, where you been hiding? You know I need my fix." A tall, dark skinned guy stood from behind the check in desk they were approaching, grinning at her.

"Liza, you know where to find me. I got what you need." He pulled a package out from under his desk and held it up. "Fresh made last night."

Liza reached for it and he pulled back. "Come on now, Little Liza, you know what it costs." She turned the wheelchair and leaned across the desk, kissing him on the cheek. He grinned and handed her the small package.

"That's more like it." Liza sniffed the package then smiled at Mason. "Heaven in a cookie. If you're a good boy, I'll share. You will die." She handed his chart across and Freddie took it. "Mr. Jerah is coming in for his first treatment in the water table. But we have to mind the plaster."

"Right on, bring him this way. I've got room two set up for him." Freddie came around the desk and led them into a room that was not a whole lot different than the one they'd just come from, only instead of a hospital bed, there was a low, shallow table with about an inch or two of water in it, a small plastic pillow at one end.

"Okay, Mr. Jerah, let's get you up and in." Liza said as Freddie closed the door. Liza helped him stand, letting him hold onto her arm as he pivoted toward the table. He held the sides of his hospital gown as he lowered himself down, and Liza pulled it off him once he was sitting in the tepid water.

Freddie offered him a small rectangle of cloth to cover his modesty as they helped him move so that he could lay on his back in the water, with Liza holding up his plaster encased leg. Once he was in, Freddie moved to the side of the room, bringing what looked like two IV stands with him, a sling between them.

He adjusted the heights of the poles and moved them into place so that Liza could put his left leg into the sling. When they were done, his broken leg hung just an inch or two over the water.

"Okay, so, Dr. Anthony will be along in a few minutes. Lay there and get comfortable. We'll be back."

Mason closed his eyes, letting the water soak into him. It was an amazing feeling, even if it wasn't free flowing water. It seemed like a lifetime ago the last time he'd been able to just relax in water.

He felt for the energy of the water, stirred it a little with his fingers to make it move over his skin.

"I see you know something about working with water."

Mason lifted his head to see Dr. Anthony coming into the room, the sleeves of his lab coat rolled up to his elbows. "Yeah, I know that much."

He smiled and pulled a rolling stool over to the table. "Good. This is a method we Shades have been using for generations, just updated and improved."

He put both hands in the water and Mason instantly felt it heating up. "Water is a natural conduit for us. Our bodies trust it and once you learn how, you can use it to affect better healing. Close your eyes and connect with the energy in the water."

Mason did, opening to the feeling of the other Shade's touch. He could trace the pattern, and some distant memory sparked inside him. There were different patterns for different needs. The one Dr. Anthony was using was specifically for burns.

The energy moved through the water, over his skin, and he could follow his body's reaction, feeling the way the skin knitted itself together and the blood in his body rushed in to feed the new tissues.

"Something tells me you like that." Dr. Anthony said, pulling his attention back to him.

"That feels amazing."

"Good. Let's see you give it a try. Do you understand the energy pattern?"

Mason bit his lip. "I think so?" He put both hands in the water and tried to replicate the pattern. It took him a couple of tries to find it, but when he did, the water stirred and warmed, just like it had before.

"Good, now try moving it to the spot on your back that is in the most pain."

He fumbled the pattern a little, but got it to the spot low on his back that had taken the most sun. The skin was hot to the touch, but began to cool as he held the pattern of energy in place. After a moment, his concentration began to falter and fatigue washed through him. Dr. Anthony touched his shoulder. "Good, good. I think that's enough for you today. Just follow along now."

The energy pattern shifted as Dr. Anthony moved toward the leg held in the sling. His hands glided up the bare skin to just before the plaster, and Mason could feel the energy travel up from the water. He closed his eyes to focus internally, watching the doctor work.

He dozed off a little and was startled when he heard Liza's voice. The doctor was gone and Liza and Freddie were back to help him up. Once he was standing, Liza gave him a towel while she shook out a fresh hospital gown.

A few minutes later she was wheeling him back toward his room. "Once you get that plaster off, you'll get some time in the soaking pools. If you thought today was good, you're going to love the soaking pools." She leaned in and whispered in his ear. "Wait until you get to try number three. Deep and cold and it tingles in all the right places, if you know what I mean."

Mason looked up at her, realizing that he had completely missed the fact that she was also a Shade and she laughed. "What? You didn't think Dr. Feel Good was the only one of us in medicine, did you? We were made for this." She pushed the chair down the hallway. "Got to take care of our own, you know?"

She wheeled him back to his familiar room, though someone had been in to change the bedding his evening meal was on the tray, along with two small chocolate cookies.

"I guess I was a good boy." Mason said joking as she helped him up.

"So far you have." She helped him stand and offered him a cane. "Why don't you take care of business." She gestured at the bathroom door. "I'll turn down the bed."

Mason limped into the bathroom, taking his time to relieve himself, stretching and testing out the improvements in his physical state. He found himself yawning, and, as much as he hated to admit it, all of the activity had worn him out. He flushed and paused to look in the mirror. The bruising was nearly gone from his face. He noticed again that his hair was too long, and he really should get it cut, before he turned and limped out of the bathroom.

Liza was right there with an arm to support him back to the bed and help him get settled with the light blanket pulled up over him. She put the cane within reach.

She pulled his tray over his lap and grabbed the water pitcher, disappearing into the bathroom to fill it. "So, what is your story, Jerah?" she asked as she emerged.

"My story?" He fidgeted a little. "I thought you already knew my story."

"I know the gossip." She poured water into his glass and set the pitcher down. "Rumors. Darvin tried to recruit you, you declined. You got jumped doing the family tradition thing and nearly ended up dead. Then you came here."

"Pretty much sums it up." Mason said, pulling the cover off his meal and making a face. "Does this place serve anything other than chicken?"

"Yeah, but trust me, it's worse than the chicken." She moved around the room straightening things. "So, going to give Darvin another shot at recruiting you?"

"I...don't know." Mason shrugged. "Not like I have a lot else going on."

She nodded, her hand resting on the end of the bed. "Just don't let him railroad you. You don't owe him anything."

"I take it you don't like him."

She shook her head. "No, it isn't that. He's a good enough guy. He likes us, trusts us. It's the government he works for that I don't completely trust."

Mason could understand that. He stifled a yawn and she patted his good leg. "I should let you rest. Buzz me if you need anything. I won't be far away."

He watched her go, feeling his face warm as she paused at the door, looking back at him with a wink. He turned his attention to his dinner, making himself eat at least some of it. She was wrong. He did owe Darvin. He owed him a lot, because this care he was getting was top of the line, and someone was footing the bill. It wasn't something he could ever hope to pay for on his own.

All he had to do was figure out how to repay the man without betraying himself. Without betraying who he was. He could hear his

Nana's voice inside him, warning him about being turned into a killer. As he abandoned the chicken for the cookies Liza had left him, he promised her he would never let that happen, the same way he had repeatedly while she was still alive.

Chapter Sixteen

"I think it's fair to say that someone knows about us." Anson said quietly.

It was just Alaric and his father. The rest of the house was empty. It had been nearly twenty-four hours since the fire. He didn't have to be an empath to know that everything had changed in those twenty-four hours.

"We have no idea what they know, or how many of us they know about... But it's becoming obvious that this is bigger than we thought it was already. The fire is being reported as an accident, that Abigail was involved in some magic ritual and some candles got knocked down."

Alaric frowned. "That isn't what happened."

His father nodded. "I know." He rubbed his temples and stifled a yawn. It was clear he hadn't slept. "Bryan and I read some of the firemen, and I managed to get a cop. The firemen had their memories altered. Whoever did it did a good job. I almost missed it. The cop, well... He was a very angry man." He sighed and turned to look out the window.

"How is Riley?" Alaric asked softly.

Anson stiffened a little and brought his eyes back to Alaric. "About how you'd expect. He's distraught; he's filled with rage. He isn't safe either. If whoever is behind this even thinks he might also be a witch or whatever."

"Witch?" Alaric asked.

"The sidewalk outside the house was painted with the words 'Burn Witch, Burn' when we finally got there."

Alaric nodded a little numbly. In his mind he could see the people outside the windows screaming the same words... Or at least that's what he'd convinced himself he was seeing. It was hard to tell anymore. His mother had used skills she seldom utilized to make him sleep the night before, and he could tell she had done some work to blur the memories so that he would be able to function.

"So, what are we going to do?" Alaric asked.

"For now, once it's dark out, you and your mother are taking Riley up to camp. We've already packed your things, and you're ready to go."

"What about you?"

"Bryan and I will follow. I've reached out to the handful of Sages I know in the area. I'm meeting with them first. It's time we do more than just pull our clan back together."

Alaric nodded. "We have to unite the tribes."

"Exactly."

"How is this happening?" Alaric asked after a long silence. "Can't anyone see what's going on?"

"I wish I knew, Son. I wish I knew."

* * *

Alaric stood naked in front of his mirror, his eyes raking over the fading scars that were all that remained as a physical reminder of what had happened. The skin on his hands and forearms was smooth and soft and his feet and legs had only the smallest marks left. There was still a red splotch on his hip where the melting drapes had landed, but even that didn't hurt anymore.

"Alaric, we're waiting on you."

"Yeah, just a minute, Mom." He abandoned his examination and reminded himself to thank Victoria for the treatments. Most of his clothes and a bunch of his personal belongings were already down in the car. He crossed to the pile of clothes on his bed. He dressed quickly, then shoved his feet into his well-worn sneakers and headed out of his room.

The house they had lived in since Alaric was six was the only home he could remember, and as he reached the bottom of the stairs, he was struck with the feeling that he would never see it again. His hand caressed over the wood of the railing and he sighed. He wasn't generally attached to things, and the people he loved were coming with him, so he knew he'd be fine. But his heart tightened a little at the thought.

The front door was open, and he could see Riley leaning against the fender of his mother's SUV, his arms crossed, his eyes closed. His grief was overwhelming and Alaric had to adjust his shields quickly. He wiped at a tear as he stepped out onto the porch.

Riley shifted as he approached, his face dropping as he reigned in his emotions. "Sorry, man...I..."

Alaric touched his shoulder. "You have nothing to be sorry for," he said softly. "I'm sorry." He tried to draw the blame, lessen Riley's emotional load for a moment. "I wish there had been something I could do."

Riley nodded, his face twisting as he tried not to succumb to the tears Alaric could feel welling up. Alaric held his arms open, and Riley gave up the struggle, his head on Alaric's shoulder as the tears came. Alaric held him and let him cry, letting calm and comfort and love seep from him to encompass them both.

After a few minutes, Riley stepped back, wiping his eyes and thanking him without words.

"Are we ready?" His parents were arm in arm beside the car. Alaric nodded and held out his hand for the keys.

His father put them in his hand, then pulled him into a hug. "Look after your mother."

"I will." Alaric agreed. "You call me if you need me."

He nodded. "I will."

"Emily, I'm going to be fine."

"I know, Anson. I'm allowed to worry." She kissed him and hugged him one more time before circling the car to get in on the passenger's side.

Riley nodded farewell and got into the back seat. Alaric sighed and got behind the wheel. "Okay, everybody get comfy, we've got a drive ahead of us."

* * *

They were well past the kinds of roads with streetlights, and his headlights cut through the darkness as he slowed down to find the turnoff to the old dirt road. It was hard to find in the daylight. In the dark it was nearly impossible. He slowed even more, his eyes scanning the left side of the road.

Beside him his mother stirred, yawning as she opened her eyes. "You okay?"

"Yeah, just looking for the road." He pointed as he found it and made the turn. They were forced to keep the slow pace by a road that was deeply rutted in places and wound its way through the trees.

She rubbed her eyes and sat up, peering out into the darkness around them. "I've always loved it up here."

Alaric drove them up to the parking lot and parked near the trail that led to the bunk house. It was the middle of the night. He could sense Sahara and the girls in one of the cabins not far away. He put the vehicle in park and set the parking brake, glancing behind him to see if Riley was awake. Riley nodded and slid closer to the door.

"We can sleep in the bunkhouse tonight." Alaric said softly. "In the daylight, we can pick a cabin."

Emily was the first out of the car. Alaric knew she was bothered by all of it and grieving along with Riley, but she shoved it aside and went into nurturing mother mode, opening the back of the SUV and pulling out pillows and sleeping bags as Alaric went up to the door. Inside there were still hot coals in the fireplace and the bunk house was fairly warm. Emily went straight upstairs to make up beds for them.

Riley stood in the doorway, his eyes sweeping around the room. "I remember the first time Abigail brought me up here." Riley said, stepping into the room and closing the door. "It was just after our honeymoon."

"I remember you hating it." Alaric said, turning to him with a soft smile.

Riley nodded, a vague smile turning the corners of his lips up. "City boy." He came closer, holding out his hands to the heat of the coals. "But I learned a lot that weekend. And I came to really like it here."

"But you're still a city boy," Alaric chided lightly.

"Always will be," Riley responded.

"Okay boys, up to bed. It's late."

Riley turned away and shuffled toward the stairs and Alaric followed. His mother radiated concern as she watched Riley head up, and Alaric stopped to put a hand on her shoulder. "*He'll be okay.*"

She nodded, slipping an arm around him. They followed Riley's back up the stairs that way, with her arm keeping him close. At the top, she kissed his cheek and pointed him toward the door to the men's bunk. "Sleep well."

She disappeared behind another door with the silhouette of a woman on it.

Riley was dropping his jeans across the end of his bunk as Alaric came into the room. He didn't say anything as he climbed into the sleeping bag spread out on the bed. Alaric left him to it, stripping off his pants quickly and settling into his own sleeping bag.

He lay still, knowing he wasn't likely to sleep just yet. He focused instead on keeping his thoughts in order and away from recent memories. He listened to the night sounds, so much different than the sounds at home.

Only, that wasn't home, not anymore. For now, this was. And it was his job to make it as comfortable and secure as he could.

* * *

Alaric pulled the last of the supplies out of the SUV, looking up as another vehicle pulled in beside him. He nodded hello to Victoria as she emerged, setting the boxes beside the suitcases near the trail.

"There are a few more cars behind me." Victoria said.

From her car emerged several people he knew by name and face, but had never really spent time with. He went to help them unpack their belongings. "What's going on?" Alaric asked as Victoria stayed by her door.

"I'm not staying. My old knees and back just wouldn't handle it."

"You aren't going back there, are you?"

She shook her head. "I'm heading back east. Going to stay with my daughter awhile. She's expecting my second grandchild."

"What about Dad?"

"He's still trying to run some damage control. He said he'd be along in a few days."

"So this is it?"

She shrugged and they both looked up as a van pulled in, followed by another SUV. "Expect them to keep coming," Victoria said. "And not just us Shadows; there's a fair number of Sages in Sacramento that your father is reaching out to."

It had been a while since he'd heard the old word for their people. It hadn't been in use much in the last century. A reference to a skill that let a trained person slip into another's mind and control them, like a Shadow inside them, the name had been left behind when the tribe made the conscious choice to regulate the use of those kinds of skills.

"I guess I better get us organized then," Alaric said. He hugged her tightly. "You take care of yourself, Victoria. Drive safely."

He stepped back as she got back in her car, moving to the trail where he could see all of the newcomers. "Can you all gather over here? Please."

Besides the three who had come with Victoria, there were two families with three children between them and two couples. Marcy and Jacob Masters and Marcy's brother and his wife, George and Debbie Casten, were relations on his mother's side. Of the four, he knew that

Marcy was a fairly adept telepath and her brother George was one of the few with the rare gift of telekinesis.

Nicole Guiilon was only in her early twenties, but her gift was even more rare than George's. She could control fire. Beside her stood Carter McDaniel, who had a knack for getting people to tell him their darkest secrets, and Jessica Melvin. Her gifts were a mystery to him.

The families he knew by reputation only. The Ollivers, Cassandra and Ethan with their son Charlie, ran the garage where Riley had worked, and there was the Sanders, Colette and Otto along with their teenage daughter Diana and their eight-year-old son, Richard. He only knew them because Diana had been in some of the classes he and his mother had taught.

"Okay, most of you know what we have here at the camp. We're fully stocked for at least the next few months, and we can supplement with hunting and fishing. There should be plenty of cabins for everyone, but we will have to share. I'd like the single folks to consider staying in the bunk house."

He made eye contact with several of them before continuing. "We will get a register drawn up so we can keep track of who is here and where they're staying, but for now, go ahead and pick out your cabins. There's also room for tents across the river if you're up for that sort of thing, but I'll remind you that winter is coming up fast. I'll have lunch ready in about an hour, so come on back to the bunk house then."

Alaric watched them scatter, hauling their belongings with them. He felt his mother come from up near the bunkhouse, so he grabbed a couple suitcases and followed the others up the trail. She was standing on the porch as he set the suitcases down. "We'll have to set up shifts to hunt and get wood," she said softly.

"Yeah, I know."

She touched his shoulder. "Let me worry about it. You have to get on that lunch." She smiled and grabbed her suitcase from beside him. "Riley's on his way for the rest."

Alaric nodded and let her go, scratching at his head as he tallied up how much food to make. He'd already inventoried the stores in the pantry and the industrial sized freezer. Jordan had done a good job getting them ready. He opted for simple, and set about making up a bunch of sandwiches and a simple vegetable soup.

Riley showed up as he was finishing to help him move trays of food out to one of the tables in the hall. People trickled in and took food to their own tables. In just a few minutes the hall was filled with conversations, and that familiar feeling of dread that had haunted him for weeks settled over him.

On impulse, Alaric stepped out onto the porch, stilling his mind and attempting to reach out across the distance to his father. All he got was static and the start of a headache. He turned his attention then closer to home. He could sense the old wards that they had erected years before, but they would need reinforcing.

"Am I interrupting?"

Alaric opened his eyes, a little surprised that Sahara could sneak up on him. "No, of course not."

She inclined her head toward the door. "Lot of new folk."

"Yeah, sorry about that. I should have found a way to warn you."

"You owe us nothing," Sahara said. She sat in one of the wooden chairs, her eyes going gold. "Do they know about us?"

He sat beside her. "They can tell that you're here. And you should probably introduce yourself."

"The girls are afraid."

He nodded. "I can understand that. But they're safe here. No one is going to harm them."

She looked at him, her eyes narrowing. "And you know that?"

"I don't *know* it," Alaric acknowledged. "What I do know is that we need to be united against our common enemy, not fighting one another."

She sat back in the chair, her hands folding together. "In my experience, we don't intermingle well. Shifters have often been targeted by the other tribes."

He nodded. "As have Shades. In reality, we've all turned on each other at one point or another."

"And now, we make peace?" Sahara asked softly.

"I think we have to try." Alaric confirmed. "I think it's the only way we're going to survive."

"If we don't kill each other first," Sahara responded, standing. She crossed her arms, staring out into the trees for a long moment before she turned to look at him. "You haven't asked, but you should know, when we were prisoners, they were trying to... I guess you could call it brainwashing. Trying to make us kill for them."

Alaric nodded. He'd already suspected that from what he'd seen in Riley's vision. "But it didn't work."

She looked at him, her eyes narrowing. Alaric could feel his cheeks flushing a little. "You've read us?"

"Not me, but yes. We had to make sure." It was something he had tasked to his mother, the one person he knew could befriend the Shifters easily.

She inhaled slowly and let it out just as slowly. "I was going to ask you to do it anyway," Sahara said. They were quiet for a long moment before Sahara nodded. "The girls and I can go hunting. Bring back a deer. Should feed the camp for a while."

"We'd appreciate that."

He watched her walk away. He knew she had a point. They would need to find a way to work together though, despite their collective histories. It was cliché to think it, but the old adage remained true. United, they would stand, but divided they would likely kill each other so the enemy wouldn't even need to try.

Chapter Seventeen

Every day, twice a day, Mason got to spend two hours in the water table. For the first half hour, he would soak, then Dr. Anthony would join him and give him a treatment similar to when he worked directly on Mason's back, but utilizing the water. Then he would leave Mason to doze in the water, letting the remaining energy work unattended. On the third day, Dr. Anthony wheeled a stool close to the table after making a few notes on Mason's charts.

"How are the burns, Mr. Jerah?"

"Almost can't even tell they were there, Doc," Mason replied.

Dr. Anthony smiled and nodded. "That is what we want to hear. Now then, shall we focus on your leg today?" His hands dipped into the several inches of water and wiggled his fingers. The water warmed and Mason closed his eyes, slipping himself along the lines of his body to watch the doctor work.

The energy moved under the plaster cast, knitting together the broken bone beneath. It was a more thorough treatment on the leg than he had done before. Mason could feel the bone fragments easing together and strengthening.

After a few minutes the doctor withdrew, his face a little red and sweaty with the strain. He dried his hands on a towel draped over his knee. "That is coming along nicely. I think we can get you out of this cast and let you have some real soaking time."

"Liza did mention you have some good soaking pools."

"We do indeed." He stood and went to the door, speaking softly to someone in the hallway. "I will check in with you later, Mr. Jerah."

Liza and Freddie came in as Dr. Anthony left to get him off the table. "Doc says we get to let you out of that plaster prison." Liza said as they eased his leg out of the sling. Freddie helped him swing the leg off to the side while Liza supported his right side. The nurse helped him get dry and handed him a fresh gown. She pulled the wheelchair closer and helped him ease back into it.

"You're in good hands, Mason." Freddie said with a smile. "Now that you're ready for the big pools, I won't be seeing you in my ward again."

Liza pushed him out of the room and down toward the elevators. "So we'll get this off and get you into a splint for support until it's healed, and then Dr. Anthony has prescribed you an hour in pool number one."

"It's been a long time since I had a good soak." Mason sighed as the elevator doors closed.

"How long is a long time?"

Mason had to think about it. His last time in the pond felt like a lifetime ago. "I'm not sure. Time is a little blurred right now."

"Here we go." She pushed him out of the elevator and into a waiting area, checking him in, before wheeling him back behind double doors and into a room. It didn't take long for the technician to show up and cut the plaster from his leg.

The technician washed his leg, then felt over the bones, nodding to himself. "This is healing well. Let me send someone in to fit you for a boot to protect it while it finishes healing."

Almost an hour later, Liza wheeled him into a room filled with small pools. She stopped beside the first one, and locked the wheels of the chair, coming around to remove his new splint/boot combo. "Pool number one." She held an arm for him to use as leverage out of the chair and helped him out of the hospital gown.

He shivered a little in just the light cotton shorts she had given him for modesty's sake once they'd gotten the cast off. "It is only about two feet deep, so you can just lay back and relax." She supported him down into the water and when he was sitting she smiled. "I'll be back in an hour."

Cool, but not cold, the water was like a companion he had left behind, embracing him as he lay back into it, covering him like a blanket. It mostly covered him, his nose stuck up out of the water, but he didn't care. It was perfect.

It took him a few minutes to realize that it wasn't just water though. It was subtle. The mineral balance was ideal, and the electric current was a gentle buzz along his skin. He had read that the right levels of certain minerals and electricity could boost the natural properties in water that contributed to a Shade's well-being, provide soothing healing that required little expenditure of energy. He had never had a place to test that.

Mason closed his eyes and let himself drift, let the energy of the water move over him and through him, refreshing skin that hadn't even realized how much it had missed the touch of water.

The hour sped by, and all too soon, Liza was helping him back up out of the water and into a robe and slippers. "Like that?" She grinned. "You look like you liked that."

"It was amazing." Mason agreed as he adjusted his position in the chair. The combination of the water and getting rid of the cast had him feeling better than he had in a while.

Liza got him back to his room where a fresh hospital gown was on his tray table with the splint. Liza parked him and set the brakes before grabbing the splint and coming to kneel in front of him. Her hands were gentle as they lifted his foot and got him back into the boot. She held up the gown and smirked at him. For a second he was half sure she was going to tell him to drop his still wet shorts right there, but she winked and handed him the gown, followed by the cane.

"Go on, get changed."

He could hear her in the room as he stood in the bathroom to change. In the last few days she had seen just about all he had to offer physically. He flushed a little at the thought, dropping the wet shorts to the floor and using a towel to dry himself off a little more.

Liza had been friendly from the moment he'd met her, but he was sure that was just part of her job. Not that he'd recognize it if it was anything else. His experience with women was largely his Nana and whatever he had seen on television.

Mason relieved himself and flushed, washed his hands, and then pulled the hospital gown on. He got most of the ties tied and opened the bathroom door.

Liza was right there, her hand sliding to the small of his back to help him balance, tucking her body in close to his on his left side. Her fingers slid through the openings in the gown, her skin warm where it touched his. She helped him toward the bed, her hair brushing his face. His face was hot with the flushing of emotion as she turned slightly, her lips brushing his cheek as she helped him across the floor.

Liza's hand slipped to his elbow and she stepped lightly out of the way, helping him pivot on his good foot to sit on the bed. That was when he noticed Adam Darvin sitting in the chair. Mason started, but Liza continued getting him into the bed, helping him lift the splinted leg and then arranging his blankets out of his way. His eyes followed her as she went to refill his water his face still hot.

She put the pitcher on his tray. "Buzz me if you need me." Liza said, one eyebrow lifting. "For… any reason."

Mason watched her go, feeling the blush on his face deepen as Darvin cleared his throat. "I was beginning to wonder when to expect you," Mason said pulling his eyes away from the door.

Adam smirked. "Oh now, she's a handful."

Mason hid his own grin behind a hand, then pulled that hand through his hair. He didn't know exactly what was going on between them, but he was starting to wonder if the friendly wasn't flirtation or something more than just friendly. "Tell me about it." He cleared his throat and forced his attention back to Darvin. He needed to be thinking clear when dealing with him, that much he was sure of.

"So the doctor tells me you're doing a lot better."

"Not ready to run a marathon, but yeah. I'm better." Mason pulled the light blanket up over his legs and shifted on the bed. His hands and back were nearly normal, his ankle wouldn't be far behind. Any day now, he expected Dr. Anthony to tell him he was being released. Which, he thought, was why the fed had shown up again. He nodded to himself, slowly looking up at Darvin. "I figure this is where you come and tell me what I owe you."

Mason had spent a lot of time thinking about it. The kind of treatment he was receiving wasn't cheap, even without the added benefit of Shade physicians and nurses and massage therapists. The debt he was accumulating wasn't small, and he owed it to Adam Darvin for making it possible.

Darvin opened his mouth, then closed it. "I wasn't going to put it that way."

"I'm not a man for pretty words, Mr. Darvin. I got nothing but what came in with me, so you know I don't have money. But I figure all this don't come with just a handshake and a 'see ya round', either."

Darvin nodded, sitting back in the chair. "Okay, no pretty words. My agency employs people with certain gifts, abilities. Our mandate is to provide the government with intelligence that might not be available by traditional means. And to police the activities of other such enhanced individuals."

Mason could appreciate the honesty. It wasn't far from what he had expected. He'd considered what he would and wouldn't do, what his Nana would approve of. "I have some conditions." He waited for Darvin to nod his agreement. "I won't kill. I won't be an assassin. No bomb planting, no engaging of any kind. Just information gathering."

He didn't have a deep understanding of the politics involved, but from what he had learned, the world was in need of someone to try to find the balance, now that Shades had been exposed. He knew that large groups of the population had no love for his kind, and that there organizations filling their need to lash out. The 8th Battalion was the most visible, but in his time here at the hospital, he'd learned of others.

He also knew he had nowhere else to go really. He could go home, back to hiding from the world the way his Nana had, but that wasn't living. He needed to do something with his life, and as long as he could hold to those principles, he figured this would be as good a job as any.

"No, we wouldn't want you to do anything against your morals." Darvin. said. He tilted his head to the side and frowned a little. "Well, we might want you to, but we won't force you. We'll train you, and some of that will include fighting, self-defense, that sort of thing. Most of the time you'll work with a handler, but sometimes things get dicey."

"I can handle myself." Mason looked down at himself and the evidence that his last fight was what had landed him in this position and rolled his eyes. "All evidence to the contrary aside. I can handle weapons, been hunting for food since I was a kid." He bit his lip. "I want time to copy and repair my Book of Line, and I want access to learn more from Dr. Anthony and Liza."

The fed stood and rested a hand on his shoulder. "All in good time, son. All in good time." He rubbed his hands together and took a step toward the door before turning back with a grin. "We'll get you sprung out of here in a day or two, and I'll take you to a training facility. We'll have you out in the field in no time."

Mason watched him leave, feeling for a moment like he'd just made a huge mistake, but then Liza was at the door and all thought of Adam Darvin or the government he worked for slipped away.

"So, you leaving us already?" She leaned on the door, biting her lip.

"Oh, I'm sure I'll be around." Mason said, rolling his eyes as he felt himself blushing.

She moved into the room slowly, her hand finding his foot and sliding up his leg as she held his eyes, her own eyes filled with mischief. "Is that so?"

Her hand was on his thigh and he cleared his throat, licked his lips. "You're the one who keeps telling me you got the best soaking pools in DC."

She nodded and her hand inched upward. "So you'll be around.... for our pools..."

His heart thundered as she leaned in closer, her mouth only inches from his. "Well...and...and...because..." Words stopped mattering though when her lips covered his and her tongue teased along his lip. He was pretty sure he stopped breathing for a second as she pulled away.

"Because..."

He snaked a hand up into her hair and tugged her back in, bringing their mouths together.

Someone cleared their throat near the door and Liza pulled back. "Ms. Datonelli, the patient in room 234 is waiting."

She smirked at Mason and rolled her eyes. "Be right there, just making sure Mr. Jerah's eye is healing up." She moved to the door and grinned at him. "Don't go anywhere, cowboy. I'll be back to check the rest too."

He flushed and rubbed his hands over his face. It wasn't like he'd never kissed anyone before, except for how, at eighteen, he'd never really kissed someone before, not like that. Certainly not another Shade.

His sheltered life with his Nana did nothing to prepare him for this kind of thing. He exhaled slowly and tried to center his thoughts. Maybe there were other reasons to stay in DC and work for Darvin. Reasons that had nothing to do with what he owed the man, and maybe everything to do with what he owed himself.

* * *

"This will be your room. You can drop your bag if you want." Darvin handed him a key card. Mason took it and swiped it through the reader on the door. The room inside was small, cramped with what little furniture there was, but it was adequate. A twin bed against one wall, a desk complete with a light and a supply of basic office supplies, and a wardrobe was more than he'd had in a while before he'd found himself in the hospital. Mason dropped his backpack on the bed, his eyes scanning around the room.

"We'll get you fitted for some basic clothes before the day is out. You'll want to wear the standard uniform around here, help you fit in." Darvin said, checking his watch. "Let's get through the rest of the tour."

Mason followed him back into the hall and down to what looked like an impressive gym set up. Various people were busy with the equipment, glancing their way before going back to their work outs.

"Just about everything you could need." Darvin said, walking him past treadmills and elliptical trainers, free weights and other machines. "When Dr. Anthony gives the okay, you'll be training with Jake Mars." He pointed to a short, but well-muscled man currently putting a petite blond through a boxing exercise. "He's our best hand to hand guy. He'll get you certified on everything you need before we put you out into the field."

Darvin took them out into the hallway again. "I'm afraid our pools aren't as good as the ones at the hospital, but we have one set up for our Shades. Good for swimming laps and the like."

"Shades. More than me then?" Mason asked.

Darvin nodded. "Yes, four besides you right now. You'll meet them soon enough." He pointed down a hallway. "Pool is down there. This is the residential level for assets we have reasons to keep on site. My office is up two floors. Tactical is down two. Onsite medical is on the floor below. Anything more than sprains and strains, we'll send you back to Dr. Anthony." He took Mason to the elevator they had just come down. "Dr. Anthony sent us a pretty thorough rundown of your physical condition, so we'll skip the usual medical once over."

The elevator took them up two floors, and Darvin led them down a series of hallways. "This is me. I have a stack of paperwork for you before I take you to meet the rest of the team."

Mason looked around the office as Darvin sat behind the desk. "Have a seat." Darvin said, making Mason turn from perusing the books on his shelf. "We get through this, we can grab some lunch and I'll introduce you to your handler, trainer, and the rest." He sat, taking the stack of papers Darvin handed him. "All of the places to sign are flagged. I'm going to grab some coffee. You want anything?"

Mason shook his head and scanned the first page. "What is all of this?"

Darvin chuckled. "Obviously, you've never had a job. Most of it is standard employment stuff, then all the added crap because it's a government job. Make sure you read it all before you sign it. I'll be back if you have questions on anything."

He left Mason there with a pen and the stack of papers to read and sign. As he made his way through it, he wondered if maybe he'd gotten himself into something he shouldn't have.

It ended up being a couple of hours before he got to the bottom of the stack and looked up. Darvin was standing in the doorway of the office, talking to someone out in the hallway. Mason set the last of the paperwork on top of the stack and stood, stretching slowly. Darvin called him over, stepping into the hallway. "Mason, this is Agent Ellen Landry. Ellen, Mason Jerah."

She was pretty, in a very buttoned up sort of way. Her hair was pulled back in a tidy knot and her navy suit was impeccable. But she was upset, Mason could feel it. "Ma'am."

"We'll talk later." Darvin said, and she nodded tightly.

"Welcome, Mr. Jerah. Sir." She turned on her heel and walked away.

"She okay?" Mason asked.

Darvin sighed. "Yeah, she will be. She just lost an asset."

"Lost..." Mason narrowed his eyes as Darvin gestured down the hall.

"She was a handler, her asset was killed in the line of duty."

Mason looked back over his shoulder. "Shade?"

Darvin shook his head. "No. Different sort of asset." He was quiet then as they walked to the cafeteria. Mason followed his lead, grabbing a pre-made salad from the cooler and a bottle of water before taking a seat opposite Darvin at one of the tables.

It wasn't like Mason didn't realize that what he was about to undertake was dangerous. It wasn't like he'd be delivering the mail. He'd vaguely understood that he could be asked to do dangerous things in places where his kind would not be well received, but somehow, Agent Landry's emotional state was bringing it home. "Were they close?" Mason asked, pulling Darvin up from some deep thought.

"What?"

"Landry and her... asset. Were they close?"

Darvin shrugged. "Hazard of the job, I guess. Sometimes it's just you and your handler, and you rely on each other." He took a deep breath and let it out slowly. "Which is why you will be getting training." He ate quietly for a few minutes, his eyes on his food.

Mason took the hint and focused on eating as well. He stifled a yawn as he finished his salad. It had been a long day. His ankle ached inside the boot, but he figured that to be the price for all the walking he'd done since leaving the hospital. He could do some healing work later.

He just had to get through his first day.

Chapter Eighteen

Alaric woke suddenly, his heart racing and his head a jumble of memories, visions, and his father's voice. He sat in the dark, listening for something to tell him what had woken him. The cabin was still and quiet. His mother shifted in her sleep in the next room, and Riley was restless in the bedroom downstairs.

He wiped his sweaty face and got out of bed, padding to the window on bare feet. The night sky was clear and a sliver of moon shined down on the valley. It seemed peaceful. He knew it was anything but peaceful.

He pulled on his pants and rummaged in his bag for a shirt to pull on as he left the room. By the front door, he shoved his feet into his shoes and eased the door open. The path between the cabin they had chosen and the bunk house was well worn, and it led him behind the shower house and what had been a vegetable garden in the years when the camp was occupied all summer.

Adrenaline was still pumping through him as Alaric approached the bunkhouse, making his hands shake a little. He wasn't sure what was happening or what he could do about it, but he knew he wouldn't be sleeping again for a while.

The bunkhouse was dark. The bunks upstairs were half filled with people who had been coming in a slow stream. More than half of the cabins were full as well.

Alaric circled the bunkhouse, moving toward the parking lot. He wasn't alone. He could feel them. He slowed his steps, listening intently, letting his extra senses add to his perception. Three animals... two on the porch, one sitting by the stairs. He came to a stop as six gold eyes turned to him. The largest of the three stood, gold fur rippling over tense muscles and he froze, not afraid exactly, but knowing that the animal could tear him apart if it wanted to.

It came toward him slowly, eyes intent on his face. Rising up on its hind legs, it shimmered a little in the wan light, features shifting until rather than a big cat, Sahara was standing there, naked and proud, her eyes on his.

"Sahara," he greeted softly.

She raised an eyebrow and turned her eyes to the other two cats, gesturing with her head for them to go. When they were gone, she turned on her heel and headed to the porch, pausing to lift a robe from one of the chairs. She shrugged it on and tied the belt before turning to him again. She lifted her hair free of the fabric and sat in the chair. "Can't sleep?" she finally asked.

Alaric stopped on the stair, one hand on the railing. "Something woke me."

Her eyes were watching the trees when he looked up at her. "Something's coming." Sahara said.

He nodded, his eyes following hers to stare into the dark woods. The wards along the property line were pulsing, as if someone had walked along them, not quite crossing them. He took a step away from the bunkhouse, then down the trail. He passed between his mother's SUV and another car. The night was still, but he could sense turmoil, pain... and it was rolling their way.

He was pulled forward, moving faster as he headed down the dirt road. The wards pulsed louder in his head, alerting him that someone was pushing against them. Alaric ran down the road, stopping when he reached the inner gate that had only been erected the week before. It marked the halfway point between the camp and the main road. It was another two and half miles out to the state road from there.

He stood at the gate panting, staring out into the darkness, trying to put something more concrete to the feeling that they were under attack.

Sahara was beside him in cat form, big paws on the top of the gate. For a long moment they stood side by side, watching and waiting. The wards calmed their warning, and settled to their normal silent watch, but still he stood, expecting something, anything to happen.

Then he felt the wards open and Sahara was up and over the gate before he could respond. He jumped the gate as well and took off running after her, pulling up short as he spotted Bryan, bloody and exhausted with a ragtag group behind him. He had a gun in his hand, pointed at Sahara who seemed poised to jump at him.

"Bryan?" Alaric asked as he reached them.

The gun lowered. In response, Sahara sat beside Alaric who was scanning the ten or so faces. "Bryan, where is my father?" He reached out for him, but like before all he got was static.

Bryan looked away. "I'm not sure. Last I knew he was alive." He shook his head. "We'd know if he wasn't." Alaric could tell he wasn't completely convinced of that, but didn't seem willing to say more. "He sent me, with these people. Said he'd be behind us."

Alaric looked at the tired, frightened faces and nodded. "Okay. Let's get you up to the bunkhouse."

He led the way up the road, leading them around the gate, which served only to prevent vehicles from continuing up the road. Sahara walked beside him until they reached the driveway. She sort of nodded to him and trotted off toward the cabin she shared with the sisters.

Smoke was coming from the chimney of the bunkhouse and a warm glow lit its windows. His mother opened the door, wrapped in her bathrobe. "*Heard the wards,*" she sent.

Alaric stepped aside and let Bryan lead the group inside. He counted four women, two teenaged boys, and four men. It was difficult to tell exactly who they were, but if his father sent them, they would be welcome. He smiled reassuringly to his mother, slipping an arm around her as they moved into the main hall of the bunkhouse. "We're going to need first aid supplies," Alaric said softly.

"I'll get them." She kissed his cheek and started to pull away, but then her hand tightened on his. "*He's okay.*"

He nodded, not sure he believed her, but turned his attention to the new arrivals. They looked a little shell shocked, clumping together in small groups. Bryan stood apart, still bleeding from a wound close to his scalp. His face was bruised and from what Alaric could see of the rest of him, he'd been through an ordeal.

Alaric approached him, pulling him away from the others. "First thing, are you okay?"

Bryan nodded, though it took him a minute to lift his eyes to meet Alaric's. "Yeah. I will be."

Alaric nodded, shifting from one concern to the next. "Okay. What happened? Who are these people?"

Bryan looked over them and shrugged. "Ahmed and Sabina, her father was the victim of a hate crime a week ago, killed because he was Muslim." He gestured at a woman in a headscarf and the man holding her. "The woman helping your mother is Keisha Freeman, Sage midwife. She worked at a clinic that got closed down with the new mandates. Those are her boys."

If he had to guess, Alaric would put the boys at fourteen and seventeen. They were both tall, the younger one broad at the shoulder. There was a challenge in the older one's eyes when he felt Alaric looking at him. The color of their skin was enough to mark them by those who seemed to be attempting to whitewash the country, and he knew he must seem like the enemy.

He was, after all, blue eyed, with blonde hair and a complexion that started out pale and deepened to a tan in the sun. He was nothing like them.

Alaric sighed and followed Keisha as she moved with the first aid supplies to a woman who was holding her arm across her body.

Bryan followed his attention. "Patty...something. I don't remember." He rubbed his forehead, frowning when his hand came away bloody.

"Okay, introductions can wait. Tell me what happened."

Bryan's shields were up and tightly shuttered, but Alaric brushed against them to let him know he was there, that he was among friends. Bryan didn't acknowledge him, just sighed and slowly sank to the bench behind him. "We met with a couple of the Sages." He gestured at Keisha. "Your father extended the invitation." He rubbed his eyes and inhaled. "The violence has gotten crazy. The National Guard presence has doubled. Not just here. Utah is all but shut down. Airports are closed, all the main roads into the state are barricaded off. Montana isn't far behind. The news is saying that Georgia and Alabama are considering similar measures. Most major cities are under curfew."

Alaric shook his head. "How is this happening?"

"Fear." Bryan heaved a heavy sigh. "Douglas is milking it like it's a dairy cow. Every appearance, every rally, every interview. His rhetoric is giving people a place to point their fear."

"Let's have a look at you."

Alaric stepped to the side as Keisha approached them, setting the first aid kit on the table behind Bryan, who tried to pull away. "I'm fine."

"I'll be the judge of that." Keisha said, lifting gauze to his bloody forehead. "You're lucky you're still upright."

"I said I'm fine." Bryan said, grabbing her wrist.

"You have a concussion." Keisha countered, pulling her wrist free. "And probably some bruised ribs. Not to mention that finger looks broken."

"Bryan, let her look you over." Alaric insisted, crossing his arms in imitation of his father's best do-as-I-say stance. "And finish telling me what happened."

"He nearly got himself killed getting us out of there," Keisha said for him as she dabbed at the blood on his forehead. "Me and my boys were being detained, same as Letta and Maria over there. They wanted to 'test us,' never said for what. They were going to ship us somewhere. Then him and another man came and got us out."

"My father?" Alaric asked, his voice tight.

Bryan nodded, hissing as Keisha's finger got too close to the wound. "We found them locked in a room at a place owned by the same holding company as owned that lab. Your dad and I got separated. I got caught, he got out. When they tried to move us, I..." His eyes met Alaric's, and he could see in them that Bryan did what he had to in order to free them. Invading the minds of others that way was distasteful, but Alaric could see the necessity. He nodded his acceptance of that truth, and Bryan cleared his throat. "I stole a truck and we ran. Picked up the others at the place your father told them to meet us. Got out of the city before they set up the checkpoints."

"So where's the truck?" Alaric asked.

"Hid it a few miles back. Didn't want it leading them here." Bryan let Keisha take his hand, yelling as she set the finger. "Damnit, woman!"

"For your own good," she said as she taped two of his fingers together to give the broken one time to heal. "You're going to have a headache for a few days, but you'll live. Take some aspirin for the pain."

"I'd rather have a glass of whiskey," Bryan grumbled as she walked away.

"So where is Dad?" Alaric asked, feeling his mother's eyes on him.

"I'm not sure." Bryan answered, refusing to look at him. "I just know he's alive."

Alaric nodded and turned to survey the room. "Okay, let's get these people settled in and get some rest." He moved away, smiling softly for the traumatized people as he drew them close. "For now, let's get you guys some sleep. There are men's and ladies' dorms upstairs. Go in quietly as others are sleeping. Come the morning we'll get you into something more private if we can."

"Bryan, we have an extra room in our cabin." Emily said, joining them. "You're welcome to stay with us."

He nodded slowly. "Thank you, Emily. I appreciate that."

"You two go ahead," Alaric said. "I don't think I'll be sleeping again tonight."

His mother kissed his cheek before she took Bryan's arm and lead him out the back door of the bunkhouse. Alaric sat near the fire his mother had started, wishing it could ease the chill that came from within.

He felt as though it was all slipping away, and they were hiding from it instead of trying to do something to prevent the end Riley had seen. Not that he knew what they could do, but they could use the gifts they had, try to challenge the anger and fear.

He sighed and scrubbed his hands over his face and up through his hair. Now he had the responsibility of these people, keeping them safe. He had to focus here, on getting them through the winter.

If he was honest, he'd rather be out there, finding his father, figuring out what was behind all of this. He could hear his father's voice in his head, telling him that a leader doesn't always get to do what he wants. A leader must think of his people first.

"I never wanted to be a leader," Alaric mumbled, though the point was moot. His father was the clan's leader, and theirs was one of the few clans that still had one. As such, the entire tribe looked to his father, and as Anson Lambrecht's son, they looked to Alaric as well. Now wasn't the time to run away.

* * *

The air was chill, even in the middle of the afternoon, as Alaric and Riley hiked along the boundaries of the property, examining the wards that had been put in place decades before. They didn't keep people out, necessarily, though they did mask the property to a degree, turning the ungifted eye away. It wasn't quite a glamor, but it came from the same sort of gift. They had started down by the road, shoring up the wards that took the most beating from those passing by, and they worked their way up onto the eastern ridge. Alaric paused them as they came to the trail that led away to the south and east.

About a day's hike down that trail was a small town that they had befriended when Alaric had been only ten or so. It was an eclectic little place that served those who lived in scattered cabins around the area. There was a small general store and a tavern, as well as a single gas pump, a post office, and the start of a paved road that cut through the forest, north of the camp, leading west and then south.

The ward there was intact and strong. Alaric put his hand on the tree that bore the marker and could sense his uncle's hand in the making of the ward.

"It's quiet." Riley said softly, pulling Alaric's attention away from the tree.

"Yeah, you'd never even know that the valley below is home to over twenty people right now."

"With more coming." Riley moved closer to the edge of the ridge, peering down through the trees. "Can't even see it from here."

"That's good though. Means we're less likely to draw attention."

Riley was quiet for a long moment, looking down into the valley. "For now anyway," he said, glancing up at Alaric. "But what do we do now?"

Alaric sighed and moved to stand beside him. "I don't know. Wait, I guess."

Riley nodded, his eyes distant. Alaric could just about see the vision come over him, and he reached out a hand to steady Riley so he wouldn't pitch over the edge. Alaric watched and waited.

Riley shuddered a little as it ended and looked up at Alaric, licking his lips before speaking. "Your father..." He shook his head. "Alaric, they have him."

"They?"

Riley nodded. "Some building, east of here. A compound." Riley's mind touched his, then Alaric was looking at a desert compound with low buildings and chain link fences. "He's not alone."

His instinct was to run back to camp and gather volunteers, but he forced himself to calm, drawing a deep breath in. There was no way to tell if Riley's vision was foretelling a possible future or if what he was seeing was happening already. "Let's finish up." Alaric said, gesturing toward the next ward. "Then we can figure out what to do about Dad."

Chapter Nineteen

Mason sat at the small desk in the crowded confines of his room. It wasn't much, but it was starting to feel at least somewhat like home. Maybe home was an exaggeration. It was safe, and he had everything he needed.

The desk was currently covered with pages out of his Book of Line, the new book sitting open where he'd been copying the family tree.

Darvin had offered to scan the old book and reproduce it for him, but Mason didn't have much in the way of tradition handed down to him. He wanted to keep this one. Besides, it was affording him time to learn. Already his control of his own body had improved, his ability to meditate and connect to the memories inside him stronger.

Of course, that was only part of how he was spending his time. The stack of books and manila folders on the floor beside the desk spoke to the amount of studying he'd been doing outside of his Book of Line.

There was history, the traditional kind he would have learned in school, and the less traditional kind he should have learned from his family. Books that told stories of the old tribes, of Shapeshifters and Sages, Shades and Shadows, folders of intelligence on those who, like him, lived in secret.

He had just finished reading deep background on current events: intelligence on the field of presidential candidates, how their rhetoric was skewing the courts of political opinion, about the wave of anti-Shade sentiment, and the bigotry that rode along with it for other groups of outsiders. The problem wasn't unique to the United States, but it was the most pronounced there. Both Canada and the United Kingdom were reported scattered violence as well.

It was worse than he had imagined. According to what he had read, multiple states were considering a move to cede from the union, closing borders and airports. Major cities were under curfew, their police forces joined by military personnel to enforce it in an effort to stem the violence.

The intel on the 8th Battalion was not nearly as coherent. It had begun in response to Senator Norman Douglas' call to arm themselves against the enemy, to defend their way of life from the ungodly heathens who sought to destroy the country from within. They were just starting to understand that what had at first seemed like individuals acting out their personal hatred was in fact being driven by an more organized power, though no one had a clue who that organized power was.

They took their name from a book, popular in the far right, conservative circles, a novel that told a story of an army rising to do the work of their god.

Darvin's agency was tasked with gathering intelligence, determining how big this army was and helping the US government determine how to respond. He had agents out west and down south, and the reports they were getting were grim.

That wasn't the end of his education either. Mason had finally been cleared by Dr. Anthony to begin his physical training, which had started with basic fitness and progressed to hand to hand combat of various kinds. For the first week, his whole body had been one continuous ache.

There was a knock on his door and Mason looked up from the page he was copying to find Darvin nodding at him from the door. "You ready? I've got something for you."

Mason dropped his pen and stood, shoving his feet into his boots to follow Darvin out of the residential quarter and past a couple of gyms where he'd routinely gotten his ass kicked over the last few weeks. Darvin led him into a conference room where he gestured to a seat.

Mason sat, his eyes sweeping the room. The agent he only knew as Raven was there, her long hair tightly braided, her dark eyes focused. He could tell she was favoring her left arm and there were fresh bruises on her neck and up onto her jaw. She nodded tightly to him, but didn't look at him squarely.

General Neal stood at the head of the table, his aide taking the seat to his right. There were others in the room that Mason didn't know, though if he was reading uniforms right, the one currently talking quietly with Darvin was an Air Force lieutenant, and the woman on the phone in the corner was a Navy Lieutenant Colonel.

The General cleared his throat and everyone immediately took their seats. "Thank you. I'll make this brief. We've lost contact with our man in Oregon. We know from his last report that the 8th Battalion has begun a campaign to control the area. From what he's managed to observe, they start by inciting violence against anyone the locals already fear: outsiders, Muslims, people of color." He pushed a remote and the screen behind him lit up with a map, red circles marking towns in the south-east corner of Oregon, into the southwest corner of Idaho and along the top of California and Nevada. The entire state of Utah was red as well. "However, our last communication from Agent Lunnal indicated that they were planning to come as far west as Tahoe and south into the Shasta mountains. He was heading south into California."

"Jerah, you ready for your first insertion?" Darvin asked.

Mason nodded, his eyes scanning the map. "I can get across Lake Tahoe, see what I can."

"I'm sending Raven to Tahoe," the General countered. "What I need is someone to go after Lunnal."

Mason frowned a little. "I'm not sure that's exactly my area of expertise, General."

"Last known location." He pointed to the map, to a body of water in the California mountains. "You know this area.?

Mason nodded tightly. "I've been through there." He didn't know it as well as the mountain where he had lived, but he had spent some time there when he was younger. "Okay, what exactly is my mission?"

The lieutenant handed him a file. "Last recon of the area, last time anyone had eyes on him, he was... here." He pointed to a spot up-river from the lake. We'll insert you in Shasta, you can make your way up river to his last known. Your mission is to determine if Agent Lunnal was compromised and whether or not he can be recovered. Recon only."

Mason nodded. "When do I leave?"

Darvin stood. "Chopper's on the roof."

"Let me grab my gear." He headed back for his room, taking the time to tie his boots before grabbing his pack and tucking a canteen and a change of clothes into it before he headed out the door and up to the roof.

Darvin met him, along with the Air Force lieutenant Mason had been introduced to on his first day. They'd attended briefings together, but they had never spent much time with each other. "You and Lieutenant Bracker will be flown to Langley where you'll take a military flight to Fort Bragg. From there, you'll be on the ground. You'll be issued necessary gear at Bragg."

Mason nodded as Bracker got into the helicopter. "You stay in radio contact."

"I will. See you when I get back."

* * *

As much as he preferred being in the water without the encumbrance of clothing, he didn't think it wise to be in what could very well be enemy territory stark naked, so he conceded to a wet suit and a waterproof pack for his map and other necessities. Mason was still getting used to the earpiece, kept safe and dry by the close-fitting hood of the wet suit. The only thing open to the touch of the water was his face, hands and feet.

"I'm almost to his last location," Mason said as he swam against the current. The water was getting shallow and he moved closer to shore. "The water is pretty shallow here, Bracker. Are you sure he was camped here?"

"I gave you the coordinates off his GPS." Bracker said, his tone cold.

"Yeah, okay." He got his feet under him and waded a few more feet into the shallows before stepping up onto the rocky shore. He closed his eyes and exhaled, centering himself and feeling around him for the presence of another Shade. It took him a minute to get past the pull of the water, and the water was everywhere, ponds and streams all around him. As far as he could tell, he was the only living thing for miles.

Mason sighed and moved further upstream. He was just moving back into the water when he felt something on the other side. He waded across and climbed the bank, following the sense of wrong that hung on the air.

The smell of death stirred up from the ground as he moved closer. Mason spotted a small fire pit and felt around him. He grimaced when he found it. "Bracker, I think I found our guy. He's dead. Judging by the smell, it's been a while."

"Can you tell what happened?"

"Hang on." Mason crossed the small clearing to squat beside the body. He reached for it, then recoiled. The stench was strong, and the sense of wrong was even stronger, the feeling that this was not a natural death. He rolled the body onto its back. "Yeah, looks like he took a bullet." Mason lifted a hand over the hole, feeling into him for the damage. "Shit." He shook his hand and pulled back. "The bullet fragmented. He would have lingered on for days while it killed him."

"Can you find his book?"

"I'm working on it." Mason spotted the man's bag and pulled it to him, moving away from the body to kneel in the dirt and open the bag. He pulled out a canteen and set it aside, then found the notebook, wrapped in plastic. He pulled it out and paged through it, nodding to himself. "Last entry is dated a week ago. It has a bunch of coordinates and numbers."

"Right, take anything that might identify him, GPS, and head back."

"What about him?"

"Leave him. We don't have time to haul him out or bury him there." That didn't sit well, but before Mason could argue, Bracker's voice changed, softened some. "Look, I know how that sounds, and he was my friend, but if we don't get you out of there now, you could be laying there beside him, get me?"

"Yeah, okay. I'll be on my way back inside ten minutes."

"Good."

Mason turned his attention to cleaning out the man's bag, stuffing the notebook, his GPS and the canteen into his own bag before returning to the body. He let his hand move in under the man's shirt, sliding along his chest until he found the talisman. Like Mason, he had been the last of his line, and that meant another Shade line was broken. He removed the talisman as gently as he could. The symbol on it was one he didn't recognize, marking it as that of the clan he'd never seen documented. He was learning there were more of those than his Nana had led him to believe, five clans, each with families and lines that stretched out around the world.

With a sigh, he tucked the talisman into his bag before securing the bag and putting it back on his back and returning to the water. He had a terrible feeling that this would not be the last time he became the keeper of another Shade's relics.

The water welcomed him as he slid into it, following the current this time, slowly sinking as it deepened. He let it wash the dark feeling away and turned his attention to getting back to his escort. The sooner he got the notebook into the right hands, the sooner he would be able to get back to the relative safety of Washington.

* * *

Mason should have known that his first mission wasn't going to just end and let him go back to his Book of Line and an education in spycraft. The helicopter that picked them up in Redding got them to Fort Bragg, where Mason handed off the intelligence he'd retrieved. Bracker told him to get some sleep in their borrowed quarters while he communicated back to Washington.

When Bracker wasn't back after Mason had slept for a few hours, he went looking for him. He was eager to get back to Washington.

"Mr. Jerah?"

Mason turned as he pulled the door closed on the quarters where he had been sleeping. A young woman in uniform was approaching him. "Yes?"

"Sir, Lieutenant Bracker sent me to find you."

"Here I am," Mason responded. She didn't smile.

"If you'll follow me, sir."

She led him out of the residential building to a jeep, gesturing for him to get in. A few minutes later they stopped in front of what looked like an office building.

"Sir, please." She held the door for him, then led him through a maze of corridors before opening a door and ushering him to what looked like a war room. He spotted Bracker and lifted a hand in greeting.

"Jerah, good. Come have a look."

Mason circled around a long conference table to a stand beside his handler, looking at a map that was decidedly more red than the last one. "It seems our friends in the 8th Battalion aren't slowing down," Bracker said. He had Lunnal's book in his hand. "Lunnal says they infiltrated the National Guard."

Mason frowned at him, then at the book. "He does?"

Bracker shook his head. "I keep forgetting how green you are. It's code."

That made sense. "Okay, so…"

"We have new orders from Washington. We're headed north. Lunnal seemed to think that Salem is under 8th Battalion control, even though it hasn't shut down its entry points. We're going to determine if that is true."

Mason found Salem on the map. At least there was plenty of water. "When?"

"First thing tomorrow," Bracker said, dropping the book on the table.

"Why us?" Mason asked, leaning back against the table. "I mean, this seems like something you'd want a more experienced agent doing."

"We're closest," Bracker said. "Raven and her handler have their hands full with their current mission. We're stretched pretty thin right now."

"Okay, so what's the plan then?" Mason asked.

Bracker nodded tightly. "The city has a National Guard presence. I'm going in as part of some reinforcements. You're riding along as a government advisor."

"And what exactly are we looking for?" Mason asked.

"Proof one way or the other. If our National Guard has been compromised…" He shook his head.

He didn't need to finish the thought though. If the National Guard had been compromised, there was no telling how far it went, how deeply into the military. Or governments for that matter.

Mason glanced around them at the various faces. It was a sobering thought. Anyone in that room could be an enemy. If they knew he was a Shade, they might even try to kill him.

Bracker's hand touched his arm. "Stay focused."

Mason nodded. "What do you need from me?"

He drew in a deep breath and exhaled slowly. "Be ready. Whatever it is you need to do, get it done."

"I'll be ready," Mason assured him. He turned to find the young woman in uniform who had brought him to the room still waiting by the door. "Take me back, please."

They didn't talk on the ride back to the residential building, and Mason didn't feel obligated to say anything as she stopped the jeep. Suddenly, he wasn't sure he could trust anyone. He let himself back into the small apartment that served as guest quarters. It wasn't much, but it included two beds and, more importantly at the moment, a bath-room with a tub.

Mason locked the door to the bathroom and started the tub filling. He stripped out of his clothes and stepped into the lukewarm water, sinking into it as much as he could. He was too tall for the space, the water only coming half way up his torso, even with his feet propped up on the edge of the tub. Still, it was better than nothing and he closed his eyes, focusing his energy on himself and being ready for what came next.

Chapter Twenty

It would be dark soon. Alaric lowered the binoculars and glanced aside at Bryan. "Anything?"

Bryan shook his head. "Nothing but a lot of static."

Alaric had found the same. "They must have some pretty heavy duty wards."

"Which doesn't make sense," Bryan said. "Seeing as they're making us their enemy."

"I told you, they've got someone on their side who is pretty powerful." Alaric lifted the binoculars again, scanning over the fence line. They didn't seem to have any guards patrolling. In fact, the only sign of life they'd seen since parking the SUV was a gray van that left from the building in the north and raised a line of dust as it left the compound.

"So, now what?" Bryan asked.

Alaric sighed and shook his head. The logical thing was to go back to the camp. Logical didn't sit well with him right then, however. He licked his lips and handed Bryan the binoculars. "Stay here, watch my back."

"Where are you going?"

Alaric moved to the back of the SUV, pulling a canteen out and clipping it to his belt.

"Alaric."

"I'm going to see if I can find one of the wards."

"And then what?" Bryan asked, grabbing his shoulder. "If you pull it down, you let them know right where you are."

"Only if he's right here. I don't think he is."

"You don't think…" Bryan growled his displeasure. "What you mean is that you're not thinking at all."

"Bryan, my father is probably in there. Now that we've seen it, I'm not walking away until I know for sure."

Alaric turned on his heel, walking down the rough dirt path that marked a line across the high desert, giving way to the west to hard scrabble brush, then trees as the ground rose to meet the mountain. It was little more than a hiking trail, but there was evidence that vehicles had used it in the past, skirting around the forest to cut through the desert to the next paved road.

Alaric climbed down the sandstone that supported the path, dropping down about four feet to the desert floor. The ground was hard baked and showed little to no sign of his passing as he moved toward the facility.

About a mile away there was a tumble of boulders and rocks that looked partially man made, as if it had started with a few boulders crashing off the mountain, and someone had decided to add to the pile. It was bigger the closer he got to it, making him reassess his idea of how they'd gotten there. The facility was at least a mile beyond that, probably closer to two. He wasn't the best judge of distances when there was little point of comparison.

Alaric kept the rocks between him and his destination. Bryan stopped following after a few steps, switching to a different tactic.

"*Your mother is going to kill you.*"

Alaric ignored him and kept moving, crouching down when he reached the rocks. They were bigger than he had first assumed from the vantage point above. In fact, there were openings big enough to hide a man in, caves formed from the jumble of rocks. He moved slower now, feeling around him for anyone who might be hiding there. He reached back for Bryan then. "*See anything?*"

"*No, you're clear. Watch yourself, that building nearest the fence has lights on.*"

Alaric acknowledged him with a thought and eased around the last boulder. The sun was sinking fast, casting long shadows that he wished he'd learned how to bend. It was a gift of his mother's that he'd always envied. He slipped along the edge of the shadow, his eyes on the building in the distance.

Half way from the rock to the fence he came to a deep ditch that looked like it might have had water flowing through it at some point. The static was louder in his head there, letting him know he was getting closer to the source. Alaric dropped the three feet or so into the ditch, crossing the four feet across, pausing in the middle to look down the length of it. There wasn't much to see in the dark, but it seemed to turn west toward the mountain not far from where he stood and ran south east in the opposite direction.

Voices lifted on the still air and Alaric crouched down, pressing himself against the wall of the ditch, listening, but the voices were too far away to make sense of. They faded as the men who were talking opened and then closed a heavy door somewhere to the east.

"*You're clear,*" Bryan sent. "*Do whatever it is you're going to do and get your ass back here.*"

Alaric eased up, peering over the edge before pulling himself up and moving away from the ditch. With the sun down, the desert cooled dramatically, and he could see his breath pluming on the air as he felt for whatever physical marker was the grounding for the ward.

He reached the fence and knew it was nearby. Alaric looked up and down the line of chain link. It was one of a circuit, set to deflect the eyes of anyone without gifts, and to deflect the minds of anyone with them. Alaric eased along the fence toward the south, until he came to a sign. It was a standard "Private Property - No Trespassing" sign, but for the company logo at the bottom.

"*This guy is slick,*" Alaric sent as he squared himself to the sign. The ward was set in the logo, like a sigil. It was similar to work he'd seen his father do years before.

"Be careful."

Alaric licked his lips and exhaled while he felt around the ward. It was obvious that whoever had set it didn't actually expect anyone that might know how wards worked to come across it. It wasn't sloppy work, exactly, but it had an air about it of being hurried and not as clean as it could be.

He felt along the lines that stretched from either side of the ward. Dismantling it would be easy enough, he only needed to snip the lines and break the sigil.

Of course, he was only guessing that whoever had set the wards was no longer in residence. If he was wrong and he broke it, he could end up on the receiving end of some nasty psychic feedback or worse.

"Be ready, just in case."

Alaric bent to pick up a rock near his foot. He inhaled sharply and raised his hands, feeling for the lines again. He snipped them quickly and brought the stone down over the sigil, scratching a small line through one of its outside lines. There was a flare of energy as the ward tried to sound its warning, but he squelched it quickly.

For a long moment he didn't move, waiting for a blow that didn't come. When he was sure nothing was going to happen, he exhaled the breath he'd been holding and turned his attention into the compound. Now that the ward wasn't blocking him, he got a strong sense of groups of people. It was a lot of emotional input, and he sorted through it as quickly as he could.

The building the furthest west was filled with boredom and fatigue, likely men who were there working the various menial jobs a compound like this would require. Closer to him, and at least two floors underground he felt discipline, focus. It felt similar to students learning or even people in a lab working. A little north from that came a wave of pain, dizzy, hurt, confusion, fear. Alaric latched onto that and let his mind follow it down two flights of stairs. The air was dry and stale, and there were cells lining the dark corridor. Several of them held prisoners.

"*Got something.*" Alaric felt through each cell until he found the familiar feeling of his father. "*Dad.*"

The thoughts that met his were sluggish and confused. There was little control once they were connected, sending Alaric sloshing around in his father's once orderly mind. There were heavy drugs in his system and head trauma, so the memories were jumbled, slamming Alaric around while he tried to find a balance. Eventually, he metaphorically planted his feet and forced everything around him to stillness, throwing up temporary walls to lock away the excess and give him room to function.

"*Dad? Can you hear me?*"

The response was a blast of pain and fear that pushed Alaric back physically. "*Bryan and I are here. We can get you out.*"

"*NO!*" The response was strong and Alaric could feel his father's conscious mind latching onto him, pulling itself up out of the chaos.

"*I'm not leaving you here.*"

The shadow of his father's hand brushed his face with warm affection. "*I love you.*"

"*Dad, stop. Let us help you.*"

Gathering his strength, Anson pushed himself up, though he didn't attempt to take back control. As he did, Alaric could see his father was not well. Aside from the drugs and head injury that together had eroded his mental control, he was physically broken. He couldn't catalog the broken bones and other injuries.

"*Can't. Won't make it. Can't walk.*"

Anguish filled him as Alaric realized what his father meant. He was dying. Even if they could figure out how to get in, he wouldn't live to make it back to the SUV.

"*Tell your mother...*"

"*No.*" Alaric shook his head. Tears spilled onto his face as he opened his eyes, determined now to find a way to get through the fence. "*Bryan, I need something to cut the fence with.*"

"*Alaric, please. There's so much to tell you.*"

He didn't want to hear it. "*Bryan, help me.*"

His father used his link to Bryan to speak to his older Keeper while Alaric pulled uselessly at the fence. "*Stop wasting your strength,*" Alaric pleaded.

"*Alaric Lambrecht, listen to your father.*" Bryan sent strongly, pulling him up short.

"*Alaric, you know I only want what is best for our people. I can't lead them now. You have to.*"

Alaric landed on his knees, his fingers twisted in the chain link of the fence. "*I never wanted...*"

His father was fading though; Alaric could feel him slipping away. Anson pushed a bunch of thoughts and images at him, things he wanted Alaric to know, to remember. He almost pushed it away. "*Please...*"

The moments drew out as little by little his presence went dark, until all that was left was the lingering scent of him. Then came the final snap as the connection between their leader and his Keepers broke. Alaric slumped against the fence, staring dumbly into the dirt, barely acknowledging the information that was now filtering through him.

The elder Lambrecht had been scarcely alive even when he had been brought to this place. The memory of the impact was thankfully a blur, but it was clear that his father had been struck by a vehicle of some kind prior to his being captured by men that wore the navy blue of the 8th Battalion.

"*Alaric. Alaric!*"

He was unsure how long he'd sat there, unmoving, arms wrapped around his stomach, but Bryan's voice in his head was urgent. He didn't respond, but Bryan knew he'd gotten through.

"*I need you to get up and get back here. Right now.*"

Alaric looked around him slowly, vaguely registering the potential danger. He staggered to his feet and started back toward Bryan. The distance seemed impossible, the world around him cold and his feet numb.

It took forever just to get back to the ditch. Bryan pulled at him mentally, keeping him moving. As he reached the rocks, Alaric collapsed in the dirt, his mind stuck on the empty place where his father belonged.

"Get up." Alaric blinked and looked up at Bryan who was somehow standing over him. His eyes were red, his face wet. "Alaric, get up. We need to move."

His hands gripped Alaric's arms and pulled. Alaric stood numbly, nodding a little. His head was mostly static and he shook it to clear it. The night had deepened around him, and a starry sky spread over him. "Dad…"

"I know." Bryan got them moving, back toward the shadowy mass of the SUV. "But we need to get back to camp. By morning, everyone will know. We need to be there for Emily."

The death of a leader was something that spread without words. As part of the ceremony that confirmed Anson Lambrecht as the clan's leader, his mind was connected to the entire clan, no matter where they were. With his death, that connection dissipated until everyone could feel the loss.

It began with those closest to him, his Keepers, his family, his friends. His mother would know before they even got back to camp.

* * *

She was waiting for them at the door to the bunkhouse, her eyes sad, her hands curled around a cup of coffee. Somewhere in the distance the sun was just beginning to rise, stretching warm fingers across the cold night sky.

Alaric got out of the SUV slowly, his body aching with his grief. He dragged himself up the trail behind Bryan. He embraced Emily before his hands took her waist and turned her into the warmth of the hall. Alaric paused on the porch in the cold air. Winter would be coming. They would need to lay in more supplies before the first snow. The only way in or out would be on foot once the snow came.

He hugged himself and let the tears fall. His father was gone, and in his absence, Alaric would be expected to take his place.

The memory of his father's confirmation ceremony drifted up inside him, but he pushed it away. It wasn't something he was ready to even consider. Instead, he turned to the bundle of memories and images his father had given him before he died. It was a jumbled mess because of the drugs and injuries, and he sorted through it for something useful, something to hold on to.

The story it told wasn't pretty. Things were worse than they had imagined, worse than anyone had imagined.

Chapter Twenty-One

Salem, Oregon wasn't a whole lot different than some other places Mason had visited since leaving the solitude of his mountain. It wasn't the sprawling metropolis of D.C., but as the industrial outskirts gave way to businesses, it reminded him of the many towns the bus had rolled into on his trip across the country. He rode in beside Bracker on a truck filled with soldiers sent as reinforcements for the National Guard already helping to hold the city together.

Or at least, that's what he'd been told.

Mason wore the same uniform they did to let him blend in a little better. They unloaded outside the command center set up by the Lieutenant Colonel in charge. Mason followed Bracker inside, hanging back to watch the people around them.

His job was to see the things Bracker couldn't, to get the measure of the land while Bracker came at it from the inside.

"Lieutenant Bracker, welcome to Salem. I'm Lieutenant Colonel Shallon."

Bracker saluted the man sharply. Mason looked the Lieutenant Colonel over. He was in camo like the rest, his brown hair buzzed short, making his face look long. His nose bore the signs of multiple breaks that hadn't been set properly. Mason instantly didn't like him, though he wasn't sure exactly why.

Shallon showed Bracker to a table with a grid map on it. "I need your men here." He pointed along a three-block area. "We've had a number of protests that have gotten ugly."

"What are they protesting?" Bracker asked.

Shallon shrugged his shoulders. "What aren't they?" He turned as an aide approached, taking his clipboard to scribble a signature. "Our job is to keep the peace and enforce the curfew. No one on the streets after six pm without papers."

"Papers?" Bracker asked, his eyebrow raised.

"Waivers. Citizens can apply for waivers for work and other reasons." Shallon glanced at Mason, his brow furrowing into a frown. "Who are you?"

Bracker stepped between them to draw Shallon's attention. "He's a government observer. Sent to get a look at your operation, see if it would serve well in other cities." That seemed to appease the man, and he went back to pointing out places on the map. "What is this?" Bracker asked, pointing to a heavily marked area.

"Prison. We're consolidating the prison population, transferring the worst offenders to one location to be dealt with. But that isn't your concern. Your concern is the protestors."

"Right. If you'll excuse me then, sir. I'd like to get the men deployed." He saluted, then turned to leave, grabbing Mason's elbow as he moved for the door.

"What is going on?" Mason asked once they were out of earshot.

Bracker shook his head. "I don't know. This city is far more fortified than I was led to believe, judging by that map." He stopped them between two big trucks. "He's hiding something at that prison. Find out what."

Mason nodded. "And what are you going to do?"

"My job." Bracker left him standing there, and Mason waited for a few minutes before he turned to find a way to get to the prison.

* * *

Mason eventually got a private in a jeep to give him a ride to the prison, but before they could reach the gates, they were forced to stop by the large crowd of people. He was fairly sure he had never seen that many people in one place before.

The noise was thunderous, a slurry of chanting and yelling, and somewhere there was drumming. He stepped out of the jeep and thanked the driver. "I'll get there on my own."

The driver saluted him and turned around, going back in the direction they had come.

Mason stood in the shadow of a building, squinting into the bright light of a sunny afternoon. The mob was a mix of men and women, young and old. It was difficult to tell what they were protesting, but they were not going to be dealt with easily.

His uniform marked him, though whether it marked him as a friend or an enemy to the crowd, he wasn't sure.

Exhaling his anxiety, Mason pulled his cap down and stepped out of the shadows, skirting along the flank of the crowd, trying to parse out their words to understand what was going on.

"Stop the killing!" seemed to be the chant closest to him, and signs held over the protesters heads bore similar sentiment. He wasn't sure what killing they were protesting, but as he got closer to the fence surrounding the prison, it became clearer.

In front of the prison a platform had been set up, metal grating with three metal poles with metal restraints that held three prisoners, their hands and feet manacled to the poles, their arms up over their heads.

The late afternoon sun was hot where it touched his skin and sweat was already beading on his forehead, under the brim of his hat. His eyes scanned the crowd, then the line of soldiers along the barricades that held them back from the prison gates.

The roar of voices was stronger the closer he came to the fence. One of the men in uniform saw him and made a hole in the line for him to slip through. "It's not safe out there," the man said to Mason as he pulled him behind the barricade.

"What?" Mason asked, turning to look at the man.

"The executions are about to begin. Two cops were nearly killed by the crowd during the last one."

Mason frowned and turned to look back at the prison. There was a man in a suit now behind the platform, talking into a microphone. Even with the amplification of the PA system, Mason could barely hear him over the crowd.

"...thereby sentenced to death by burning. May God have mercy on your souls."

From beneath the platform, flames sprung up through the metal grating, instantly engulfing the men in fire. The crowd surged forward. From random places in the crowd there was cheering. Behind him the burning men screamed until they couldn't.

Mason wanted to cover his ears, to run from the sounds and smells, but he couldn't. The crowd was churning, fights breaking out. The soldiers stood at attention around him, their guns held at the ready.

The sound of gunfire echoed from the left and the crowd seemed to undulate, breaking into groups as more gunfire sounded. The soldiers all raised their guns, but instead of firing into the crowd, one of them shot off into the air, pushing the protesters back.

Chaos swirled around him. People ran, shoved, pulled each other away. Inexorably, the crowd thinned, dissipated, and ultimately there was only the soldiers and Mason, and five people bleeding into the concrete.

He moved toward the closest of them, his hands already reaching out, but he pulled up short. There was nothing he could do without exposing himself as a Shade. He knelt beside the man anyway. He was bleeding from a head wound.

A hand touched Mason's shoulder. "Leave him. Medics are coming."

"I can help-"

"He's an agitator. Our orders are to leave them for the medics."

Mason let the soldier pull him away, blinking a little at the realization that they really weren't going to do anything for the fallen until medics arrived. He turned away from them, but that just left him looking at the blackened bodies of the dead on the prison's pyre. He was trembling and he knew he needed to get out of this scene.

There were sirens, and the arrival of medical units in army green that allowed Mason to pull away and distance himself. He moved toward the man who seemed to be in charge of the medical unit. "Can I catch a ride back to ops with you?" Mason asked.

The man grunted and pointed to one of the ambulances. As they loaded the last of the fallen protesters into the vehicles, Mason climbed up into the cab. The woman behind the wheel looked very young, her blond hair pulled back into a knot at the base of her skull.

She nodded to him, her eyes straying to the blackened corpses beyond the fence. Her face paled and she swallowed hard, pointedly turning her face away from him and the sight outside his window.

"You okay?" Mason asked.

She nodded. "I will be." She shifted uncomfortably. "I'm not used to it yet."

"Used to what, public execution?" Mason asked, the distaste in his voice strong. "I didn't even know that was legal."

"Depends on your interpretation of legal," she muttered. She didn't look at him as she followed the ambulance in front of her onto a side street.

"Killing people like that..." He shuddered and shook his head. "I've never...I thought..."

"Lieutenant Colonel Shallon says that lethal injection is too fast for people to really take as a deterrent."

"So he orders them to be burned alive in front of the prison?" Mason asked. "How is that even his decision?"

She looked at him sharply. "Be careful who you say that to. Lieutenant Colonel Shallon doesn't take kindly to questions about his authority."

"His authority? Has anyone actually told him he isn't the one in charge?"

Her face drained with color. "The last man who did ended up dead."

She was quiet the rest of the way back to the command center. Mason wanted to ask her a dozen different questions, but he could tell she was terrified. He helped them unload the patients and move them into the medical unit, and even though he wanted to stay to help them, he knew he needed to find Bracker.

* * *

Mason moved through the sandbags creating a path along what looked like the front line in some war movie. Razor wire and barricades blocked the command center off from the rest of the city.

In the hour or two since he'd left medical, the sun had set and he'd worked his way along the line, listening to the soldiers as he moved through them. He was anxious to find Bracker and get them out of Salem. The sentiment among the soldiers seemed to be split into two camps. The bigger of the two was very supportive of Lt. Colonel Shallon. Some of them sounded downright bloodthirsty. The smaller group were confused by their duty to their commander when everything he seemed to be doing went against their actual mandate.

The streets beyond the barricades were empty and quiet, the buildings closest to them dark. The only movement seemed to be the soldiers themselves as they rotated shifts on the line.

Mason found Bracker organizing some men nearly ten blocks away from the compound, and he waited in the shadows for him to finish. Bracker seemed to know he was there, turning and nodding. Mason approached and Bracker clapped a hand to his shoulder, guiding him back away from the line and behind a jeep.

"This place is insane," Mason said quietly. "Did you know that they're executing inmates? Not even death row inmates any more. They've already killed them." Mason kept his fists clenched to keep them from shaking. It had taken a lot of careful questioning to learn that much. "That's not the half of it, Bracker. They're burning them. Publicly."

Bracker's eyes were dark, but he didn't seem surprised. "Not just here. I've hear rumors of it happening in other states too. I just got word that they'll be closing off the city in the morning. No one in or out without approval."

"This is crazy." Mason said, scanning the dark around them. "That Shallon guy thinks he can do whatever he wants."

"And as long as he controls this city, he can." Bracker said. "We should get back to Bragg and report."

Mason nodded his agreement. The sooner the better, as far as he was concerned.

* * *

"I think it's safe to assume that there are a number of men and women within our military who have already sided with the 8th Battalion, sir," Bracker said as they sat in the briefing room at Fort Bragg.

The big screen on the wall connected them to a similar room in Washington where Mason could see familiar faces lining the table.

The door at the other side of the room opened and Mason looked up, eyes widening as Raven and her handler entered the room. She sized up the room quickly, her eyes darting from Mason to the screen. "Sir, we have a problem."

"So we're learning." Darvin said on screen.

"They're moving more quickly than we had anticipated." Raven looked tired, her face paler than Mason remembered. "The military has been compromised, sir. And not just a handful of units. We've seen evidence of it in Utah, Idaho, even Nevada."

"And Oregon." Mason added.

She looked at him, then back at the screen. "Right now, they're mostly moving to consolidate the big cities, isolating them, but in doing that, they're choking off the small towns. If we don't act, and act now, they'll have the entire western coast locked down."

"That's a bit alarmist, don't you think?" General Davis said, standing up.

"No, sir, I don't." Raven responded.

"If it was as bad as all that, we'd know," a lieutenant said from beside the General. "The media would have this plastered all over the news."

"They're controlling the press." Raven countered. "What press does get in, they're actively suppressing. Journalists are getting arrested, their recordings seized. We need to act." Raven said.

"Gentlemen, let us consider this carefully." General Davis said. "We're talking about men who have taken oaths to defend this country. Not some crazy terrorists."

"What else do you call people who create terror?" Mason asked softly.

"Excuse me, Mr. Jerah?"

Mason took a deep breath. "I can only tell you what I saw, General." He looked around the room, then back to the General. "Those people were afraid."

"I thought you said they were angry."

Mason conceded the point. "They were, but they were also afraid. That man up there in Oregon, he's murdering people publicly. I saw it with my own eyes."

"Our intelligence says that the men you saw killed were murderers themselves." The man who spoke wasn't military. Mason wasn't sure who he was.

"Does that justify burning them at the stake?" Mason asked, not really wanting to know the answer. He felt eyes on him and looked up, meeting Raven's gaze.

"*Can you hear me?*" Her mouth didn't move, but Mason heard her all the same. He nodded a little. "*Be careful. Don't trust them.*"

He wasn't sure which them she meant. He turned back to the General who was wrapping up the meeting without actually deciding anything. Bracker was shaking his head and muttering about bureaucracy.

"So they aren't going to do anything?" Mason asked quietly.

"No, they will, once it's been discussed to death by men who will read our reports and determine we are blowing it out of proportion."

He stood, pulling his cell phone out of his pocket. "Don't get too comfortable. I'm going to call Darvin."

Mason stood, watching Bracker leave the room while pressing his phone to his ear. The room was nearly empty but for him and Raven and a couple of aides. She came around the table, grabbing his elbow and dragging him out into the hall. "What are you doing?" Mason asked.

She looked around them and pulled him down the hall and out a side door. She kept her hand on his elbow, even as she met his eyes and touched his mind with her own. "*I meant what I said. Don't trust them, not even your handler.*"

Mason frowned at her. "*What? Why?*"

"*He's military, just like mine. I think she tried to sell me out. I almost didn't get out.*"

"Are you sure?" Mason asked out loud.

"Not sure." Raven conceded. "But that's how it looked." She sighed and rubbed nimble fingers along a bruise that ran the length of her jaw. "Listen, I'm seeing a pattern. As they move into a city, it starts with anti-Shade, anti-Muslim, anti-everything incidents... graffiti and op-eds in at least a few places that was followed by what was made to look like Shade revenge."

Mason wasn't sure he could frown any harder than he was. "Like what?"

She inhaled sharply. "I forget how green you are. In Sacramento they found a couple of bodies drained of blood with the Zelena clan's emblem carved in them. Darchel was a Zelena. In Salt Lake it was a virulent flu virus that hit primarily affluent neighborhoods. Then come the violent acts and protests, then the police call for military help. Once the army arrives, the city gets locked down. Then they can do pretty much what they want."

"How do they get away with it? Why aren't we seeing it on the news?"

"The military controls press access, and they're suppressing cell phones. Some of it is getting out online, but... I can't tell how much is getting to the people it needs to. You saw what happened in there."

Mason nodded, but he was having trouble believing her. "So what do we do?"

"I'm going back to DC, without my handler. Told her I have family in San Francisco I want to visit before I head back. I'll get on a commercial flight and get back to Darvin." Mason's head was spinning through everything he'd seen. He didn't want to believe her, but a lot of what she said jived with things he'd seen. "Watch your back, Jerah." Raven said. "And don't trust anyone in uniform."

Chapter Twenty-Two

"We need to go back and get it, before the snow comes," Bryan said, standing against the wall with his arms crossed.

"It's a suicide mission."

Alaric Lambrecht let the argument swirl around him, his eyes on his mother's face. When the voices settled into silence he looked up. They were all looking to him. He was supposed to step into the place his father's death had left empty. He let his eyes sweep over the gathered group of people. They were a ragged bunch, city folk who had no idea how hard it was to live rough like they'd been forced to do since leaving Sacramento.

The camp was nearly full. Most of the clan that had come together when his father had taken the leadership role had either come here or headed back east to more ancestral grounds. Bryan, Riley, Jacob, and Jordan represented the clan at the camp. In the chair near the fire, Keisha Freeman was watching him, representing her own family, and Sahara was watching him from the corner nearest Bryan. Ahmed sat on the couch beside him, speaking for the group of people that were not of the tribes.

It had been nearly a week since Anson Lambrecht had died. Alaric had stumbled through the days, focusing on the work of making the camp function so that he didn't lose himself in his grief.

"Alaric, your father–"

He held up his hand to stop Bryan. This was where he was supposed to step up. Alaric stood, circling around to stand behind his mother, his hands on her shoulders. "My father is no longer with us, Bryan."

"All the more reason we need to get back into Sacramento and get the orb."

Alaric turned to Riley, surprised a little that he was agreeing with Bryan. It was confirmation to him that it was the right thing to do, but unlike the others, Alaric had knowledge of his father's last days, of just how much the enemy knew. He sighed and nodded. "I agree, but we can't just go in blind. We need to plan."

"I have a plan; we go in and get what's ours." Bryan said.

"It's not that simple." The youngest person in the group stood. Jordan was barely eighteen, small in stature with no active gifts of the clan that spawned him but able to use the passive to his advantage well enough. He had only just returned from taking some family members back east, and he was the last one to have passed through Sacramento.

Jordan leaned over the table and put a finger down on the map. "See this? They have a checkpoint set up here. And here." He pointed again. "They haven't locked down the city like some other places, but they have a military presence, and no one gets through the checkpoint without being stopped, in either direction."

Jordan looked up at Alaric, his eyes filled with concern. "I mean, I got around them, but I just had people with me. Carrying the orb, even crated, is going to raise alarms."

"What if we used one of their trucks?" Bryan said, coming to look at the map. He pointed to a place on the map. "I hid the truck I stole here. It should be big enough to get the orb out."

"The problem is, we don't know what they know." Alaric said. "We could be walking into a trap."

"So we go in with teams." Riley said. "We have two teams ready to run interference, and one to get the orb out."

Alaric nodded slowly. "That might work, but we'll need volunteers with active gifts." He glanced around the room, mentally tallying who could do what. They probably needed some who could handle themselves in a fight too. "Jacob, I need a skills inventory by morning. We'll need people who can do more than reading people."

"Not everyone is going to like us using those skills." Jacob said.

Alaric knew that. "I think we're past the point where it's an option not to use them." Alaric squinted at the map, trying to imagine how it would play out. "Three teams of two, plus Jordan and Riley. You two will go in after the orb. The rest of us provide cover, and distraction if necessary."

"Us?" Bryan asked, crossing his arms.

Alaric nodded. "Yes, we. I'll be involved."

His mother touched his arm, her concern filling his mind. "I'll be fine," he responded, rubbing a hand over hers. His eyes swept the group. "Bryan, I want you with me." He didn't voice his reasons, but he suspected that Bryan knew them anyway.

"We don't have your particular gifts." Sahara said, moving closer. "But we have talents of our own. I don't know what this orb is or why it is important, but we're quick and good in a fight."

"There's a strong chance of getting caught." Alaric said. Sahara had been adamant that their troubles were not hers, so he was surprised by her volunteering. Her skin rippled and gold filled her eyes, a sign he was coming to learn meant she was not amused.

"I will consider our debt clean," she replied, meeting his eyes.

"Okay." Alaric accepted. He looked up and around the table. "That's a start. Jacob, get back to me in the morning with that list, make sure anyone on it is willing to get their hands dirty. We'll meet back here after dinner tomorrow to rough out a plan."

His mother stood to walk people out and Alaric sat on the couch, staring at the map.

"You know this is stupid, right?" Bryan said when only he and Riley remained. "You know someone's going to get caught."

Alaric nodded. From the moment they'd started talking about this, he'd had the idea in his head that he was supposed to be involved. The face of a Shade filled his mind. If he believed what he had seen, he would need the man. He wouldn't meet him hiding away in the woods. "Probably. And more than likely you and me."

"You shouldn't be risking yourself." Riley said, crossing his arms.

"Well, it's a risk I have to take," Alaric countered. "Besides, we already know where they'll take us if we get caught. We can build an escape plan around what we know. You and Jordan get the orb, and once it's secure, you come get us."

Bryan shook his head, pacing away. "This is stupid," he repeated. "I have no desire to have those assholes poking me for days while we wait for Riley to come get us."

"So you go with Jordan. I'll back Alaric up," Riley countered.

Bryan snorted and looked up at him. "Yeah, how you going to do that, with your sporadic ability to know the future? How is *that* going to do the job?" There was a reason Alaric picked Bryan and he knew that. "I'll do it; I'm just making it known that this is a stupid plan."

"It's going to be fine." Alaric said, standing and clapping a hand on Bryan's shoulder.

Bryan shook his head, and pulled away, but Alaric felt the sudden memory of Anson and the spike of pain it brought. "I'm going to go get some sleep. I suggest you both do too." Bryan said a little sadly as he headed for the door.

Alaric could hear him saying goodnight to Emily, who then came in, rubbing her hands over her arms. "Getting cold out there."

"It will be snowing before too long," Riley responded. "Which means, we need to do this if we're going to."

"I know. We will." Alaric rubbed his hands over his thighs before standing. "I have the feeling this is the next step in uniting the tribes."

Riley raised an eyebrow at him. "How so?"

"Three of the four are represented here now. I think this is when I'll meet the fourth."

Riley's eyes narrowed. "The Shade?"

"I keep seeing his face. But Bryan is right, we should get some sleep." It was going to be a rough week.

* * *

Bryan sat behind the wheel of the stolen truck, and Alaric could feel his discomfort with the plan. In the back of the truck, Alaric sat with the rest of his team. They would scatter once they were inside the city, but for the moment they huddled in silence in the locked cargo area of the Omega Labs truck.

They were slowing down and Bryan's heart rate increased. He could hear Bryan talking with someone, using the cover story they had created with just the right pushes on the untrained mind, and within a few minutes, they were moving again.

"Okay, that's the second checkpoint. Does everyone understand your objectives?" Alaric asked, looking around. They all seemed determined and somber. "Remember, keep your senses open, we need as much information as you can gather."

"What about people?" Cassandra asked from her spot beside Sahara. "What if we find more of our people?"

Alaric licked his lips and considered the answer. He knew the more people involved, the larger the risk, but he was loathe to leave anyone behind who wanted out. "As long as it doesn't compromise you or them, bring them with you."

Relief rippled around him. "Remember, meet up with Jordan and Riley before three or you're on your own getting back to camp. And be careful."

They were nearly to the center of downtown the next time the truck slowed. Mila and Matthew stood up. Matthew was going to try to determine how much information the 8th Battalion had and use his particular skill set to lay a few traps that would obfuscate that information where he could. Mila was there to protect him.

Cassandra and Sahara were next as they moved out toward the storage facility. Cassandra was a solid reader with a gift for glamors. Sahara, well, Alaric could imagine that like Mila, Sahara was prepared to tear apart anyone that threatened them. Their job was to ensure that Riley and Jordan would be clear.

At the gate to the storage facility, Bryan stopped the truck and got out, coming to the back as Alaric, Jordan and Riley got out. Alaric pressed the key to their unit into Riley's hand. "Be careful. Don't take any unnecessary risks."

"Same to you," Riley said.

Bryan took off the navy blue jacket that had been enough to fool the guards at the checkpoints with a little subtle nudging and handed it to Riley. "You're covered as long as you're wearing this. I tagged all the guards I could as we came through. They should see this as an 8th Battalion uniform jacket."

"Thanks," Riley said, tossing the jacket into the truck before they pulled it closed. "You two sure about this?"

Alaric looked at Bryan. "Well, he's not, but I am. You two going to be okay?"

"We got this," Jordan said. "You better get going."

"Meet you at the rendezvous spot at three," Bryan said.

"Just watch your back."

"Let's go." Alaric headed for the busy street corner. He wanted to go to the last place he knew his father had been prior to the accident. As they headed away from the storage place, Alaric could feel Bryan laying down a field of confusion that would waylay almost anyone who ran into it. It should help keep any curious onlookers from noticing Riley and Jordan.

They cut across a side street and headed back toward downtown. Bryan and his father had discreetly made the rounds of those they knew as belonging to one of the four tribes, and after they had gotten split up at the Labs, Anson had taken refuge with someone.

Alaric pointed as they rounded a corner. "There, it's down that alley." He led the way out of the bright sun and into the alley. There was a small, unobtrusive sign on the door with Chinese characters in black and under them an English translation that just said, "Acupuncture."

He lifted a hand to the door, setting his palm just below the sign. "Dad was here." He tried the knob, a little surprised when it turned under his hand. Behind the door was a small, cramped front office with several chairs. The place was dark, and it felt like no one had been there in days, maybe longer.

Bryan moved around him, stepping into the waiting room. "Yeah, he was. Came here for help." Bryan was frowning as he moved toward the door to the back office. Alaric could feel him straining for the strands of information left behind.

"Shade. Ran when your father did." He put his hand on the door, slowly pushing it open.

There was an audible pop and Bryan jumped back. "We have to go." He shoved Alaric toward the door.

"What was that?" Alaric asked.

"Someone came looking for them, left a land mine of sorts. It's a good bet he knows we were there." Bryan led the way to the street, his eyes scanning around them. It seemed a normal city street, if a little underpopulated. The sun glared off nearby windows, making Alaric squint.

"Now what?" Alaric asked.

Bryan responded by pulling on his elbow. "We move." He pointed to the left at a black SUV coming toward them. "I think they're looking for us."

They hustled away from the oncoming vehicle, their speed increasing as the SUV did too. It felt far too familiar for Alaric's taste, echoing the memory of his father's attempt to escape them.

They dove around the corner, and Alaric aimed them toward a familiar door. It was a little early in the day for the bar to be crowded, but Alaric and Riley had frequented the place and the owner was friendly. He burst through the door with Bryan behind him, stopping cold once inside. The man behind the bar was unfamiliar, and so were the two men sitting on bar stools.

"I help you boys?" the bartender asked.

Alaric ducked down to look out the window. The SUV was slowing down. He shook his head and nodded Brian toward the two men on the stools while he approached the bartender. "We're just passing through," Alaric said as his hand snaked across the bar to grab his wrist. He pushed himself into the man's mind, laying false memories that didn't include him and Bryan.

Then Bryan was grabbing his elbow and pushing him toward the back door of the place. The door let them out into the alley, which snaked between two buildings to let them out around the block.

"We need to get cover," Alaric said, trying to catch his breath.

"Or become people we're not. How's your glamor?"

Alaric groaned. "Not great."

"You shouldn't have to hold it long, just long enough for them to assume we found shelter somewhere. Come on." He darted down to the next alley, turning into the shadowed lane. Alaric followed. By the time Alaric reached him, Bryan didn't look a lot like Bryan.

Alaric could pick out the details, of course, but the dirty blond hair had gone dark brown, his beard shot through with gray. His bad eye looked normal and his clothes had gone from blue jeans and a button down over a t-shirt, to a business suit, complete with tie.

Alaric took a deep breath and calmed himself, reaching inside. He decided to make the glamor simple, nothing too complex. He made his hair black and a shortened it to above his collar, then opted to change the color of his clothes to black as well.

"How's that?" Alaric asked.

"Not bad. Can you hold it?"

"I think so."

"Okay, you go first. Head to the rendezvous point. I'll meet you there."

"We shouldn't split up," Alaric countered.

"They're looking for two men together. They'll see through the glamor quicker if we're together. Go."

Bryan gave him a little push, and Alaric moved carefully to the street. He forced himself not to hurry, even as the SUV rounded the corner. They drove past him slowly, through the intersection. Alaric crossed the street and headed in the opposite direction, holding the glamor until he had put a few blocks and another two turns between them.

He was sweating with the exertion by the time he let go of the glamor. He paused at a bus bench to catch his breath, reaching out to track Bryan. He was a few blocks away and still moving. He acknowledged Alaric and sent him the path Bryan expected to take to get to the rendezvous.

Alaric took another minute to reach the rest of the team, at least those he could. Riley and Jordan were making good time. They had the orb loaded up and were getting ready to leave the storage place. Cassandra and Sahara were almost to the rendezvous, having set things up for Riley and Jordan to not even be noticed.

Mila and Matthew were harder to get to, and Alaric got the immediate sense that they were hiding. Satisfied for the moment, Alaric started the long walk.

He had crossed from streets filled with business buildings and retail stores into residential streets before he felt the pursuit again. There was an adept with the men in the SUV now, tracking them far more efficiently.

Alaric relayed the information to Bryan, even as he sped up his pace, trying to stay ahead of the SUV. Bryan was altering his course, moving away from the rendezvous point now so they wouldn't give away the others. Alaric did likewise, running for an industrial area where they might be able to lose their pursuers among warehouses and equipment.

"*Head east,*" Bryan sent. "*I have an idea.*"

Alaric didn't question it. He could feel the SUV bearing down on him, but they weren't alone now. There were two police cars coming from the north and a military vehicle coming in from the west.

He ran between two buildings, hoping the shadows provided him at least a little cover. There was an explosion off to his left, then another, and Bryan was racing toward him, leaving behind a wave of confusion and a haze of conflicting images. For the moment, the pursuit was following Bryan's false trail, coming at them at speed but focused on a point further west, near the fires now raging where Bryan had somehow made things explode.

Bryan yelled at him to get moving as he came, his legs pumping as he ran. He was approaching the end of his stamina, the illusions starting to slip. Alaric shifted his course to match Bryan's as they headed south in an effort to further draw the cars and men away from the rendezvous point. Hopefully Riley and Jordan had picked up the others and were headed out of town.

"Move." Bryan grabbed his arm and together they took off running.

Alaric grabbed Bryan's shoulder as they ran, feeding energy into him to bolster his illusions. They followed along some train tracks that fed into the industrial area. It would make them easier to follow once their pursuers broke through the illusions, but it was the only direction left to them. Bryan stumbled and Alaric tightened his grip on his shoulder. Gunshots rang out and he spared a glance behind them.

"Too close," Bryan said, gesturing to the sound wall to their west. On the other side was a housing tract. If they could get to the housing to the west, they might be okay. Maybe they could even steal a car or something to get away. Bryan dropped all pretense of holding the illusion and they turned to cross the tracks.

Alaric felt a bullet whiz past his face, whipping his head around. He lost his footing, pushing Bryan clear as he fell. His right side slammed into the iron track, knocking the wind out of him. Bryan pulled on him, trying to get him up, and Alaric held his side as he found his feet.

"Move." Bryan pulled him off the tracks, and they headed for the sound wall that separated the housing tract from the railroad tracks.

His body protested as they ran, his breath coming in heavy gasps that made running difficult. Bryan leaped at the wall, grasping the top and pulling himself up. He reached down to help Alaric, but even as Alaric lifted his left hand and felt Bryan clasp it, he knew they were done running.

A bullet slammed into the wall beside him, and Alaric let go of Bryan's hand, falling back to his feet and down onto his knees. "*Go,*" he pushed into Bryan's head as he turned to face the drawn guns that were starting to surround him. Instead, Bryan dropped down beside him, holding his hands up in surrender. Alaric did the same, holding his hands up as he got to his feet.

The men surrounding them were a mix of local police and men dressed in the unadorned navy blue of the 8th Battalion. A man wearing blue shoved his way past the guns. "Where are the others?"

Alaric did his best to look bewildered. "Others?"

Dark eyes narrowed at them. Alaric could feel him, his mind pushing against his shields. Bryan's hiss beside him told him he felt it too. Alaric took a chance and tried to read the man, but he bristled and took a step back. "There were no others, were there? Just the two of you poking your nose where it doesn't belong." The man stepped in close. "That place was known to harbor Shades." He turned his attention to Bryan, less than an inch from his face. "But you're not Shades."

Bryan held his tongue, but Alaric could sense the thoughts he didn't speak. "Cuff them; get them in the car. I will take them to Captain Hagg. He knows how to loosen tongues." He turned to look at Alaric, his eyes threatening. "Sometimes he even lets you keep them."

Bryan bristled beside them as men pulled their hands behind their backs and put them in zip cuffs. "*Easy.*" Alaric sent. "*Let's not give them a reason.*" They had planned for this. They just had to stay calm and not give the men any reason to kill them. Though having the adept find them wasn't ideal. He knew what they were.

They were manhandled toward a police car and shoved into the back seat. After a few minutes a soldier got behind the wheel and they started moving. Alaric watched out the window as other vehicles fell in behind them and in front, a small caravan of police cars and military vehicles.

"*You're awfully calm.*" Bryan sent.

Alaric nodded, looking at him. "*It's going to be okay.*"

"*You don't know that.*"

Alaric inhaled and slowly let it out. Somehow, he did know. No matter what happened between that moment and when Riley arrived to break them out, it would be fine.

Better than fine.

Chapter Twenty-Three

Mason wasn't happy. Bracker wasn't either, he could tell. They had been stuck at Fort Bragg for days trying to convince them to send more troops up to investigate Salem, with little success.

Darvin had finally sent them on a new mission, this time with a military escort that neither Mason nor Bracker thought was necessary. There were promises made that an investigation was ongoing, but Mason found himself doubting the entire thing. They had flown into Sacramento where they had met with a pretty chilly reception. Bracker had refused additional men from the National Guard troops stationed in Sacramento, which seemed to piss off all the people involved.

Mason rode in the back of a canvas covered truck, re-packing his bag. Bracker came to sit next to him, his face tight. "Did Darvin tell you this mission had been attempted before?"

Mason shook his head, frowning at him. "No, why?"

Bracker gestured with his chin. "Colonel Handon just told me the reason they put us in a caravan instead of just giving us a car was because the Shade they sent in after Raven's mission went south was killed with his handler a week ago."

Mason sighed and shook his head. "How?"

"He wasn't specific," Bracker said. "I thought you should know."

Not that it changed anything. Mason would still do what he was told needed to be done. "Who's left?"

Bracker looked away, out the open back end of the military truck. "Of the Shade agents? Just you and Raven."

The truck was slowing down, making Bracker look up. "What's going—"

The truck rocked as something nearby exploded. Bracker pushed at Mason and shoved him deeper into the truck. "Get down." The men around them started jumping out of the truck, weapons at the ready. Another explosion came, this one close enough to send the truck careening off the road. It started rolling and Mason grabbed at the walls in an attempt to keep himself from bouncing around.

His head slammed into the floor and he blacked out briefly. He blinked his way out of the stupor to find himself alone in the truck. He could smell oil burning, and another, more foul smell that flashed him back to that scene in Salem.

Mason crawled toward the opening and the bright sunlight of a late afternoon. He stopped just before the light that spilled in from the ripped canvas covering of the truck, listening to the noises and voices around him, trying to figure out exactly what was happening.

Voices screamed and gunfire burst all around him, and suddenly the canvas above his head was ripping open and there were hands dragging him out into the sun. He fought to get loose, but there were more of them than he could get free from. Suddenly he was kneeling on hot concrete, eyes squeezed shut against the glare of the sun. Someone had a hold of his ankles and two men held his arms.

A man in a blue uniform with the fiery cross emblem of 8th Battalion on his sleeve blocked the sun for a moment, his face a snarl as he grabbed Mason's hair and yanked his head back and to the side, back into the sun. His hand closed around the talisman that was visible through the torn shirt. "Hold him tight, boys. We don't want this one getting away." He let go of Mason's head and turned. "Lieutenant, radio ahead. Tell them to call in Colonel Shallon. We caught ourselves a Shade."

He turned his attention back to Mason. "Get him up and strip him down. The more skin exposed to the sun, the less danger he is to us.

The rest of you, finish cleaning up this mess. I want us on the road in ten minutes or less."

Mason was pulled to his feet and rough hands tore through buttons and knives cut through denim until he was standing in nothing but his boxers. Mason breathed through the pain. He had learned to take a little heat, some direct sun. Sometimes it was just necessary. He could stay out in it for a few hours or more as long as he kept moving, got enough water and managed to find shade from time to time.

The men were laughing as Mason hissed and involuntarily attempted to twist away from the heat as the sun found his skin. Through it all he could see flashes of what was happening around them. Bracker lay bleeding a few feet away, his eyes glassed over. If he wasn't dead yet, he would be soon. The others he managed to spot were in the same condition.

Then came the ropes. They bound his hands and looped a rope around his neck, using it to drag him away. He was shoved and man-handled into the back of one of their trucks. The man who had pulled his hair handed one of the others a flashlight. "Keep that on him. Sun's going down and we don't want him trying anything."

Mason was pushed down to lay on his stomach in the middle of the truck. His skin was burning and his head pounded with his heartbeat. He fought to keep awake, aware even, but between the head injury and the growing pain of the sun kept him slipping into a haze where he couldn't focus. When the truck finally stopped, the sun was mostly down, and he could breathe a little easier as the flashlight's artificial UV light left him. The respite was short lived, however, and they started shoving him out of the truck, dropping him to the ground and yanking until he found his feet and got upright to follow the pull of the rope.

They went into a door and down, the cool blackness soothing, though it didn't last long. Someone cut the ropes that bound his hands and he was shoved into a chair with force. A light was turned on, and he blinked at the intensity of it. The UV wasn't enough to burn him, just enough to make him uncomfortable and sap his strength.

He tried to remember when he'd last had water. Bracker was good about keeping him hydrated, but for the moment, he couldn't remember drinking anything on the road. All he could think about was the way Bracker's eyes had stared out at him, vacant and empty.

"We had been told that the disgusting Federal government was using heathens and abominations to attempt to poison us." Mason looked up to find the man who had identified him as a Shade towering over him. "You are the first we managed to take alive."

"Lucky me," Mason muttered, earning a strong backhand across his face.

"My reward for capturing you alive will be substantial. Even more so when you give me the information I need."

Mason lifted his head, looking at him. "I have no information. I was just riding along." He was hit again, harder the second time.

"You will tell me what I need to know before Colonel Shallon arrives."

That confirmed what he and Bracker had believed. Shallon was no longer working for the US army. But, it didn't make sense that he was the first, not when he knew there had been others doing his job, not when so many killed in the random acts of violence were supposed to be Shades.

"I've got nothing to tell you." Mason exhaled slowly, knowing that what was likely to follow was going to hurt, a lot. He wasn't wrong.

The beating that came with the questions was measured, producing a lot of pain, but not much permanent damage that he could tell. More than once he blacked out, telling him his head was not in good shape. The concussion wasn't helped by the blows that snapped his head to the side. He wasn't sure how long it went on, or even if he ended up saying anything before it suddenly stopped.

The room emptied, and he was alone for a few minutes, though the light made sure he wasn't comfortable. The door opened again and three men came in. One blindfolded him while another bound his wrists in metal manacles. The rope around his neck was tightened and once again they dragged him until he could get his feet under him.

If he had any sense of direction, it was gone by the time they dragged him down at least one staircase and around several corners. The only respite was the darkness. Finally, they came to a stop and his hands were dragged up above his head where the manacles were locked to something and he was left there, his feet sweeping the floor. The balls of his feet barely made contact with the cold concrete if he tried hard.

He didn't try that hard.

The blindfold was ripped off, and a light like the one they had interrogated him under came on. Mason blinked in the sudden light, quickly closing his eyes. Even like this they were afraid of him.

His head pounded out the rhythm of his heart in stereo behind his ears, which, in his experience, wasn't a good thing. He could taste blood, but it was sort of an aftertaste, like the actual blood was hours ago. He didn't recall bleeding though.

He shivered, making his body sway, the cool air kissing over skin damp with sweat and tender with bruises. He needed to take stock of his current situation, but the constant UV was a distraction and it kept him unfocused, dazed.

There was a movement in the shadows; he heard it, cracked open an eye just in time to see a foot withdraw into the dark. He licked his lips and looked for his voice.., but it was cracked and broken and sounded like he had swallowed white hot sand. ""lo?" Something moved in the shadows, the sound of skin on concrete. "Someone there?"

"Shh... not so loud."

This time the sound was behind him. Hands touched his feet, hot and dry and almost too much. "Easy, just let me..." Those hands traveled up his bare legs, over the filthy boxers that were all he had left of his modesty. They spent time exploring his ribs, then a tanned face rose in front of Mason. One dirty finger pressed to his lips. "Quietly, or they will come back. You don't want to draw their attention back to you. Here."

He held out a hand and a small tin can appeared in it. "I don't have much to give you." He lifted the can to Mason's lips and tilted it, dribbling warm water into Mason's mouth. "I'm Alaric Lambrecht. You are a prisoner of the 8th Battalion. Just like us."

"Mas-Mason." He hated the way his voice sounded, the way he must look hanging there in some dirty cell in some god-forsaken nowhere.

Alaric's hand was gentle as it caressed his face. "It will get worse, Mason, before it gets better. But it will get better. I hope you are strong." His eyes were soft and blue like the deep water of a mountain lake, his blond hair long and disheveled around his deeply tanned face. He held the water to Mason's lips again and Mason swallowed greedily. He was parched, dry through to his toes, weakened by the sun and the light and the hours of beating without any respite.

"You know he's one of those freaks." Another voice came from the shadows and a face followed it. He was taller and his voice was dark, his face hidden behind facial hair and dirt. As he came closer, Mason could see he had a scar that whited out his left eye.

"Bryan." Alaric turned to him, but the new man lifted the talisman still hanging around Mason's neck.

"I'm just saying, don't get too attached, Alaric. They like his kind even less than ours. He won't live long enough to be of use to us."

"Bryan, you can be an ass, you know?" Alaric held up the water and tilted the cup, pouring the last drops into Mason's mouth. "Don't mind him. We're going to be here a while and he's not a closed-in places sort of guy." His hand was gentle, ghosting over Mason's face. "Just be strong."

Mason swallowed and closed his eyes. Strong... He wasn't even sure that was possible any more. The pain from the constant exposure to light was too much, his injuries more so. He figured by now Darvin was looking for him, but there was no telling how far he'd been dragged or where they had ended up.

He had to consider he was on his own.

The stale air around him reeked of human bodies, sweat and excrement. These men didn't seem to be U.S. government, and they weren't Shades. He didn't know what to make of that.

He had no idea why these men were here, or why Alaric's touch was so soothing, despite the chilling tone of Bryan's words. Idly, Mason wondered what Bryan meant, about who they were and why Alaric would offer him the kindness of his own water, which was probably in short supply. The 8th Battalion was not known for treating their prisoners well.

* * *

The door to the cell opened and a man in uniform entered, followed by two other men who Mason recognized from the earlier interrogation. Mason felt his eyes as he looked Mason over, circling around him and coming back to look him in the eye. "I am Colonel Shallon and I will be taking over this interrogation."

He lifted a gloved hand to Mason's face, squeezing and turning it to see all of him. He lifted an eyebrow as Mason lifted his eyes. "Mr. Jerah. How intriguing. Had I known you were a vile, disgusting Shade and not just a government trouble maker, I might have saved some time. But no matter, you're here now." He let go of Mason and stepped away.

"I have a confession to make here, Mr. Jerah. You are the first of your kind we've managed to take alive. Fragile creatures you are. This is very exciting, as you might imagine." He unbuttoned his uniform jacket and slid it off.

"I'm not all that excited," Mason managed to say.

Shallon turned back to him, the smile gone from his face as the lieutenant next to him took his jacket. The punch landed solidly on Mason's jaw, snapping his head to the left and filling his mouth with blood. "Oh, but you should be, Shade. Together, you and I are going to learn everything there is to know about your kind."

He watched Mason for a moment, then glanced into the shadows around him. "The rest of you would do well to take note of this. Your turn will come. I have a transport in route to take all of you to a more permanent housing situation where you will all be tested and examined."

He turned his attention back to Mason, gesturing over his shoulder at the lieutenant. "Now, the lieutenant here believes that you are not worth my time, that I should kill you and be done with you." He paced around where Mason hung in the center of the cell. "As a Shade, you are, after all, a son of the devil. Evil. Your very existence is an affront to morality."

Mason resisted the urge to spit the mouthful of blood at him and swallowed it instead. He needed the fluid urgently, and wasting it on this asshole would do him no good. "Look who's talking," he growled, knowing it would just earn him another blow. Nor was he disappointed.

Colonel Shallon made a "tch tch" sound at him. "Now, that is no way to talk to the man with your life in his hands." He walked to the door of the cell and when he came back he was holding a small can. "Perhaps we can begin with a simple test. Open his mouth."

On either side of him men held him and two hands pried his mouth open. He panted and struggled, not sure what to expect, but then the Colonel was pouring salt into his mouth. He struggled harder, tried to spit it out, but then water was pouring in and his liquid starved body swallowed reflexively. The hands holding him let go.

His throat burned and he thrashed around on the end of his chains, feet dragging the ground. They let him be as the salt worked its way into him. He could feel it burning down his throat and into his stomach, which was already starting to cramp and seize around the salt.

Behind him he could hear Alaric's whispered curse. "Fucking bastards." There was a scuffle, then a thud, then Mason's face was slapped.

"Now, Shade... I am not interested in your work for your government, or what spies you might know of. All of that is secondary to the information you can offer us about you." His hand squeezed Mason's face, forcing him to look up. "Is it true that you can only be killed by beheading?"

When Mason didn't answer, the Colonel held up the salt again. "I have to admit, I don't really know what the salt will do to you if I keep pouring it in. Will it kill you?"

Mason knew it would, though it would be a slow and excruciating death. "Yes." He forced the word out. "Yes, it will kill me and no, beheading is something Hollywood made up."

The Colonel smiled. "See now, that was easy. I'm certain Hollywood made up many things, but you and I, we will uncover the truth, and before you die, perhaps even discover if a filthy, evil, non-human like yourself can earn God's grace."

He handed off the tin and put both hands on Mason's ribs, feeling along them for the broken ones. "There. I am told you can heal yourself. Is that true?"

Mason closed his eyes and inhaled, anticipating the pain. Thumbs pressed in against broken ribs, bringing tears to his eyes. "Yes, fuck. Yes."

"And yet, these have not healed." He pressed in a little harder. "Why?"

His stomach burned with the salt and he imagined he could feel it sucking fluid from his body. He blinked his eyes to keep the tears from falling, tilting his head back. "Too...much...light..." Mason gasped out around the pain. "No strength."

"An honest answer. I like a man who can admit his weaknesses. For that a reward."

Hands fumbled overhead and the Colonel dragged his face back. "I will offer you a few hours' respite. Rest. We have much more to discuss."

He turned on his heel and Mason was dropped to the floor, his arms still bound in front of him, but free for the first time from the chains overhead. His shoulders screamed in pain as he tried to move. The Colonel's men left the cell, and suddenly there were hands, pulling him back into the shadows, out of the artificial sunlight.

"Come on, stay with me." Alaric said, pulling Mason's face up. "You have to empty your stomach, Mason."

"Need the water." Mason argued, but Alaric shook his head.

"Not as much as you need to get rid of the salt." He supported Mason's upper body and stuck fingers into his mouth, past his gag reflex. "Come on."

Alaric's fingers tasted like dirt and sweat and together with pressing into his throat it was enough to make him start to gag, then his stomach lurched and he was spitting out a pile of watery grains that had a pinkish hue to them. He realized distantly that they were like that because he was bleeding somewhere inside of him, but Alaric was pulling him away, and there was something wet on his lips. Mason swallowed, pulling back a little when he realized it wasn't water. He shook his head, licking the taste of blood from his lips. Even as his body craved more, he turned his face away, longing for sleep to take him away from the pain.

He closed his eyes, relishing the cool darkness. Inside him, memories whispered and his Nana's voice echoed, telling him he should have stayed where she left him.

He couldn't say she was wrong.

Dear reader,

We hope you enjoyed reading *Through Shade and Shadow*. Please take a moment to leave a review, even if it's a short one. Your opinion is important to us.

Discover more books by Natalie J. Case at
https://www.nextchapter.pub/authors/natalie-j-case

Want to know when one of our books is free or discounted? Join the newsletter at http://eepurl.com/bqqB3H

Best regards,
Natalie J. Case and the Next Chapter Team

The story continues in:

In Gathering Shade

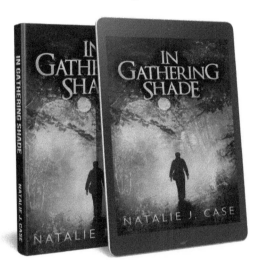

To read the first chapter for free, please head to:
https://www.nextchapter.pub/books/in-gathering-shade

About the Author

Natalie Case was born telling stories, or so she says when asked. Words were her first love and she grew up finding new ways to put words together to tell stories. Known to occasionally commit random acts of poetry, Natalie primarily dabbles in worlds where magic exists, where vampires and shape-shifters share page time with gods and demons and the characters that are born inside her head find themselves struggling in a world made real through the magic of words.

Refusing to be confined to a single genre, Natalie's current works in progress span, and sometimes combine, horror, fantasy, sci-fi and more.

She currently calls the San Francisco Bay Area her home, splitting her time between her day job in the city and writing and photography in Walnut Creek.

Through Shade and Shadow
ISBN: 978-4-86752-856-3

Published by
Next Chapter
1-60-20 Minami-Otsuka
170-0005 Toshima-Ku, Tokyo
+818035793528
12th August 2021